to forgive and hold safe

THE BROKEN MEN CHRONICLES

book four

carey decevito

DEDICATION

To those who have loved and lost. May you find peace in the memories you hold, may you find happiness in the smallest of things, and may you live to love just as fiercely.

ACKNOWLEDGMENTS

I may be the queen of words when it comes down to writing a novel but it seems that words are never sufficient enough in expressing my love and gratitude to those who've been on this unforgettable ride that is *The Broken Men Chronicles* series.

Without a face, there is no story, so a massive thank you goes out to Eric David Battershell and his amazing talent in capturing Ben's character in a way I couldn't dream being any more perfect. 'Thank you' is never enough when it comes down to our collaborations. Your amazing talent and professionalism aside, I'm proud to be able to call you 'friend'. I look forward to more collaborations in the near future.

As with a photographer, there usually comes a subject. Joshua Scott Brown, thank you for agreeing to grace the cover of *To Forgive & Hold Safe*. Your support, your hilarious Facebook posts, and your undying love for pizza will forever be appreciated.

Once you have a photographer and model, who else could I thank but the design guru in my life? Clarise Tan, I've had an amazing time designing covers with you. It's our fourth together and I can't imagine ever doing this with anyone else. You may be half a world away but you're a sister of my heart.

No good book happens without an editor. Marissa Caldwell, lady you are a mastermind at finding those tiny little faux-pas that seem to evade my sight. Your attention to detail and constructive feedback, not to mention your excitement and professionalism have been addicting. I know we'll have more fun in the future as new stories come to light.

To Laurie and the Pub-Craft team, you ladies and gents do it best! Boy am I ever glad that I stumbled into that ORWA workshop in 2015! Having you all as virtual assistants has been a blessing and a huge load off of my shoulders. You're awesome!

And finally, to my wonderful readers, without your words, reviews and support, I'd be nothing but a vessel of words. Thank you for sharing, for enjoying, for taking this ride with me. I hope that you fall in love with Ben as much as I did while writing this!

CHAPTER 1

The day had arrived where I watched as Mike vowed to love, honor and cherish the woman standing before him for the rest of his life. He couldn't have chosen a better partner, in my opinion.

Nicole was a phenomenal woman. Over the last few months, during their nuptial preparations, I had grown to appreciate her matter-of-factness and no-bullshit attitude. In fact, I loved her for it. She knew not to sugar coat things, told you like it was, yet her softer, more empathic side was never too far behind.

I couldn't be happier for my best friend, despite the subtle pangs of jealousy that arose throughout the week while I performed my best man duties. The more time I spent with them, the more I was acutely aware that something was missing in my life.

Something I couldn't bring myself to try and attain.

Not yet, anyway.

Hell, maybe never.

"To the bride and groom!" Danica toasted the happy couple, effectively bringing me back to the present.

And now, it was my turn to deliver my well wishes to the bride and groom. I had no idea what I was going to say, but I spoke from the heart, hoping that it would be good enough.

Apparently it was.

Mike was the first to approach me, a grin that couldn't be erased etched on his face, and a ready man-hug awaited me. Nicole waited her turn at her husband's side with tears in her eyes.

I squeezed the woman tight, pulling back to wipe the stray droplet from her cheek and kissed the other in a brotherly fashion.

"We love you, Ben. Whoever lands you is in for one hell of a treat," she whispered in my ear before kissing my cheek.

My chuckle was a dry one. "I'd have to find her first."

She reached up to wipe the smudge of gloss off my face, then held my hands in hers. "At the risk of sounding like a nagging mother, you know you deserve to be happy again."

I knew I deserved the happiness that Nicole spoke of. It surprised me that it had taken my best friend's woman to make me realize that I had erased most of the good, and held on to all the bad memories of my late wife Candace, and our daughter Karen.

In truth, it was hard to remind myself of the greatness that once was my life, when nightmares of the night that altered my existence haunted my subconscious as I succumbed to sleep every night.

At times, I was overcome with so much grief, while at others I blamed Candace for leaving me, giving into the anger and bitterness instead of the sadness.

Suffice to say on more than one occasion, I wished that my tragedy had claimed me instead of them. The guilt of being the lone survivor was crushing—no, debilitating.

I don't give a damn how some think that God has an alternate plan for every one of us. Truth is, I stopped going to church and turned my back on The Big Guy shortly after the funeral. If there was a God, he wouldn't have allowed for something so horrible to happen in the first place.

Man and wife danced and I played my part quite easily, finding that I even enjoyed myself at times.

Despite my having fun, the exhaustion caused by my regular bouts of insomnia had me taking my leave when the crowd began to thin.

Mike grabbed my hand in a shake and patted my shoulder. "Thanks for being here, buddy."

"It wasn't exactly a hardship." I turned to Nicole. "And you…" I moved to kiss the newly-appointed Mrs. Withers' forehead. "Take care of him."

"You know I will," Nicole whispered and kissed my cheek.

I pulled away, holding the woman's hands in mine and looked over at Mike. "I can't believe you married Little Nikki, bro."

The man laughed and Nicole slapped my chest playfully. Mike wrapped his arms around his wife and held her back to his chest where she relaxed into him.

As I eyed their picture perfect demeanor of contentment, that all too familiar pang of jealousy made a resurgence. Clearing my throat, I hoped that my expression didn't give away my envy.

With a forced smile, and a pat on Mike's back, I took my leave.

The winding country road was dark, the night sky lacking light, with the moon's absence, loaning to the allure of eeriness.

I was almost to the city limits when something off to the side of the road caught my eye, causing me to stop whistling to the tune playing low on the radio.

But I didn't stop the car.

I hated this stretch of road. The one I had travelled nearly three years before. The one that had altered my life for the worst. There was a reason why a vast majority of the residents of Jacksonville dubbed it Dead Man's Way.

A few seconds later, the niggling in my gut had only worsened.

I was hell-bent on getting home, but that unsettling feeling begged me to turn around and check things out.

Making a U-turn, I headed back to investigate.

The closer I got, apprehension grew.

I pulled over, putting my four-ways on so my vehicle was visible to oncoming traffic, then left to check things out.

There, in a deep ditch lay an upturned SUV. It was so badly mangled that I wouldn't have been able to tell you what make and model it was had it not been for the insignia labeling the rear hatch.

Smoke billowed from somewhere at the front and I knew that it was only a matter of time before the vehicle went up in flames.

I grabbed my phone and dialed 911, requesting the slew of first responders. Then, I hurried to the vehicle to check on its occupant.

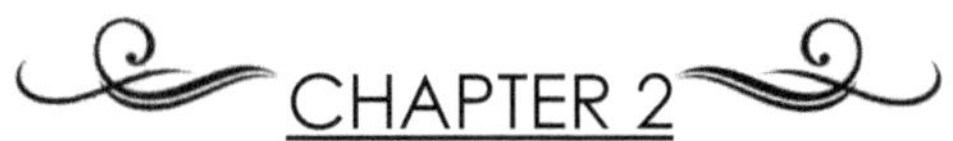

CHAPTER 2

It was my worst nightmare come to life. Two people hung upside down by their seat-belts in the front of the vehicle. At first glance, I could tell that the male passenger wasn't faring well. Having received some basic paramedic training, with closer inspection, it was evident that if the medics weren't on scene in the next ten minutes, his chances of survival would be slim.

I heard a groan coming from the driver's side. The female occupant was coming to. Due to her positioning, it was hard to make out the extent of her injuries with the abundance of blood and my lack of lighting. The dash had been pushed in, and it looked as if it pinned her legs, but without a flashlight, I couldn't tell for sure.

"Ma'am," I said when I got to her side of the car. I could smell fuel and, not knowing where the possible flame was in relation to the leakage, I was weary of staying so close to the vehicle.

"Help me," she pleaded, her bright green eyes met mine.

It was a sucker punch to the gut.

In that moment, I knew I couldn't leave her—*them*.

She tried to turn her head to the side.

"Don't move," I said. "You're hurt and we don't know how bad yet."

She tried to laugh, but it came out as a wince. "What was your first guess?" Coughing, a spatter of blood from her mouth made contact with the side of my face. "God, it hurts!"

I wiped the secretion from my cheek. "Can you tell me what hurts? What's your name?"

"H-hannah. Just call me Hannah. Everything..." Her eyes closed and silence consumed the darkness of the night.

"Hannah, I need you to try and stay awake. Can you do that for me?"

"Mmm." She mumbled drowsily. Seconds later, her body stiffened and her eyes shot open. "Lee! Where's–" She abruptly tried to lift and turn her head to the side. She must have been met with excruciating pain, what with the tortured cry she emitted.

"Help is coming." I reached to squeeze her hand. "I'm just going to go to the other side and check on him, okay? Just...don't move."

She capitulated with a weak, "Okay."

I went back to the other side of the car to check on Lee. As I felt at his carotid, despair filled me. No pulse.

I peered at Hannah and that's when I noticed their matching wedding bands.

Hanging my head, cursing internally, I did my best to stifle the surge of potent memories as well as emotions that surged to the forefront of my mind. I sat in silence, grieving for the loss she had yet to know of, flashes of my own past threatening to consume my very sanity.

"How is he?"

"H-he's okay," I lied. "He's in rough shape though."

"It's my fault. It's all my fault. I should have listened to him. Lee, I'm so sorry." Her hand searched for his, but with the way they were positioned, they were too far apart for her to make contact.

"You need to stay calm, Hannah."

She began to pray, and I went back to her side of the vehicle. I listened as she begged, bargained and pleaded with God that they walk away from their nightmare.

"What's your name?" she asked when she finished reciting her pleas.

"Ben." I couldn't help but reach for her hand again.

"He's not going to be okay is he, Ben?" Her voice held so much despair, making me want to lie again, but I couldn't bring myself to say the words.

"Hannah," I sighed, "let's just concentrate on getting you both out of here, okay?"

"Just say it! Why won't you tell me?"

I looked away from those bright green pools of hers that searched for hope where there was none. "I'm sorry."

She slipped her hand from beneath mine and began to cry silently. Overcome with her grief, her weeping gave way to sobs.

In that moment, I wished that I could take the pain of her loss away. I knew how it felt—what she was about to face—having been there myself.

In a flash, the front of the vehicle went up in flames, causing me to duck to the side to avoid the burst of hot air and debris.

Time was of the essence, and I had to act fast.

I looked around us and took action. "Change of plan, Hannah. I need to get you out of here. Can you move anything else other than your arms and head?"

"I'm stuck pretty tight, but I can try moving my legs." After a few seconds, she said, "I can feel my toes."

"That's good. That's really good. Can you try and slide your legs toward the door?"

I couldn't hear any rustling what with the crackling of the flames. "I-I'm stuck." She let out a tortured cry. "Oh, God, it hurts!"

My optimism of getting her out of her car took a nosedive.

"Dammit!" Despite knowing it wouldn't help, I punched my frustration on the side panel of the rear door.

As if they knew of Hannah's worsening predicament, the sirens in the distance could be heard, then the flashing lights to the emergency crews came into view.

"Hannah, they're coming." The woman's head slumped sideways. "No Hannah, open your eyes."

"Can't..." Her words were slurred. "So tired."

"You've got to try." I reached for her hand again. "You've got to fight."

"Please don't leave," she said. "I'm all alone."

"No, you're not." I squeezed her hand. "I'm right here. Just...just stay awake, okay? Talk to me."

Next thing I knew, I was pushed to the side. The crews went to work on dousing the flames that had grown in intensity far too quickly.

The door was pried open and we discovered that Hannah's legs were in fact pinned too tightly for her to dislodge herself on her own. They brought in a jack and extra lighting. The spotlight illuminated her bare legs, giving away their mangled state. Judging by the couple's attire, they had been on a night out.

The car's dash gave a loud creaking groan under the jack's pressure, but it was enough.

"Ben, we need to check you out," one of the medics said. The other medic was putting a c-collar around Hannah's neck, prior to removing her from the vehicle.

Seeing as Hannah was conscious and able to move her legs—barely—I gave into the man's request, sitting to the side as he checked me for signs of smoke and fume inhalation. I knew I was fine. Even if I weren't, Hannah was in worse shape, and I was more concerned about her getting the care that she required over me.

Extricated from the car, Hannah was carried to a gurney. When she spoke next, I realized that not only were her words slurred, but they no longer made sense.

"She's crashing," the female attendant said. "Let's load her up. We'll work on her on the way."

I got up quickly and grabbed the driver's arm before he could jump into his seat. "Will she be okay, Craig?" The man and I have had our share of calls together in the past.

He seemed surprised at my concern. We were trained to remain somewhat detached with those we rescued, and for the most part, I didn't have much of an issue doing that. Except this once. The man's lips formed a thin line. "I don't know. You're welcome to follow us."

I shook my head. "Just keep me posted, all right? I need to get home."

His brows furrowed, but he nodded after giving me a long assessing gaze. "Sounds fair."

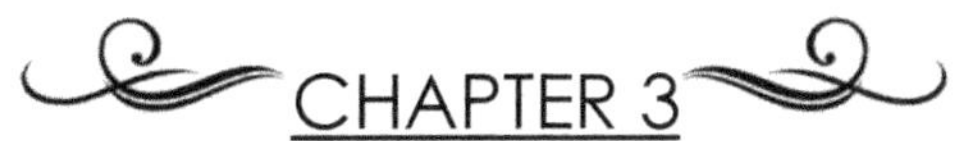

CHAPTER 3

I'm not sure why I went home. God knows I wasn't going to be able to sleep, due in part to the adrenaline coursing through my veins, but also because of Hannah's piercing irises.

Hannah.

I paced the main hallway to my home wondering why I felt so guilty.

You promised her.

I paused mid-step and ran my hands over my face letting out a loud sigh. I never uttered the oath, but I did say that I wasn't going to leave her. Those words, on the side of that treacherous stretch of road, had been as good as a promise in my book.

With rough hands, I undid my tie with a jerk, chucking it on the back of the leather sling-back chair in my study before I proceeded to unbutton the collar of my shirt. I allowed my butt to collapse onto the seat behind me.

So why wasn't I with her?

Simply put, I didn't know anything about Hannah other than her first name. *And those eyes.* Yes, those pleading eyes that seared my soul. So helpless, so desperate…so familiar.

For whatever reason—maybe it was the similarity of our situations—the night's events had shaken me to my core.

The longer I sat there, pondering the reasons, the more I grew apprehensive.

"I don't even know her full name," I said to the walls surrounding me. What if she didn't remember who I was and what she'd asked of me when she woke?

What if she does?

That thought alone had me getting to my feet and reaching for my keys.

You've got to be losing your ever-loving mind, Ben.

Locking the front door, I jumped in my car for a destination at which I wasn't quite sure I belonged—but I was going to live up to my word.

I lost count of how many times I circled the parking lot after I arrived. When I found my resolve, I put my car in park, turned its engine off, and sat there staring out the windshield.

Craig, the paramedic I'd spoken to earlier, walked out of the ambulance bay door. I made a mad dash toward him, hitting the key fob to activate my car's alarm from across the lot.

"Hey, Craig!"

The man turned to face me. His face was grim and I felt my heart sink to the pit of my stomach. My feet came to a dead halt a few feet from him.

"Is…is she…" I couldn't finish, but what surprised me was the tremendous relief I felt when Craig shook his head.

"No. She's alive, but we ran into complications on the way. She went into full arrest, but Lindsay managed to resuscitate her."

As if once wasn't enough, by the time the rig had arrived, Hannah had crashed a second time. She was now in the OR.

"She looked in rough shape, but…" I ran my hand through my gelled brown hair and down my face, releasing a loud sigh.

"Hey man, you okay? You're all bent out of shape."

"It's nothing. Long day."

"Listen…" His gaze turned, assessing much like it had at the scene. "I've got to get this rig back to the garage, clean, and restock it."

"Yeah, you do that." I blew out a puff of air. "Hey, Craig?"

He paused before getting into the ambulance. "Yeah?"

"Did you manage to get her last name? I mean…"

His brows drew together. "Parsons."

My nod was curt. "Thanks."

Craig paused before turning his key in the ignition and gave me one last once over. "Are you sure you're okay?"

I waved my hand as if to brush his concern off. "I'm fine." I wasn't, really, but he didn't need to know about the turmoil I felt inside. So, I chased my words with a quirk of my upper lip, hoping it was enough to appease Craig.

It worked.

CHAPTER 4

When Craig retreated, I turned toward the Emergency Room entrance, observing the chaos of an unruly weekend night through the floor-to-ceiling windows.

I wondered if any of Hannah's relatives had been contacted, if any of those people sitting in those waiting room seats, at the very moment, were there for her.

I walked through the sliding glass doors to be met by crying babies and an assortment of worried, sickly and irritated people. I smiled when I saw Marie at the triage desk. Her familiar face helped assuage the small bout of nerves that suddenly consumed me.

"Hey, Marie, I need a favor."

The woman looked at me with an arched brow, her eyes travelling from my face down to my toes and then came back up to stop at my shirt.

"What the hell happened to you?"

I followed her gaze and peered down at myself. My front was covered in soot, dirt and dried blood. Not once had it occurred to me to change my clothes before leaving the house.

"That's why I'm here. A woman was brought in not too long ago. I was the one who called 911 and stayed with her until they came."

"Her name?"

"Hannah Parsons."

"You know I shouldn't be doing this, right?"

"I promised her. She lost her husband tonight. I-I promised her that I wouldn't leave. I just want to know if she's okay." With those words, and the desperation in my voice, the look in her eyes shifted to one of recognition, then sympathy. She had been there that night when my family and I were brought in.

Marie gulped and nodded. "Okay," she whispered. She paused before her fingers made contact with the keyboard in front of her. "Ben, are you okay?"

"Why is everyone asking me that?" My sudden burst of frustration caught me by surprise.

"It's just…" She was bringing up the past. "Look, I'm sorry, okay?"

"No, I'm sorry. I'm fine, really. It's been a long day. I guess I'm just a little tired."

She nodded, gave me a forced smile and proceeded to find the information I'd requested. "She's still in surgery, there's no room assignment yet."

"Can you tell me if her next of kin has been contacted?"

"She had nothing with her when they brought her in, but the police are looking into it." I nodded. "I'm not supposed to do this, but–"

"Is Hannah Parsons' family here?" I heard behind me.

"Here," I said without thinking and turned to the voice, dismissing the arched brow and tight-lipped expression that had made its way onto Marie's face.

The man in surgical scrubs eyed me from top to bottom. "Well you look like you've seen better days," the mid-fifty year old doctor said before presenting his hand. "I'm Doctor Caruthers. I'm the surgeon who operated on Mrs. Parsons. What's your relation to the patient?"

"I found her."

"You're family?"

"No, not exactly, but–"

"They can't seem to locate her family, Doctor," Marie interjected.

The man nodded.

"How is she?" I asked.

"I'm afraid I'm not at liberty to discuss that with anyone but her family," the man said.

"But–"

"Excuse me, but we got a call about our daughter being brought here?"

"Name?" Marie asked.

"Hannah Parsons?"

"Mrs. Parsons' parents I presume?" Doctor Caruthers said, and I turned to stand beside him.

The older couple turned toward us and looking into the woman's face, it was unmistakable that she was Hannah's mother. I'd recognize those emerald eyes anywhere.

"Yes," the man said as he squeezed his wife into his side in an effort to support her. The woman stood there, her eyes fused to my shirt and then meeting mine, her expression one of inquiry. Her husband must have noticed her diverted attention because he addressed me next. "Who are you?"

"I was–"

"He was on the scene with your daughter," the doctor supplied.

"How are they doing?" Hannah's father asked.

"You haven't heard?" Caruthers's tone sounded so robotic I wanted to hit the man and let him know that he needed to brush up on his people skills, despite his obvious years of practice.

Hannah's mother's eyes were still on me and I could no longer hold anyone's gaze. With my eyes set on my feet, the woman's whispery voice asked, "He's not okay, is he?"

"No, ma'am," I said before the doctor had the chance and lifted my gaze back to hers. "He died before the emergency team got there."

The woman emitted some sort of squeak, seeking refuge in her husband's chest, where he held her tight, her body shaking with quiet sobs.

"How's our daughter?" he asked, his voice quivering.

Doctor Caruthers escorted Hannah's parents away from me before providing them with an answer, which I listened in for regardless. "Hannah's status is critical right now, but she is stable."

"She's going to pull through though, right?" Her father's tone of desperation had me gulping down the surge of emotion that burned my throat.

"It's too early to determine that," Caruthers said. "Your daughter lost a lot of blood. She arrested en route and crashed once more upon her arrival. For all intents and purposes, she should be fine physically."

"What do you mean she should be fine?" he inquired.

"She was unresponsive to our efforts for longer than I would have liked." Regardless of that dire news, the health professional had the audacity to continue his mechanical speech. "We're not sure if she'll wake up."

"No," the man whispered.

I saw the signs before anyone else.

Before he could collapse to the floor, his wife nowhere near strong enough to hold him up, I rushed to the man's side and stabilized him before leading him to a nearby chair, crouching down beside him along with his wife.

"But she can wake up, right, Doctor?" I asked. I'd be damned if I let this quack leave these folks without an ounce of hope or optimism.

"Well, sure." The man met my stare. "It's always good to remain positive about these things."

I straightened to my feet, then faced off with the man who held all the answers. "What did the neurological tests say?" I questioned again.

"They…they showed some activity," he sputtered, but regained his composure. "Listen, I understand that you were there to help, but I believe that this matter should be—"

"Can we see her?" Hannah's mother cut in, her hand squeezing my forearm in a gesture of appreciation.

"Right this way." Caruthers made an abrupt turn and proceeded to walk down the corridor without waiting for them.

My feet stayed glued in place as I watched the sixty-something couple get up and walk away, clutching at each other like they were each other's lifelines.

My ass made contact with the nearest chair, and my head hung in my hands as I leaned my elbows on my knees.

A relieved breath escaped my lips.

She's alive.

It could have been a minute like it could have been hours, I don't know, but when I felt a gentle hand on my shoulder, I looked up. Hannah's mother stood before me and offered her hand.

"Thank you for being there," she said with a tearful gaze. "What's your name?"

"Ben Carpenter, ma'am."

"Benjamin," she said, and somehow I didn't cringe at my full name being used like I had so many times in the past. Only my parents got away by calling me by my birth name. "Would you like to see her?"

"I…" I swallowed the ball of dust that had formed in my throat. "You and Mr.…" I realized that I had no clue if Parsons was their name or Hannah's married name.

"Donner," she supplied, with a sad smile. She wrapped her arm around my elbow and started tugging to get me to my feet.

Standing in front of her, I said, "You and Mr. Donner should take this time with Hannah."

"But you promised her."

My head snapped in her direction. "How'd–"

"The nurse at the desk." She looked toward where Marie had been. "I came back to ask her for your contact information to thank you for all that you've done. She said you hadn't left yet, and pointed me in your direction." I nodded. "Call me Anne." She paused just outside a door and looked at me as if she was waiting on something. "Well, aren't you going to go in?"

My mind was so far off that I hadn't even realized we'd been walking. I looked at the room's number and took a fortifying breath. Gesturing with my arm, I said, "After you."

When my feet crossed the threshold, I came to a halt. The tubes, the wires, the bandages, the mechanical beeps from the monitoring machines—they all brought back so many horrible memories.

"Benjamin?" Mrs. Donner said.

I forced my eyes from my feet, Hannah's parents both fixing me with worried gazes. I managed to put one foot in front of the other and made it halfway to their side before I caught sight of Hannah's sleeping face. And I froze again. "I–" I shook my head. "I'm sorry, I can't. I can't do this." I turned and hightailed it out of there with no further explanation.

CHAPTER 5

I've never run away from anything or anyone so damn fast in my entire life.

When my eyes fell upon Hannah's face, a wealth of emotion overwhelmed me. Fear for her life, empathy for what she and her family were going through, sadness for the loss and guilt.

Guilt for not being able to do more to save her husband.

Guilt for not stopping right away when I knew I'd seen something.

Guilt…guilt…guilt!

Was this how I was destined to live my entire life? Feeling guilty for shit that I wasn't responsible for, for things that were out of my control?

I snorted.

Funny how one can rationalize how they should and shouldn't feel, yet they can't seem to control the end result.

I sat in my car, pondering my reasons for running, for caring. Finding an answer as to why I seem to end up in situations where I'm forced to relive my past.

I looked up. Had I been sitting in my car that long? Mr. and Mrs. Donner walked out of the hospital's front entrance with Anne turning to and collapsing into her husband's arms. Her shaking shoulders indicated proof to her sobbing. He kissed her hair as he wrapped himself around her. It was an intimate moment that shouldn't have been shared, but there I was taking it all in, wishing that I had a pillar of strength at my side.

With Candace gone, I would never have that kind of support.

Hannah won't have it either.

The Donners walked toward the parking lot, and instead of starting my car to leave, I took the keys out of the ignition and jiggled them in my hands. I could forget sleeping for tonight. Too much had happened within the last twenty-four hours to ensure that. With a sudden bout of determination, I got out of the car, locked it, and marched my way toward the building. Visiting hours were over, but I made like I knew where I was heading and no one bothered to stop me. There were perks to a busy night.

Despite my nerves, something filled me with resolve during my earlier pondering session in the car.

Hannah and I had suffered similar fates. It's hard to explain, but it bonded us, somehow.

I walked through her room's doorway and instead of being consumed with old memories, this time I forced my brain to remain on the present, to focus on the fact that this wasn't about me—it was about Hannah.

I stood by her bed, looking down at her battered body.

A memory flashed in my mind. The image of those petrified eyes of hers that had looked at me, the sarcasm that had come out of her mouth despite her predicament and pain, the trust she had put in me to stay with her.

Would she remember this night when she woke up?

For her sake, and from personal experience, part of me hoped that she didn't.

But that would mean she wouldn't know who you are. Somehow, the thought of that possibility saddened me.

"I've got to be losing it," I said aloud. "Hannah, if you can hear me, I'm still here." I allowed my fingers to skim the tips of hers before I sat down on the chair next to her bed.

CHAPTER 6

I woke to a hand on my shoulder. Jumping up had been a bad move as I felt the painful stiffness in my neck.

Where the hell am I?

Looking around, taking in the rhythmic beeping of machines, the medicinal scent of the air, I remembered. Embarrassment filled me the moment I looked up into Anne Donner's eyes.

"You came back?"

"I…uh…" I didn't know what to say, so I nodded.

One look out the window and I realized that it was morning. I never meant to spend what little that was left of the night there, but for some reason sitting at Hannah's bedside had filled me with a sense of calm I hadn't felt at night in a long time.

"Benjamin, are you all right?" Anne asked.

I nodded and got up, feeling foolish. The woman was sweet, but how could she not be worried about a total stranger spending the night at her newly widowed daughter's bedside?

It had been a mistake.

I cleared my throat. "I should go."

"Wait!" She grabbed my arm as I tried to make my way past her. "Will you be back?"

I looked down. "I don't know." *I want to.*

I looked up once more into the older and wiser version of Hannah's eyes and felt like the woman saw through me. It was as if she could see my deepest and darkest secrets; the ones I wanted to leave dead and buried. The longer she looked at me, the more I wanted to put distance between us.

As I made to move away, she wrapped her arms around me.

My arms went from limp at my sides to giving her an awkward pat on the back.

She pulled back, smiled and reached up to cup my cheek. "You're a good man. I hope you come back, Mr. Carpenter."

"Ben. Just Ben, ma'am." I forced a smile. I turned and Mr. Donner was walking into the room. "Sir." I nodded my head.

"Son, I know my wife said it last night, but thank you." The man stuck out his hand and I looked down at it for a few seconds before I took and shook it.

"I'm glad I was able to do anything at all." I looked toward their daughter. "I better go."

I drove home from the hospital absentmindedly, not realizing where I was headed until I looked up.

It was a stop I had made far more times than I cared to count, but seeing as I'd already been this week, I was confused as to why I had ended up here.

The cemetery gates loomed before me as I drove through them and parked the car on a drawn out sigh. I got out and walked the solemn and lonely path to the two plots that awaited me like they did every week.

Kneeling before the tombstones, I ran my fingertips over their names.

Candace.

Karen.

My two girls.

The habitual ball of emotions clogged my throat. I missed them both so much.

For however long I stayed, my peace was interrupted by a car door slamming shut behind me.

I paid it no heed. It was a public place after all.

"I love you, my girls," I whispered before getting to my feet.

Turning to leave, my body halted first with surprise—then trepidation took hold.

"Ben."

The incessant lump in my throat grew and brought forth a very familiar feeling of suffocation. Candace's parents stood before me.

"How are you, Ben?" Betty asked.

"I'm okay." I knew my appearance sure as hell didn't convey that. Why had I ended up here instead of at home where I should have been all along?

Don's gaze took my appearance in. His eyes showed worry. "You look like you've seen better days."

"I've been getting a lot of that lately." I tried my hand at smirking. "I should get going, it's nice seeing you both. Take care."

I should have known that Don wouldn't let me make my escape in a quick and painless fashion. He rarely did these days.

He followed me to my car. "We have some things of Candace's that she'd want you to have, Ben."

I took a deep breath and paused with my hand on the door before turning to face the man. "Not now, Don."

"You know, there was a day when you used to call me Dad."

I couldn't look him in the eyes. "I-I can't. Not anymore."

In a rush to get out of there before he said something else, I opened the car door and paused to look back at the man that had been as much of a father to me as my own.

"It's been three years. You need to stop blaming yourself, Ben. No one else does."

That was it.

I got in my car without acknowledging his words, started it, and peeled out of there.

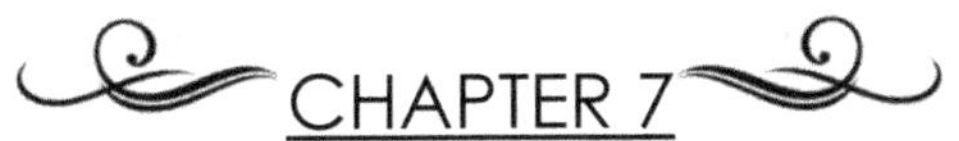

CHAPTER 7

I called my bar manager, Derek, on the drive home, and told him that I needed him to look after Fairfax for the day.

I walked out of the shower stall, my towel hanging around my waist. The good thing about daytime was the fact that I was able to sleep whenever the opportunity presented itself. I shed my towel and crawled naked under the sheets.

A smorgasbord of thoughts ran through my head as I settled onto my back.

Candace.

Hannah.

Hannah some more.

Then, back to Candace.

The more I thought about my wife, however, the more my mind flittered back to thoughts of Hannah. Knowing her pain, I worried about what she was about to go through. It wasn't going to be an easy journey. Hell, after three years I was still struggling.

I woke with a start.

Those piercing green eyes had been there, pleading with me.

If one thing was for sure, that dream had me resolving that I needed to abide by my word and stay at Hannah's side.

At least until she wakes up and tells you to get lost, Carpenter.

I got up, headed to the bathroom, and splashed some cold water on my face. Staring back at my reflection, I took in my light brown hair laying in all sorts of directions, the dark circles under my eyes, and my pale complexion. My stomach rumbled, and that's when I realized that it was nearing dinnertime and I hadn't eaten anything since the night before at Mike and Nicole's reception.

Grabbing a quick bite after dressing in jeans and a t-shirt, I headed out the door. Before I could take my first step, however, my foot ran into a box, nearly sending me tumbling down the front steps.

One look at the brown cardboard and there was no question as to what it held.

I don't need this right now!

Bending over, I picked the box up, turned to drop my keys on the small table by the front door, after kicking it shut, and set the load down on the coffee table in my living room. Staring at it, I backed away from the cardboard container as if it might contain a communicable disease of some sort.

I knew what I would face if I lifted that lid, and I was terrified that the hell I had been living these past few years would worsen to an unbearable level if I did just that. Fighting through my weariness, I sat down and made to peek inside.

In that box, I found notebooks—five of them, to be exact. They matched others I had found around the house after Candace's death. Why they hadn't been kept here, I don't know. Upon opening them, I found Candace's neat scripture.

"I love that man…" This made me smile.

"He's asked me to be his finally…" This made me remember.

"Chris is…"

Hold on!

I re-read the last few words of the passage I was scanning.

My heart began to pound. My eyes bulged at what I read—twice!

That's when I realized that this was a whole new set of journals. Journals I was never meant to see. Journals written by a woman, that up until moments ago, I thought loved me.

No, it's not possible.

But then, masochistic curiosity struck, despite my wanting to deny what I had just read. My eyes flittered to the top of the page where I knew I'd most likely find a date.

My heart sunk.

The book dropped to the floor.

Chris.

That name had come up before.

And then something clicked.

"You've got to be fucking kidding me!" I bolted to my feet and flung the box and sent its remaining contents crashing to the floor.

Glass shattered, but then again, so did more of my heart.

Anger simmered at a low boil, my temper barely in check, but I hadn't finished sorting through the items, and now I had a mess to clean, forcing me to do just that.

Crouching down, I turned the box up and peered inside. In it, there was a glass figurine. I remembered it. Candace had it since college. She'd kept it in her office.

That's when I realized that this stuff must have come from work.

As I lifted some folder from the box, something slipped out of it and landed at my feet. I bent down to pick it up.

A photograph with the following caption:

> *One year and I love you more everyday.*
> *Love,*
> *Candy*

I flipped the photograph over and there he was in Technicolor. Chris.

The ex who had given her the figurine.

A man I'd invited over for dinner, along with his wife—a man I had shaken hands with on numerous occasions.

Candace's boss—*no*—lover.

My hands shook with rage, my fingers releasing the piece of paper as if it had singed me.

I looked down at the notebooks, and then at the fallen photograph. Dropping the file folder on the table, I backed away.

The air around me was getting too thick, my lungs felt like they were closing up.

I need to get out of here.

Grabbing my keys, I locked the front door, jumped in my car, and headed for…well, I'm not sure where I was headed, but far away from home sounded pretty damn good right about then!

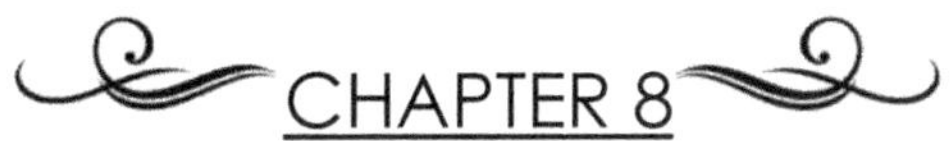

CHAPTER 8

I pounded on that door so hard my hand felt as if it would be bruised from my efforts.

"What the hell is your problem? I've got–" Danica's face went from furious to concerned in a nanosecond. "Ben, what's going on?"

"I-I don't...I didn't..." I couldn't find the words to explain myself for coming to her, but she was the only one I could think of with Mike being off on his honeymoon.

Danica grabbed my wrist, pulled me in, and closed the front door before ushering me toward the kitchen.

She made me sit down and went to the fridge to get me a bottle of water.

I'm not a man who drinks to excess, but I sure as hell could have done with more than aqua right then.

"Ben, you're scaring me. What's going on?"

"She cheated," I choked out.

"Who?"

"Candace."

"What?"

I snorted. "My thoughts exactly."

"With who?"

I ran a hand down my face, swallowing the taste of bile in my mouth. "Her boss."

"What?"

My head bobbed up and down, my gaze failing to meet hers.

Jake entered the kitchen. "Hey, man, you look like shit."

"Thanks."

Jake looked between his wife and I. "Something's wrong, I can smell it." He crossed his arms. "Why do I feel like something big just happened?"

I looked at Jake, then met Danica's eyes. The room remained silent for a moment until I gave her the nod that granted permission for her to inform her husband. Jake looked at me with shock strewn across his face as he received the news.

Shock was only the icing on the cake for me. Beneath that layer was one of betrayal, and another of worthlessness. Oh, and let's not forget the embarrassment, too. It was like I had married a stranger, like I had loved someone I had never known.

It had all been a lie.

Was Karen even mine?

A new wave of fury built with that lingering question.

I got up to leave without a word.

"Where're you going?" Danica asked.

"I think I'll find my answers if I sit down and read those journals."

"Are you sure that's smart?" Jake asked.

"I think it's time that I get past all of this, don't you?" I eyed them both, far from enthused at my surely self-imposed torture. "I can't…" I sighed. "I can't believe I've been stuck like this for so long and all of it was a lie."

"Not all of it, Ben." Danica walked up to me and grabbed my hands. "That beautiful baby girl you had. You know that Karen was yours even if she wasn't. The love you had for both of them was real too."

My chortle lacked any humor. "It clearly didn't mean much to her."

"Promise me that if you need anything, you'll call." I gave her a curt nod. "But I think you're right. You should read those journals."

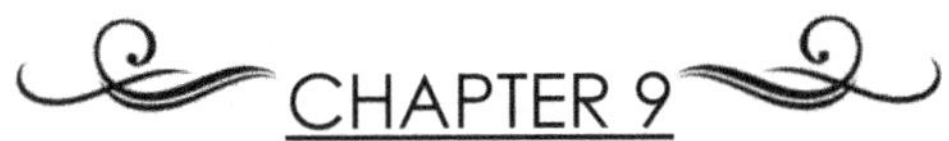

CHAPTER 9

After stopping by the house to grab everything I needed, I walked into the hospital as if I belonged there.

I had a plan.

One that would spare me a few grey hairs from the stress I was under, some bald spots from the anger that simmered, and an aneurism from the shock factor that was bound to make my blood pressure rise until something burst.

Again, just like last night, no one made to stop me from entering Hannah's room. Aside from my home—which didn't feel like much of a peaceful place right now—this was it.

I felt nervous, worried even.

Hannah lay connected to a variety of machines. Some of her color had returned even though she was still unconscious.

I approached her bedside, careful not to make too much noise as if I'd wake her.

The bruising was more pronounced as I took in the sight of her arms, shoulders, and the bit of bare skin on her chest and neck. Her face, aside from a slight scratch on her left cheek, was intact, perfect even.

My hand reached out to touch the side of her face. When I realized what I was doing, I snapped it back. I had no right. Instead, I took the seat by her bed.

For a few minutes I sat there watching over her in silence. And felt like a total idiot while doing it, too.

I wanted to talk to someone for the first time in years and

I mean *really* talk. Bare it all, as they say. It baffled me that the one person I wanted to talk to was a stranger who'd thrust herself into my life in the most unconventional of ways. Someone who couldn't talk back, someone I wasn't sure that could even hear what I was about to tell her.

"Hi Hannah, it's Ben," I said. "You look better." *You look better?* "If you can hear me at all, I bet you're wondering why I came back, huh?" Despite feeling ridiculous, I never made to leave. "I know I said that I'd stay, but you probably figured that with your parents around that I'd be long gone by now."

Something told me that if she were like every other woman I probably would have been. But she wasn't. Don't ask me how I knew it, I just did.

"I-I don't know what to do with myself anymore, but I do have a story to share with you."

I went on, telling Hannah about my wife and daughter. Our wedding. Our life together. The day I found out I was going to be a father. How much I loved them both, despite the boiling anger in my gut where Candace's betrayal was concerned. And then I talked about that awful night where I lost everything, but my very own existence.

The more I spoke, the more the weirdness of speaking to a comatose person faded. If anything, it felt right. Like somehow, in the recesses of her mind, Hannah was indeed listening, processing and supporting me with no judgement.

I didn't stop myself for grabbing the tips of her fingers in my hand this time. "I know what you'll be going through, once you wake up." I cleared my throat. "Hannah, I'm so sorry I couldn't do anything to save Lee. You two should be together right now, enjoying life, making babies, laughing. Maybe if I'd stopped when I first saw you…I should have." I sighed.

"There's more." I took in a preparatory breath. "When I left here this morning, I went to visit Candace and Karen's graves. Her parents were there. They've been pushing for me to stop blaming myself for what happened that night and move on for years now." That's when my hand took hers completely and squeezed it. "I ran away, Hannah. I ran from them like a coward.

"They've been trying to get me to talk to them. They had some things of Candy's to give me." I paused to get my thoughts together. "You see, not too long after she passed, I found journals of hers while I packed up her stuff. Today, her parents left another box of her things on my front doorstep." I squeezed her hand again. "This is hard to say." My voice had grown hoarse.

"You know when you think life is perfect? Well, I'm not claiming that Candace and I didn't have our share of issues, but I thought that we were happy." I sighed. "I never thought…"

For the first time, I felt the tears come, and I let them fall unchecked.

"It was all a lie, Hannah. Everything was. I'm not sure why I'm telling you any of this. Maybe it's because I know you'll listen, since I've heard that talking to someone in your state can help bring you out of it. Personally, I think it's because coma patients just get sick of hearing the same people over and over again so they wake up to tell them to shut up." I chuckled, wiping the few stray tears on my cheeks with the back of my free hand. "The truth is that somehow this is where I feel most comfortable at the moment.

"I've spent the last three years grieving for a woman who was my whole life only to find out that I was never hers. Not if these journals I brought with me today are anything to go by." I ran my hand through my hair and bowed my head to stare at the leather-bound notebooks on my lap. "I know I need to read them to really know what was in her heart, but I can't do it at home." On a long exhale, I continued. "Honestly, I'm not sure I can read them at all, but being here makes me feel like I might be able to."

With that, I opened the first one and began to read aloud. Call me crazy, but it felt odd yet right to share something so private with Hannah.

I managed to read the first two entries. They dated back

to right before I'd proposed to Candace. After those, I wasn't sure if I could go on with my reading, nausea making my gut churn.

I closed the book, put it on Hannah's bedside table and leaned forward on my knees, running my hands over my face.

"I wish I knew what you were thinking right about now," I said. "You know what's surprising? That despite the anger, all of this actually makes me feel better. Finding out that my wife loved another man makes it easier, Hannah. How can that be?"

"Because you're angry," I heard, making me turn, eyes wide that I had been discovered.

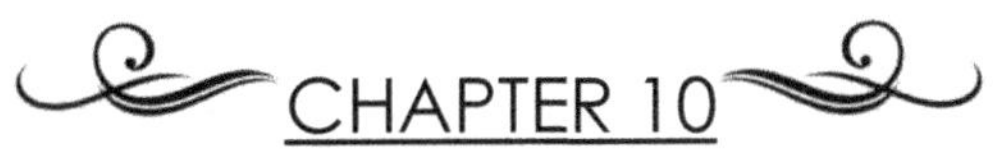

CHAPTER 10

"**A**nger can help you move on, sweetheart."

"Mrs. Donner." Mr. Donner walked in behind her. "Sir."

"I'm sorry for your loss." Her voice was soft, compassionate. "It explains why you hesitated last night." I nodded. "I'm glad you came back."

"How's our girl doing?" Mr. Donner asked.

I spent the next few hours sitting in Hannah's hospital room, talking with her parents. I was glad that they hadn't asked much about Candace, especially after they'd overheard some of what I had told their daughter.

There was an odd chemistry between the three of us that had me feeling comfortable, despite us having only met less than twenty-four hours before. The conversation flowed. It was almost as though we had known each other for years.

Anne and Adam Donner were wonderful people. They loved their daughter without reservation. I found myself wishing that I had the same support from my parents after my loss.

You did.

Instead of accepting their help though, I had pushed everyone aside, friends and family alike.

Through most of my life, my problems had always been my own. The pity and sympathy that rolled off of friends and loved ones in waves made me run from them.

When everyone seemed to back away and give up, Mike was the only one who hadn't. The man had never pitied me. Instead, he chose to be there, helping me pick up the pieces and lend a listening ear.

My parents had done the same at first, but I guess they never quite had as much resolve as my best friend did.

I've kept in touch with Mom and Dad, but nothing had ever been the same since. There existed a chasm between us now, where before I used to be able to go to them and talk about anything. I knew my distance broke my mother's heart, leaving my father to put her back together when my appearances at family gatherings were always so short-lived. But I didn't know how to cope, despite my trying.

I was a crap son.

Guilt rode me for that, too.

"You've been through a lot, haven't you?" Anne finally asked after I told them about my family situation.

I held her eyes. "That's an understatement."

"You have time to make things right. Things are never perfect, Ben," she said. "Hannah would agree."

"What do you mean?"

"Anne?" Adam said.

"I think it's time we all came to terms, Adam." Her gaze came to me quickly before heading for her husband and locking. "Lee might have been the son we never had, but the man was far from perfect."

I was confused. What were they getting at? "I'm not sure if you should be telling me this." Despite disliking gossip, I felt intrigued by the information and couldn't help wanting to hear more.

"Nonsense," Anne said and took a deep breath, letting it out slowly. "Lee was no angel."

I nodded. What man truly was? Life would be too boring if we didn't have a little bad boy nature in us. Some guys just happened to possess more than others, and turned it into a lifestyle.

"Lee may have appeared put-together, but he had a dark side," she said.

"Anne." Adam shook his head. "Let's not–"

She snorted before ignoring her husband and turned to me to explain. "Lee loved to drink. Hell, he loved to party. I didn't think it was that big of an issue, mainly because we only saw him at large family events and everyone enjoyed themselves, Hannah included."

"That's hardly anything bad," I said to which Adam snorted and that gained my attention. There was something more to this story.

Anne's next words came out with a growl akin one of motherly protection. "True, but it is when he became an ungrateful and abusive bastard."

"What?" Adam exploded. "If that–"

"Honey, please let me explain," she said.

Adam and I listened as Anne told us about Lee. The more she went on, the more I found myself looking at Hannah and wondering why she had ever stayed with him. She had a heart—a good one at that—but she was naïve and it had cost her some happiness over the years.

Lee, as it turns out, was an alcoholic. The only time he drank was for work and family functions, which pretty much was all of the time. Soon enough, he'd quit hiding his need for his vice altogether.

"It wasn't until he got charged with a DUI a month ago that Hannah called me crying. I made her come clean." Anne brushed a tear from her cheek. "He was an abusive drunk when provoked. I didn't know for sure, but I'd suspected something the last few times we got together."

"Why didn't you–" Adam's fists were clutched at his sides, anger evident.

"She didn't want you to know everything yet because she was terrified of how you'd react," she told her husband. "She has such a big heart. You know our Hannah. She didn't want to leave him because we taught her that when you love someone, you don't desert them in their greatest time of need. After she told me about what was going on though, I think she'd figured out that there comes a time…I think she was planning to leave him."

I nodded and looked over at Adam whose gaze was upon his daughter, his lips in a thin line, his eyes soft and sad.

"As bad as it may seem, maybe this heartbreak might give her the chance to start fresh," Anne said and locked her gaze on me. "She needs something good in her life, just like you do, Ben."

My heart began to race. "What makes you think that I don't have that?"

"Have you truly moved on in the last three years?" Her eyes were locked with mine in that maternal gaze of assessment mothers often have. "I may be happily married to Adam, but I'm not blind, Benjamin. You should have a woman by your side, and you don't."

"She's right, you know," Adam said.

"I just haven't found anyone." Truth was I didn't want anyone until very recently. "I'm fine here talking with you folks."

"That's nice of you to say." Anne smiled. "But you need–"

"Look, I can't give my heart to anyone when there's barely any of it left to give," I said. "No one wants an emotionless monster who can't love them right. I may want to find someone, but after today's blow…I couldn't even keep the woman I loved happy. What makes you think that I can with someone else?" I took a deep breath. "I'm sorry."

"For what?" Anne's hand squeezed my upper arm. "For feeling? For telling us exactly how you think of yourself? You have far too small of an opinion of yourself, boy. Your mother may not be here to tell you because you've pushed her away, so I see fit to tell you like it is. You're a good man. A man who promised something to a stranger, and kept his word. From where I'm standing, you're as good as they get. You're no emotional cripple. You feel just fine. You're still grieving because you haven't allowed yourself to go through the process. You haven't fully committed to the grief. Your feelings of guilt are for things that were out of your control. You're mad because–"

"Because everything over the last ten years has been a lie," I whispered.

Anne nodded. "It's a huge blow and I get that, but Ben, don't you want to be happy again?"

Did I want to be happy again?

Now that was a loaded question!

Leaving my home and cell numbers with the Donners, so they could call me if they needed anything, I chose to ponder Anne's words on my way home.

Except I never went home.

Parked on the street, I grabbed Candace's journals and got out of the car, relieved that the lights were still on. I walked up to the door and knocked rather than using the doorbell and waited.

"Benjamin!"

"Hi, Mama."

CHAPTER 11

My mother held me as if I were her little boy again. With my head buried in her neck, I soaked up the comfort she offered and allowed my reeling emotions to take over, despite us standing there on the front porch for the neighborhood to see.

"Son?" I looked up to find my father standing in the entrance. He seemed just about as shocked as my mother had been to see me standing there.

I didn't have to say anything. My father hurried to my mother and me, and wrapped his arms around both of us.

"What is this?" Dad asked when we pulled apart and he was eying the notebooks in my arms.

Mom pulled me through the threshold as Dad closed the front door behind us.

"It's a long story is what it is, Dad."

My feet carried me to the living room and I plopped myself down on the couch, leaving the books on the coffee table.

I held the bridge of my nose between thumb and forefinger and sighed, resigned to tell my parents everything I knew; to talk to them like I was once able to. "It was all a lie according to these." I motioned toward the brown leatherbound books.

For the first time since before the accident, I was able to open up quite easily. My father listened with his face studious and lips in a thin line with my mother at his side, crying silent tears as I delivered a play-by-play of what had transpired since the night of Mike and Nikki's wedding.

As I finished, I sighed. "I feel so foolish."

"You shouldn't," Dad said. "She hid it well from everyone. Have you talked to Betty and Don about this?"

"No, but now I think that's why they've been around more lately."

Mom cursed under her breath. "So you think they knew and never told you?"

"I have a feeling that they've known and wanted to tell me for a while now. They must have given up on waiting. They dropped the box of her office stuff on my doorstep this morning."

I was beginning to think of Candace's parents' intrusion as somewhat of a blessing in disguise. How much longer would I have denied them the transfer of those belongings had they not forced it? How long would I have been in the dark, before knowing that my marriage was a sham?

"I think you owe them a visit," Mom said. "Give them a chance to explain things, and if they don't know about these diaries, then I suggest that maybe you tell them."

"I don't know, Mom."

"They're your family too," Dad said. "Just because she's gone doesn't mean that–"

"I know, all right?" I said. "I just…I don't know what to say. This news is going to hurt them."

Mom nodded, but Dad said, "It might, but the truth needs to come out for everyone involved. I think it's time to put the past to rest, don't you?"

I spent the next half hour uttering profuse apologies for my pushing them to the side, and explained all that was going on in my life. Mom had moved to my side and held my hand.

"I told you that he'd come to his senses," Dad said to my mother.

I hated to think as to how much longer I would have

remained withdrawn had that box never appeared and forced me to start accepting things.

"So how's that lady doing?" Mom asked about Hannah.

As if I hadn't shared enough with my folks, I launched into more details about Hannah, how her accident had made me feel, how worried I was for her—both physically and emotionally—and her folks.

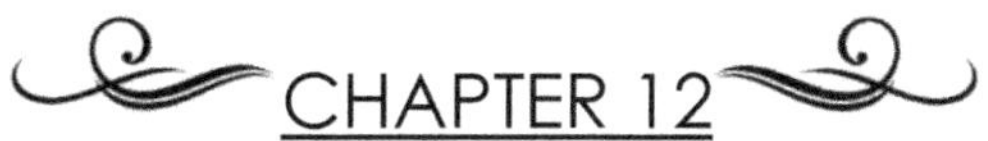

CHAPTER 12

I woke in my childhood bed, having been unable to return home last night, too exhausted, both physically and emotionally.

The smell of bacon, eggs and the slew of fixings Mom was cooking made my mouth water and stomach rumble.

I didn't care that I needed to be at the pub in half an hour.

Checking my cell, a sigh of relief escaped me that I hadn't missed a call from the Donners.

Straightening my hair, I headed downstairs to find Dad at the table, reading the morning paper with a coffee, and Mom rushing about. The sight of them made me smile.

"Glad to see nothing's changed."

"Good morning, baby," Mom said as I brushed by her, kissing the top of her head while reaching for the coffee pot. "How'd you sleep?"

It was then that I realized that I had actually slept. No insomnia. No night terrors. Nothing. "I might move back in if I can sleep as well as I did last night."

Dad looked up from his paper. "Don't give your mother any ideas."

I chuckled. "Don't worry, I'll be out of your hair after breakfast."

Leaving my childhood home had taken a bit longer than predicted, but it was well worth it to see both my parents beaming with joy, to feel the warmth of our connection filling me once again.

Mom held on to me much longer than necessary.

"I'll be back this weekend, I promise." I kissed my mother's cheek.

She backed away and looked up at me and grinned. "In that case, I'm cooking your favorite."

My stomach rumbled again despite it being full.

"Leave now before you bleed my fridge dry," Dad said, giving me one of his man-hugs.

I laughed. "I doubt you'd complain, old man. It would get you out of the house and away from Mom long enough for you to miss her."

"Shh," he said in my ear. "She's not supposed to know that that's how I feel when we're apart."

"I heard that," Mom said and wrapped her arms around my father's waist after he released me.

"I love you guys." I felt the ball of emotions lodge in my throat. "I know I haven't–"

"We know." Mom cupped my cheek. "Now go. I have some business to settle with your father." She winked.

I opened my car door to get in, and turned toward them one last time. "Good luck, Dad."

"Lucky is exactly how I feel." He smacks Mom's butt good naturedly.

I shook my head at their antics, regardless of the jealousy I felt at the playfulness between the two. They seemed younger-looking since last night. That alone offered me comfort. I'd done the right thing—for once—by letting them in again.

I got in my car, started the engine, and bid them a final goodbye with a honk of my horn as I drove off.

CHAPTER 13

Over the next few days, work dragged on, despite it being busy. I shocked my employees by handing them extra shifts as I took my evenings off, coming back to help close down at the end of each day.

I knew I didn't have to—I had staff I trusted explicitly—but I didn't want to be an absentee boss all of a sudden. I had more than enough having to explain myself to Derek who had taken a sudden interest in my life, labelling me a workaholic. He was all too pleased about my sudden need for personal time as he delivered his latest diatribe on enjoying life.

With my newfound free time, I'd made a habit of dropping by the hospital to check up on Hannah. During this time, if we were alone, I'd read her passages from Candace's journals, as well as talk to her.

When Anne and Adam popped in, I'd chat with them, learning more about their daughter as they reminisced about her childhood, the things she'd accomplished, and what her hopes and dreams had been. They were so very proud of her.

The more I heard about her, the more I liked the woman who still had yet to wake. She had more substance to her personality, even still unconscious, than so many women I had come across over the years.

It was Thursday when I got the call before I left work, and headed to the hospital. I had taken the entire night off, Derek offering to take care of the close. Peering at the number, my heart escalated to a thunderous rhythm.

"Hello?"

"They took her off the ventilator," Anne said in place of a greeting.

I was glad that I was sitting down. "They're not giving–"

"No, silly!" She added what sounded like a teary giggle. "She's ready to breathe on her own!"

"That's great!" I smiled at her excitement, feeling some of my own bubbling up. "Did they say anything about her waking up?"

There was a pause. "No, nothing as of yet, but I'm not giving up. *We're* not giving up."

"That's good. That's really good, Anne. I'm sure Adam is relieved as well."

She hummed confirmation. "Will you be by later? Adam wanted to take me out to celebrate but I don't want to leave Hannah. What if–"

"I'll be there."

W hen I entered the hospital room, Hannah had never looked better. Most of the visible bruising had faded to the point of being barely noticeable. I could see her entire face now, no longer occluded by that breathing tube and the ties that had held it in place. I'm not sure what it was, but she radiated beauty today.

I only realized that the Donners were in the room with me when Adam broke the silence. "A sight for sore eyes isn't she?"

"Very," I said, and then turned to face the man whose wife was smiling at me. "What I mean is–"

"We know what you mean," Anne said.

I changed the subject. "You two look like you're fit for one heck of a night." I gave Anne a curt nod, smiling. "You look beautiful."

Hannah's mother blushed. "Aren't you a charmer!"

"Well, he's right." Adam kissed the top of her head.

I couldn't help but smile at them.

"My mother taught me to pay a beautiful woman a compliment when due." I shuffled my foot in a bashful way.

"You two will be the death of me." She swatted at her husband playfully. "We need Hannah to wake up already and even out the playing field. Did you hear that, honey?" She walked up to Hannah's bedside and I backed away to give her more room. "Why don't you open those beautiful eyes for your mama? Your father and I would love to have loads more to celebrate tonight. We'll be back, baby girl, first thing in the morning."

"Just in case you're wondering," Adam began, "Hannah's been twitching. The doctors said that it's a reflex because the sedative they gave her, while she was on the ventilator, is wearing off."

I nodded. "Enjoy your night out. You two deserve it."

Anne took me into her arms and hugged me nice and tight. I'd grown used to it by now and I hugged her back, dropping a kiss on her cheek as she released me.

"You deserve so much more than what you were handed, Ben. I hope you see that soon."

I'm beginning to.

CHAPTER 14

I started on the second journal. Despite my growing anger, I forged onward, forcing myself to digest every new tidbit of information, piecing together the puzzle that had become my life. Hannah's presence aided in keeping me calm, soothed me.

Time flew and before I knew it, I had finished the second notebook and moved on to the third.

I looked down at my watch and was surprised to see how much time had passed. It was midnight and no one had made a move to make me leave. I didn't want to, either. Wide awake, I wanted to push through as much of Candace's words as I possibly could. It was as if I was making a mad dash for my freedom—to move on with my life.

The more I read about Candace's other life, the more it felt as if I was reading about someone I never knew.

Together, Hannah and I discovered that Candace's first act of infidelity had been when she and I had our first argument following our engagement. I remembered that night quite clearly.

Candace had told me that she'd gone out with the girls. In retrospect, I should have suspected something when she never turned up that night, but I gave her the benefit of the doubt because I loved her so much. The saying held true then as it does now: love is blind.

Upon her college graduation, she had been hired on right away. I had been so proud of her for getting a position right out of school. The job market was a bit tough as an editor, but her dream had come true just as I'd told her it would so many times before.

This is around the same time Chris' name started being dropped around the house. I knew him as her boss and whenever a work function happened—where spouses were allowed—he'd always have his wife with him. I never questioned it. Why would I? I mean, aside from the occasional arguments, life was pretty damn normal for Candace and me.

"I don't know this person, Hannah. Why would she lie? All I ever wanted was for her to be happy." I dropped my head onto the side of Hannah's bed. "Am I that gullible? I mean, do I have 'sucker' marked on my forehead or something? God, I feel so stupid for not seeing it!"

Hannah's hand twitched, her fingers nudging the hair at my temple, but I paid it no heed. It was one of those twitches like Adam had warned me about.

I sighed. "I wish you could wake up and tell me what would possess a woman to do what she did. I would have done anything. I would have let her leave if it meant that she'd be happier. Christ!"

Her fingers moved once more, but this time I couldn't ignore it.

I lifted my head and found green eyes looking back at me, tears sliding down the sides of her face.

My breath caught in my throat and came out with a whoosh. "Oh, my God, Hannah!"

I rushed to the wall and buzzed the nurse's desk.

I knew it hadn't been an involuntary reflex of her eyes opening because those tears told me that she was back.

"B–" she tried say, but I shook my head.

"No, don't. You've had a tube for nearly a week, just wait it out. Someone will be here in a minute." I grabbed her hand and squeezed. "Your parents are going to be so happy."

Nurses and doctors came rushing to the room as I stepped back and let them do their thing. They ran a few tests, mainly the reflective lights in her eyes, reflexes, eye tracking, and so on, all the while jotting down various notes in her chart.

While the health professionals tended to Hannah, I grabbed my phone and called Anne and Adam to give them the good news.

CHAPTER 15

I hadn't thought about the possibility that Hannah might not recognize or remember me from almost a week ago when her life had changed.

I listened in at her bedside as the nurse explained that she shouldn't overdo it with trying to talk, but that throat lozenges and lots of water would help get her voice back.

The doctor came in to speak with her quickly and to assess where her memory was at. She looked around the room, seemingly confused.

"Where's Lee?" she asked.

She doesn't remember?

She reached out and grabbed my hand. My head snapped in her direction and my eyes widened. "Ben, where's Lee?"

My heart soared because she remembered me, but my delight took a nosedive just as fast with the news the doctor would have to tell her. Honestly, I'd rather it be him than me this time around.

"I'm sorry, Mrs. Parsons but…"

Her hand squeezed mine almost to a painful degree. I watched her confused face register shock, but instead of panic, she looked up at me and asked, "Why do I get the feeling that I already knew this?"

"Your memory might be fuzzy for the next little while." The doctor put a comforting hand on her shoulder. "It's normal, and I would look at it as a good thing that you're already remembering things."

"What about…" she gulped and looked up at me with a tearful gaze, "my baby?"

The doctor's eyes widened and he quickly went through her chart.

"There's nothing here about a pregnancy," he said and turned to the nurse. "Get an ultrasound machine in here stat! Can you tell me how far along you are?"

My legs felt like jelly. Why hadn't Anne or Adam said anything to me about a pregnancy?

"Ben, we didn't know," Adam said as he came out of Hannah's room, evidently reading my thoughts. I was waiting out in the hallway, while the doctor performed an exam. "You look like you just found out that you're going to be a father." The man patted me on the back with a chuckle.

My worry for her and the child made my voice come out husky. "Is she?"

"I don't know, I walked out before they got started."

"I hope to God that baby's okay."

"You and me both, kid," he said as he let himself drop in the seat next to mine.

The nurse came out ten minutes later and both Adam and I turned to face her. "You can come back in now." Her neutral expression didn't give anything away.

Aside from the rhythmic beeping of machines, there was nothing but silence to greet us.

"So?" Adam asked first.

"Hannah wanted us together when she found out," Anne said.

I made to leave the room once more.

"Ben?" Hannah's voice was raspy.

I stopped and turned to her. "Yeah?"

"Please don't leave."

That line transported me back to the night we met, and I felt my heartstrings tighten at the terror in her eyes. I walked back to her side where I covered her hand with mine. "I'm not going anywhere. I just thought that you'd like a moment to find out in private with your family." I went to remove my hand after reassuring her, but she grabbed it and squeezed tight.

We waited on the ultrasound technician to spill the beans.

"I'm sorry," the tech said with a grim tone, "I'm so very sorry. I can see the fetus, but there's no heartbeat. I'm recommending a dilation and curettage. Seeing as you've been out for nearly a week, we have no idea how long it's been since…We don't want to risk sepsis. The procedure will be booked for some time within the next twenty-four hours."

"No!" Hannah broke down into sobs, rolling onto her side, facing me, clutching my hands into her chest as she rocked herself in the fetal position. "No, no, no!"

The technician left the room allowing Hannah to deal with her devastation. Anne and Adam hugged their daughter from behind, trying to soothe her.

"I'm so sorry, baby girl," Anne said in her daughter's ear, smoothing her hair back, kissing her temple.

"Just go," Hannah said in a broken voice. "Just go away."

Her words took her parents by surprise.

"Honey–" Adam started.

"I said go!"

I attempted to pull my hands from her grip, but she only tightened her hold. *Oh God!*

"You, stay."

"But–" Her pleading eyes only shut me up, and I nodded.

"Are you sure, sweetie?" Anne asked.

"Yeah. You guys go home. I need time to process this. I need to talk to Ben before he leaves."

Call me crazy, but it felt like she flat out lied to her parents. This made my stomach flutter with nerves.

"Okay, baby girl," Adam said.

He bent over and kissed his daughter's cheek. Anne did the same, then looked at me with a silent plea that I look after their daughter. I shared a small nod in the couple's direction, which seemed to work at reassuring them.

CHAPTER 16

Hannah let go of my hands the moment her parents left the room, but her sobbing grew in intensity.

My heart broke for her.

"Hannah," I said with gentleness.

"Just shut up," she said as she lay on her side still facing me.

Despite the pain that I was dealing with, I wanted to take some of hers away so she could breathe a bit easier, to lighten the load, if only for a little while.

Her long auburn hair had fallen into her face. I just wanted to see her. Crouching down, I pushed her hair back to tuck it behind her ear.

"How do you do it?" She gasped. "How do you make it h-hurt less? I mean…" Her voice cracked and she launched herself at me, wincing in pain and sobbed some more.

I had no choice but to sit on the mattress beside her, one arm wrapped around her waist to hold her up, while the other attempted to soothe her by rubbing light patterns on her back.

"I haven't done anything," I mumbled into her hair. "It's been three years and I'm still hurting, but it hurts less every day."

She nodded into my shoulder and continued to cry, her body shaking.

"Shh." I began rocking us back and forth. "It'll be okay, I promise."

Her hysterical crying subsided enough and she sighed.

"That's what I thought." She pulled away. "Before I found out about the baby, I mean. It's all I've ever wanted, you know?"

Hot tears continued to fall as I continued to watch her and those sad eyes of hers. Her hand came up to touch my face and when it came back wet, I realized that I had shed a few tears along with her.

"She was crazy, you know," Hannah whispered. I looked at her in confusion. "Your wife, she had it all and she was blowing it for some old flame."

It wasn't the subject change I was expecting, but it did make her tears slow down which I was thankful for.

"Yeah, well…" I let my words hang.

"I heard everything, you know. I know you think you've done something wrong. I may not know you past you saving me or the fact that you've bonded with my parents over these past few days, becoming some kind of a friend to them, but you're worth something, Ben. Thank you for being here."

I was choked up. Her eyes were peering so far into me that it felt like she could see my innermost secrets.

"I couldn't stay away." My gaze met hers. "Not after I told you I wouldn't leave you."

She hugged me and held on with a death grip. Her tears had dried for the time being.

"You should really try and get some rest," I mumbled into her hair.

"I don't think I can sleep right now."

"How about you try? I'll stay."

"Will you keep reading to me?"

I tensed and knew she felt it just by the hand that began to rub my back in an effort to soothe.

I thought about her request for a short moment. Hadn't I wished for her to wake up so I could hear her thoughts? Why was I hesitating?

Because she's awake now and she might just tell you what she thinks whether you want to hear it or not.

Despite my hesitation, I knew that I would most likely

never finish reading those journals unless Hannah was be-side me.

"Are they that boring?" I asked in an attempt to lighten the mood.

"Nah, the story's fine." She pulled back to look at my face. "It's that voice of yours that makes me sleepy."

I harrumphed. "Your dad warned me about your wit. Saw a bit of it the night I found you. I kind of like it."

"Yeah, leave it to the injured girl to crack a few when she's bleeding out." She rolls her eyes. "You should see me on a good day."

The thought of that had me smiling. "I'd like that."

Hannah shifted to lay on her side, watching me as I sat on my usual chair, Candace's latest journal in hand. I don't know how long I read for, but when I finished the journal, I looked up, finding a silently crying Hannah and a window filled with sunshine behind her.

It was morning.

"Please don't cry." I reached over to grab her hand.

"You're right." She wiped at her cheeks and sniffled. "She's not worth the tears. I'm crying for you, dummy." She hugged my hand under her chin with her free hand.

"That doesn't make me feel any better. You have your own stuff to deal with."

"How about this," she began. "I'll cry about yours if you cry about mine?"

I laughed, but it was more out of melancholy than humor. "I'd like it if neither of us cried at all." Silence filled the room as we looked at each other. I cleared my throat. "I should go."

"Okay." She squeezed my hand before releasing it.

"Are you going to be okay?"

"Mom and Dad will be here soon. I could try and sleep for a bit until then."

"Sounds like a smart idea."

"Will you be back?"

"Only if you want me to." I looked at my watch. "How does five o'clock sound? I'll bring dinner."

She nodded. "I'd like that."

I got up, grabbed Candace's journals and paused before aiming my feet toward the door.

"What, no kiss?"

I felt my face heat up, but turned to her. Pressing my lips to her forehead, like I had done on my last visit, I said, "I'll catch you later."

CHAPTER 17

It was just about lunchtime when my cell rang in my pocket and I was rushing to complete orders with the suppliers that Derek had forgotten to place yesterday. When I looked at the caller ID, I began to panic.

"Is everything okay?"

"Ben, it's Hannah."

"Are you okay?"

"Not really. I know you have a life, and Mom and Dad are here, but–"

"I'll be right there."

"I'm sorry," she said. "I can't do this alone. They want to do the D & C right now and I just…I can't, Ben."

"It's okay." Damn, I hated hearing her sound like that. "I'm on my way."

Hannah wanted me in there with her when the doctor went through the procedure's description prior to having her sign the consent forms.

It wasn't the longest procedure from what we were told, but the wait was unbearable nonetheless. I found myself pacing the waiting room, wondering when the doctor would come and announce that Hannah was back in her room. Anne and Adam were there with me too.

Hannah's mother stepped in front of me, halting my

mission to wear out the floor. "Thank you, Ben. She was damn well near catatonic when the doctor came in."

"It's nothing. I meant what I said when I told her that I'd be here."

"Are you sure that this isn't too much for you?" she asked.

I thought about it for a split second. "It may be hard to understand, but being here, feeling needed…I actually feel like I'm at the right place for once in far too long."

She smiled.

I returned her gesture and reached out to rub a comforting hand on the side of her arm when Adam spoke. "Guys…" His wife and I turned to find the doctor walking toward us.

"How is she?" Anne asked.

"She's a little groggy, but she did great. We've put her on a heavy course of antibiotics to ward off any possibility of infection and, aside from slight cramping, she should be fine."

"What about scarring?" Anne asked.

I looked over at the woman whom Adam now had his arms firmly wrapped around. Her sad eyes looked as if she had seen her fair share of hardships in this area.

"She'll be fine. We didn't find much scarring and what's there isn't cause for concern."

Hannah's father breathed out a sigh of relief, but I noticed that her mother didn't seem completely convinced.

"When can we see her?" I asked.

"You can all go right in if you want. Be mindful that she really should be getting some rest. As simple as the procedure was, she's still healing from the accident."

I nodded. "Right."

"Thank you, doctor." Adam shook the physician's hand.

After Hannah's procedure, I checked up on her. With her reassurances that she was okay, Hannah sent me on my way, thanking me for being there.

I went back to Fairfax to finalize my orders and tend to a few bills that required approval and payment. I worked on payroll, signed some cheques, and dropped them in their respective employee slots for pickup. All this before I headed back to the hospital for the dinner I promised Hannah.

"Hey," the woman in question said as I came in with a large brown paper bag filled with food for us. She pushed herself to sit upright with a slight grimace. "What have you got there? It smells great."

"I own a pub," I said. "I figured that I'd bring something from there. After my accident, I remember the lackluster menu options and the hankering for a good burger and fries."

Hannah laughed, but just as suddenly, her face lost all of its humor. "I don't eat meat."

I froze at her statement. "Oh…" Well this was awkward!

Just as my discomfort began to show on my face, Hannah burst into a belly laugh. My eyes narrowed right then. "I'm just kidding! It's like you read my mind, actually."

I shook my head at her. I'd been had. "I have a feeling that no one gets bored around you, do they?"

"Not that I've witnessed first-hand, no." She winced as she attempted to lean forward and pat the mattress of the bed. "Sit."

Instead of sitting on my usual chair, I sat at the foot of the bed, my legs crossed as if we were having a picnic.

"I wasn't sure what you wanted on it so I brought everything on the side." I began to pull out everything. "So what'll it be?"

Her eyes widened when I finished putting her burger together and handed it over. I grabbed my ready-made one and set the container of fries with its separate containers of ketchup, mayo and one of gravy between us.

Her laugh was light. "What, that's it?"

"I had to cover my bases, but I can't say that I'd be shocked that you wanted something that I–"

She put a hand on my knee. "Still kidding, Ben. Thank you. This is great."

I shrugged my shoulders. "We've got to eat, right?"

"So tell me about that place of yours," she said, while lifting her burger to her mouth.

CHAPTER 18

I was delighted to find out that Hannah had a penchant for cooking…well, baking, really—an art in itself that I lacked talent and patience in, but I did enjoy its consumption.

It was serendipitous that she and I had crossed paths numerous times over the last few years without even realizing it until now.

As it turns out, the bakery that was a few blocks down from Fairfax was hers! For the life of me, I had no recollection of ever seeing her in there before, and I've been there often.

What I'd noticed though, was that business had been good for her. Within the first year she had expanded, taking over the place next door. The café had a library, where customers were able to come in and checkout various literary works. On a few nights, throughout each month, she also had live entertainment. Every time I'd been in there, it always hit me how refreshing and homey the place felt. There was something there for everyone, making her business sense impeccable…not to mention her desserts—they had you coming back for more.

"Lee thought that I was crazy for starting Cake It Up," she blurted between bites. "I guess he forgot that I was one of those women hell-bent on proving anyone who thought my notions ridiculous that I could do it."

"What did he say when you expanded within the first year?"

"You noticed?" I nodded. "He said nothing at first, and

then he came in one day and told me the place actually looked smaller than when I'd opened it." Her eyes met mine and I saw the sadness there.

I was angry for her. With what Anne had told me, Lee's alcoholism hadn't painted him in the best of light, but he was becoming more and more of an asshole in my regard with what I was hearing straight from Hannah's mouth.

"I'm sorry."

"It's nothing." She shrugged her shoulders. "I built Cake It Up from the ground up and I'm proud of it. Nothing or no one can take it from me. Pipe dream, my ass!"

"But it would have been nice to share in the joy with someone, right?" I gave her a solemn smile.

"I had my parents. But you're right, it would have been nice to have my husband's support."

"He had a lot on his plate, huh?"

She nodded. "He was…God that feels weird," she said with tears in her eyes. "He was an alcoholic."

"I know."

"Things weren't very good."

"You don't need to explain." I stuffed a fry in my mouth.

"Mom and Dad don't know this yet, but a little over a month ago, after Lee got a DUI, I left him." She kept her gaze lowered, as if she were ashamed of the strength I knew it took for her to do what she'd done. "The night of the accident, he'd convinced me to go out for dinner to see if we could work things out. After the stunt he pulled at the restaurant, ruining our evening by first being belligerent with our waiter, and then…" her face contorted. "Well, let's just say that that's when I knew there was nothing to save."

That went a long way to explain why the grief of losing her husband didn't seem as profound as that of losing their baby. To say she was unaffected would be one hell of a stretch, though.

"I'm sorry."

"He was getting worse, and I might have had great intentions of remaining by his side, but every promise he'd ever made to sober up and be more supportive, he broke. I couldn't bring our child into this world to have them stuck with a brutal father."

"Did he ever hit you?" I'm not sure where that question came from, only that her mentioning the word brutal had prompted the inquiry to form in my head. I suppose Anne's mention of abuse didn't help with my concern either.

"Once. On the night he got his DUI. He was livid with me for showing up late. The second he struck, I made the decision to leave."

I snorted. "Instead of rushing to pick him up, I would have let him stay in jail overnight."

"Maybe I should have done that," she pondered aloud. "So what about you? How'd you get to open Fairfax?"

Evidently, Hannah thought the topic change was a smart one. I couldn't argue, so I told her about how it had been a shared dream of sorts for Candace and me. It just hadn't been fully realized while she was alive, but it had been on its way.

"So you opened it in her memory?"

I nodded. "But it feels tainted now with my recent discoveries."

"I bet. How are you doing with everything?"

"I should be asking you that question. Your wounds are fresher."

"It's hard, but you make it easier somehow." She blushed.

"So I'm not the only one to feel like that?" I asked. "Listen…I feel like I owe you an apology."

"For what?"

"Because I came in here after promising to not leave and I dumped–"

"Stop it!" She crossed her arms over her chest. "I'm going to tell you this in hopes you don't go running all freaked out." I nodded and held silent. "I don't know if it's the circumstance of that night or…" She took a deep breath. She set her burger down and wiped her hands on her napkin. Was she nervous? "There's just something. That night, you saw me at my worst. I was broken before the crash. When you showed up, I don't know what it was. But I knew that I could trust you.

"And then you actually came back. I know what I said. I remember your answer, but I never thought that you'd follow through after the crews came and took me away.

"I was confused when I first heard your voice, but I feel that if it weren't for you dropping by, reading, talking…your voice…" She shook her head. "I don't think I'd be awake right now. Part of me felt like I needed to wake up and say something to you."

I popped the tab on my soda can and took a gulp to wash down the food that had lodged in my throat from her words.

"We're connected," she whispered.

"Yeah."

"It's like you know where I'm coming from, and where I'm heading. It's easier to look at you and deal with things than it is to look at my parents who can't relate at all."

"I think that's another reason that kept me coming back, aside from my promise," I confessed.

She smiled and grabbed her burger, taking a large bite. "This is delicious! Remind me to repay the favor when I get out of here."

I grinned. "I may have something in mind."

"You do?"

I nodded. "Those Italian pastries you make. They seem so simple, but they're my favorite."

"Crustuli you mean?"

"If you're talking about the braided ones dipped in honey or sprinkled with powdered sugar, then yeah."

"Those things may look simple, but they're a nightmare to make."

"It explains why you don't make them that often." She

nodded. "Okay, well how about your strawberry cheesecakes with the chocolate cookie crust instead?"

She giggled. "My favorite."

"Really?" She nodded. "Mine too, and it's a perfect offering at gatherings. Everyone asks me where I get it. Now they ask me to get some whenever I agree to show up for a dinner because I refuse to tell them where it comes from."

She laughed. "Wouldn't it be simpler to just tell them?"

"Yeah, but then it wouldn't be my signature contribution that everyone seems so hooked on." I smirked.

"Tell you what…" There was a gleam in her eyes. "When I get out of here, I'll have you over and we can make both desserts." She took the final bite of her burger before patting her belly.

I laughed, but in an instant, her hand halted, her face screwed up and she began to cry softly, wrapping both arms around her torso.

I was quick to wipe my hands off on a napkin and go to her side.

"It's my fault." She sniffled.

"Look at me." I reached for her chin, but she kept her eyes closed. "I need you to look at me, Hannah." She opened her eyes, and those gorgeous green globes stared back. I grabbed her face in my hands and allowed my thumbs to wipe away her tears. "It's not your fault and you know it. You didn't choose to start the argument. You didn't let him drive because he was drunk and without a licence. You're not the one who caused the loss of control. Now say it, Hannah! Say it's not your fault!"

She shut her eyes and with vehemence, she shook her head. "I can't."

"You can and you will. If you can't say it for yourself, say it for me, Hannah."

"It's…it's not…"

"…my fault," I finished for her. "Now look at me and say it, sweetheart."

Her eyes opened, but I was pretty sure it was the shock of my endearment and not my request that made her do it. To be honest, I shocked myself. Regardless, I nodded my head for added encouragement.

"It's not…my fault," she managed.

"Good." I tilted her head to kiss her forehead. "And again."

"It's not my fault." There was more strength in her words this time.

"Again." I pulled away to see her face.

"It's not my fault! It's not my fault! It's not my fault!" she said, every succession getting louder, firmer with resolve.

"Well now you just sound like a kid having a tantrum." I got the desired effect. She smacked my arm, but her lips quirked up with a small smile. "Come here."

I hugged her to me. Her arms found their way around my waist. I waited until her hold on me loosened before I allowed myself to release her. She pulled back slowly with a hand rubbing up my chest to cup my cheek.

Quick as a flash, she leaned back in and I felt the slightest pressure of her lips to my cheek before it was gone. "Thank you," she whispered.

I reached up and pushed some of her hair to the side. "Are you okay?"

"I can't believe I'm saying this so soon, but I will be." She lowered her hand from my cheek to grab my hand and interlaced our fingers before giving it a squeeze. "And so will you."

CHAPTER 19

My weekend had finally begun, and I got up and found myself feeling happier than usual, and looking forward to my day.

After getting ready, I headed out. I drove downtown and stopped in to get a little something special before heading to the hospital. I sent a text to Anne and Adam before leaving in hopes that they could help me out.

Paying for what I needed, I made my way to Hannah and the Donners.

I walked through the hospital doors as I always did and by then, some of the staff waved, knowing exactly where I was heading. I had become somewhat of a regular. Marie was working triage again, and I nodded my head in greeting, smiling as I kept trucking on.

The box I held in my hands hit the floor as I turned the corner down the hall that led to Hannah's room. I was met with bright green eyes and a beaming smile.

"You're walking!"

"Key word is trying," Hannah said.

"Oh, hush now, you're doing great," Anne encouraged her as she held on to one side and her father the other, both acting like crutches. "The doctor told her that the sooner she got to walking again, the sooner she'd be able to leave. If it were up to her, she'd attempt running if that's what it took to get her out of here faster."

I laughed at the eye roll only I could see. "They had to find something for me to do since I didn't get my green jello and stale box of cereal this morning." She pouted. "I wonder why that is?" Her eyes narrowed on me and her brow arched as she peered down to the box I had brought. "You better have brought enough to share, white knight."

I laughed. "Is that my new nickname?"

"Why not, you like it?"

"It'll do." I laughed. "For now." I bent over and picked up the box, hoping that everything inside it was still intact.

At a turtle's pace, we made our way back to Hannah's room where she made herself comfortable on her bed.

"I have to say I was surprised to hear that you'd be here so early," Anne said.

"I have plans tonight and I wasn't quite sure if I'd be able to make it over afterward, so I brought some breakfast." I presented the box to Hannah.

"Thank you, Ben!" Her smile seemed to only get brighter. "This is a good way to make up for your later absenteeism."

I laughed. "I'm glad you approve." She squealed in delight when she saw the assortment of croissants, muffins and scones, all from her shop. "I figured that if you couldn't be there, that I'd bring part of it to you. There's enough for everyone, and I brought some butter, jams, knives and napkins." I pulled out the small bag with the added lot that had been tucked in my jacket pocket.

"It's a good thing I'm married or I would have tried to snag you for myself a long time ago," Anne said.

"Mom!"

"What?"

"I'm right here." Adam's exaggerated annoyance made the rest of us laugh.

"It's okay, Anne, I think you'd be too much for me." I winked at her, making her blush.

Adam chortled. "I like you more and more with each vis-it, son, but you're right. She's a lot to handle. It took me years to whip her into shape." He kissed his wife's annoyed look off her face and she cuddled into him.

My eyes found themselves on Hannah who was watching her parents. She must have felt my gaze because hers met mine and I couldn't help but grin.

CHAPTER 20

"So, you finally agreed to a hot date for tonight, huh?" Hannah asked after her parents had left. Thanks to her bluntness, my current sip of coffee nearly went down the wrong hole.

Sputtering, I took the tissue Hannah handed me and dabbed at my mouth. "If you call dinner with my folks a hot date, then yeah." I chuckled.

I told her about how I had gone to see them and let them in on my life earlier in the week.

"I didn't realize how much I was hurting them or how much I missed them. I'm hoping that we can get back to how things were before. It wasn't just the journals, but more what your mom told me while you were asleep. She reminds me so much of my mom, it's uncanny."

Hannah smiled. "You seem to have made quite an impression on them. Tell me about your parents?"

A conversation detailing my folks and childhood led to the discovery that we had grown up with similar backgrounds.

"Do they know about me?"

"About the accident, yeah."

Next, Hannah asked about Candace's journals, or their lack of presence specifically, and I shrugged my shoulders. "I guess I haven't felt the need to bring them along." I wasn't quite ready to tell Hannah that I would rather enjoy her company more than ruin a good mood with stories of the past that continued to paint my marriage in a darker shade.

"Um…"

"What is it?" I asked, noticing Hannah's blush. The look had my heart thumping wildly.

"I need help with something."

"Anything."

"I kind of have to go to the little girl's room." She bit her lip. "Never mind. I'll call the nurse to–"

"No," I said a little too breathless. "I was just…distracted."

Her brows furrowed. "Distracted?"

I didn't want her knowing that I had been taken with the way her skin flushed with her embarrassment. "Come on." I extended my hand to her, changing the subject. "Let's get you there before the nurses slap a pair of Depends on you."

She harrumphed. "Oh, you're funny!"

"I can be." I smirked down at her, while she grabbed my forearms to get to her feet.

At her full height, she was a head shorter than my six foot two stature. I made sure she was stable and swiveled so that I could wrap an arm around her waist as she wrapped hers around my neck.

I escorted her to the bathroom. "Are you sure you'll be okay in here?" I asked when we stopped just inside.

"I'll let you know if I need help with my underwear in a sec." My jaw dropped. "I'm kidding!" She gave me a once over and bit her bottom lip. The look bordered on seductive. "Well…" My eyes widened. "Still kidding! Well, kind of." She winked and giggled.

"You, my friend, are…" I let my words hang.

"Funny?" I shook my head indicating the negative. "Gorgeous?" I laughed and reached for the bathroom's doorknob to shut the door and give her the privacy she needed. "Smart, attentive, special…"

"Crazy!" I said through the door, laughing loudly at her antics. "But I like you that way. Let me think on those others."

She snorted. "Wiseass!"

"I heard that!"

"You better not be listening to me tinkle, mister."

"Or what?" I was growing to love this back and forth banter of ours.

She took a beat too long to answer, which I took it to mean that I had stumped her. "I don't know yet." Another boisterous laugh came barreling out of me. "But I'll come up with something."

"Did you fall in or what? You've been in there for a while," I said after I hadn't heard anything from her in five minutes. "Hannah?"

I knocked on the door and when she didn't answer, I went to open it. The thing flew inward, revealing a proudly smiling Hannah.

"What are you looking at?" She brought up a fist and chucked me under the chin playfully. "Shut your mouth, you'll catch flies."

And then her knees buckled.

Catching her before she hit the floor, I said, "You should have let me know that you were done."

"I'm going to have to do this on my own some time."

"Had you wanted to, I would have let you, but what if something had happened?"

"Nothing did."

I held on to her with my hands on her hips and her hands lay flat on my chest. The air filled with silence as I peered into her eyes. Something was shifting, and if I willed myself to admit it, it had been shifting over the course of days.

"You can let go now." Her voice had a raspy sexiness to it until she cleared her throat. "Or are you itching for another hug?"

"You're the one who fell, not me. I just didn't want you to land on your face and hurt that cute nose of yours." I flicked it with my finger, making her scrunch up her face before she stuck her tongue out at me.

Yeah, I really could get used to having Hannah around…

CHAPTER 21

I walked into my parents' home with a cheese-eating grin on my face, finding Dad in the kitchen helping Mom out, or more like helping himself.

"Company present!" They both jumped. "It smells great! What's cookin', good lookin'?" I moved to kiss my mother on her cheek, while Dad laughed and slapped me on the back.

"Someone's in a good mood," he said.

I nodded. "It's a good day."

"So you mean to say that you won't be dodging us after you've inhaled your meal?" I knew Dad's words were meant as a joke, but they still carried an undertone of hurt, which made my guilt surge up a notch.

"Not tonight. Unless I get a call that the business is burning down or–" I stopped myself right there.

"Do I detect the subtlety of a woman?" Dad nudged me with his elbow when I came back from the fridge with a beer for him and me, and an opened bottle of wine to refill my mother's goblet. I shrugged my shoulders in answer. Mom and Dad shared a look.

"Spill." Mom dropped the spoon onto the counter and turned to face me with her arms crossed at her chest. Dad assumed his rightful position: behind her, wrapping his arms around her waist and resting his chin on her shoulder.

Dad started with, "Is it that girl from–"

"Hannah." I nodded. "Sort of."

Dad grinned but Mom appeared confused.

"You said she was in a coma," she said.

I smiled broadly. "She woke up a few days ago."

As I set the table, I told them about everything that had transpired since I'd last stopped by. Like it always was, my parents remained silent as they listened to everything I had to say.

The more I spoke, the more I questioned myself on why the hell I had pushed them away to begin with. I hadn't seen one single look of pity from them as I explained what it was that I had read in Candace's journals. If anything, I saw anger, frustration and complete devastation—especially from my mother—at the reality that the only thing close enough to a daughter she had come to know had been nothing more than a farce. The look of betrayal on my parents' faces from the truth reinforced that I was right in feeling what I had been feeling.

Throughout the week, I was grieving less for Candace and more for the losses Hannah was suffering through.

Don't get me wrong, I was still dealing with my losses, but I no longer felt as lost as I have for the last three years. As it was, three years was a long time to wallow over the loss of someone you never truly had. I basically found myself moving forward without even trying.

"Seems like that girl's helped you more than you thought possible," Mom said when I finished rambling. "And it looks like you've been helping her through her own things too."

"Just be careful," Dad interjected.

I turned to look at him. "Why?"

"Because you've had three years to process things and move on, and it's still fresh for her."

"I know." And then I added, "We're just friends."

"But you're falling for her." Dad looked at me with that all-knowing gaze of his. "I know you, son."

"I agree with your father," Mom said. "Regardless of what you decide, take your time, Ben, and listen to your heart. You deserve to be happy."

A soft laugh escaped me. "That's what her mom told me."

"Smart woman." Mom winked.

"You'd like Anne and Adam," I said. "They remind me so much of you two."

Mom and Dad shared an odd look I couldn't quite place, but as quick as it appeared, it was gone.

"And what of Hannah?" Mom asked.

"Seeing as you enjoy putting me back in my place, I think you'd love her." I grinned. "She's challenging, sweet, and funny. I haven't laughed as much in the last three years as I have in the last couple of days."

"I think we'll have to meet this Hannah." Dad shared another one of those mysterious looks with Mom. "I don't care if she stays a friend or not. I owe that girl for bringing me my son back."

Mom only nodded.

CHAPTER 22

It was late when I left my childhood home, Hannah never straying very far from my thoughts. I wondered if her parents had kept her company since I couldn't be there with her like I normally was. I found that I missed our late night chats, seeing as tonight had been the first where I hadn't visited since her accident.

As I drove home, the urge to see Hannah was still potent, but the time on the clock told me that she'd be sleeping. I'd check in on her in the morning.

Arriving at the hospital around lunchtime, imagine my shock when I got to Hannah's room and the sheets were being ripped off of her bed. Her flowers and gifts from friends and family were nowhere to be seen either.

"Where is she?" I asked.

"Who, sir?" the cleaner asked.

"The patient that was in this room."

"Gone."

Gone?

"Gone where?"

The cleaner shrugged her shoulders, then pulled a piece of folded paper from her scrub's pocket and handed it to me. "This was left behind. I was going to leave it at the nurse's station. Are you Ben?"

I breathed a sigh of relief, nodded and took the paper. "Thank you."

The woman nodded and I walked out of the room to sit in one of the hallway chairs.

I looked down at the page, reading my name in fancy cursive. Unfolding the paper, I took in the words.

Dear Ben,

By now, you've noticed that I'm not there. The doctor came by this morning and told me that I was able to go home. I'm excited, but I'm scared. I'm inching toward normalcy again, and I'm not sure how I'll deal when I get home.

I'm staying at Mom's and Dad's for a few days until they're happy with how I can handle myself physically. I think they're still worried that something will happen and I'll snap.

I wanted to say thank you for all that you've done and I hope to see you again.

I finally heard back from Lee's parents. They've taken it upon themselves to handle the funeral arrangements without me. There's a backstory there, which I'm sure, when I see you next (if I do), you'll get a full rendition.

If this is it and I don't see you again, I'll forever consider you a friend. Ben, what you've shared with me, what you've helped me through, makes you matter more to me than some I have spent an entire lifetime getting to know. I only hope that I've been as much a source of comfort to you as you have been to me.

Look me up when you're ready for that baking session. It's the least I can do when I already owe you my life for everything you've done.

Love,
Hannah

And there it was, in plain black and white—her phone number.

I stopped myself from dialing her up right then and there.

Hannah was home. She had a life to get back to. She needed to settle in and I didn't know where I fit in.

She'll call you if she needs you.

As I made to leave the hospital, my phone rang.

Recognizing the number, I smiled into the receiver. "Buddy, how was Italy?"

"What's this about trying to break down my sister's door?" Mike barked.

Oh shit! It had completely slipped from my mind to reassure Danica that I was fine. I sighed. "Name your place and time and I'll tell you the whole story."

"Mine and right the fuck now, Ben."

"Give me twenty. I'm just leaving the hospital."

"The hospital? Is everything okay?"

"I'm fine. I'll explain when I get there."

CHAPTER 23

Mike and I have been best friends since our formative years. He was the one person that knew everything about me, other than my parents. Hell, we'd been through it all together: women, sports, business school, marriage, death…you name it.

So twenty-five minutes later, my knuckles were about to meet the wooden front door to my best friend's home only to find the newly appointed Mrs. Withers opening it for me. She crossed her arms at her chest and tapped her foot. A grin broke out on my face. She was a perfect match for Mike, and one hell of a person to spar with in a battle of wits. The man would never be bored.

She smiled, then launched herself to give me a hug. "Get in here!"

"How was your trip?" I set her down on her feet.

"Great! But you wouldn't think my husband enjoyed it after he spoke with his sister. What's going on?"

"That's what I'd like to know," Mike said and I pulled away to find him leaning on the wall next to his wife with a serious look on his face. "Beer?"

"Sure." I ushered Nicole ahead of me, following them toward the kitchen.

Mike popped the top and set the bottle in front of me before taking a seat beside his wife, their drinks in hand. "So, you managed to freak my little sister out," he said.

I gave him a guilty look. "I'm sorry I did. Did she tell you anything?"

Mike shook his head. "She said I needed to get it all from you. Ben, she was pretty upset, so I know it's big. You could have called me, you know."

"And ruin your honeymoon?"

"What the hell could ruin a honeymoon?" Nicole asked.

A snort escaped me. "How about finding out that your wife had a whole other life?"

The look on Nicole's face was one of complete shock, while Mike's was a mask of blankness.

"She was having an affair, Mike." And I moved into storytelling mode.

By the time I was done, I was on my third beer and Nicole refused to let me leave until I had some food in me.

"How can you be so calm about this?" Nicole asked. "What did her parents have to say?"

"I've had a little help getting over some of it," I started. "And I haven't talked to Candace's parents since before they dropped off the box. I've been to see Mom and Dad, though."

"How'd that go?" Nicole asked.

"Things are better with them. I'm not saying I'm anywhere near over what's happened, but Hannah–"

"Wait a minute, who's Hannah?" Mike asked as he flipped the burgers on the barbecue.

"You guys know about the accident out by Dead Man's Way, the night of your wedding, right?" I asked.

"You could hear the sirens for miles, so yeah," Mike said. "Wait a minute! You were there?"

I nodded. "I saw something and stopped to check it out. It was bad. There was a couple…"

"Are they okay?" Nicole asked. "How does this Hannah fit into things?"

Once more, I explained Hannah's story. I felt the rolling emotions of anger about what Lee had done to her with his alcoholism, how she'd wanted me by her side, how her parents helped me understand that I needed my folks, all the way up until why I had been at the hospital when Mike had called.

The two sat there, baffled, and then Mike's signature all-knowing grin made its appearance.

"Wipe that smirk off your face. I know what you're thinking."

"What?" That mock innocence of his didn't fool me.

Nicole giggled. "You've got a thing for her."

She was right.

"It doesn't matter. It's too soon to start anything." Sighing, I continued. "She needs time. I need time."

Nicole let out an unladylike snort. "So what?"

"So what?" I repeated.

"Yeah, so what? It seems to me that she was well out the door before the accident."

"That doesn't mean she's over her idiot husband, Nicole."

"It's not—"

"She's bitter about things. Her emotions are all over the place, and I can't blame her. But—"

"But?" Nicole urged me.

"Would you let him speak, woman?" Mike said.

"But there's something about the letter she left me at the hospital, that tells me…" I sighed. "I don't know." I ran my hands over my face. "See for yourself." I took the letter out and handed it to Nicole. "I know she loved her husband. I mean, there's no other reason as to why she'd want a family with him, or why she'd stuck around for as long as she did."

"The decision to leave him couldn't have been easy on her if she was pregnant," Mike surmised.

I shook my head. "We've talked a lot about everything. I know it wasn't."

"You know that she feels that same connection you do, right?" Nicole waved the page around, her eyes meeting mine. Mike grabbed it from her and began to read it for himself. "It's not spelled out, but if you read between the lines—"

Mike cut his wife off. "She definitely wants to see you again."

"As friends." A subtlety of disappointment wormed its way into the pit of my stomach with my words.

Mike winked at his wife. "Sure."

CHAPTER 24

I arrived home strangely feeling like I needed sleep. I took advantage of the exhaustion, seeing as although rest had come a bit more easily over the past week, it was still sporadic.

By the time my head hit the pillows, my cell began to ring on the bedside table.

I grabbed it, reading *unknown number* on the display. Something urged me to answer because no one called me that late unless it was from work, which in this case, it wasn't.

"Hello?"

"It's Hannah." I felt the smile spread across my face. "Oh God! It's so late. Did I wake you?"

I laughed. "You can wake me up any time, Hannah, but I wasn't sleeping. How was your day?"

She groaned. "I think I'll be hurrying to get out. This porcelain doll treatment is a bit much."

My tone was soft. "They're worried about you. They almost lost you, you have to understand that."

"I know."

Silence hung in the air.

What had she called for?

I heard her take a deep breath and exhale.

"Is everything okay?" I prompted her.

"I'm fine."

I wasn't convinced. "You don't sound too sure."

"I guess I just need time." She sighed. "It just feels weird you know?"

My head began to bob in agreement. "I remember that feeling. Little things like that are bound to creep up for a while yet. Still does with me."

"Yeah. Right…"

I had the feeling that there was more. "Hannah?"

"Can you come over?"

And there it was.

I sat upright, the sheets falling at my waist while I rubbed the back of my neck with my free hand. "You should be sleeping." I wanted to smack myself in the face for that one. She didn't answer me with words, only with a sigh. "What's the address?"

"No, it's okay. Never mind."

"Hannah, what's the address?" Sleep could wait. Hannah needed me.

She provided me with the directions. "Don't ring the doorbell. Just walk around the side, to the back of the house."

Anne and Adam lived a mere fifteen-minute drive from my house in a beautiful two-story home that resembled that of my parents, who lived a few blocks over from the Donners.

I laughed and shook my head at the irony of it all. So close yet so far. What would have made it all the more hilarious would be if we had gone to the same school. She wasn't all that much younger than me, of that I was sure.

I made my way around to the back of the house as she'd instructed me to and found her on the cushioned patio swing with a thick blanket. Her eyes were aimed up at the sky. Pausing to look at her, I smiled. "Wishing on a star?" I asked, which made her jump. "I'm sorry."

"No worries. I hear it's good to get the blood racing every now and again."

Without an invitation, I sat beside her on the swing with my hands on my lap. I felt like a nervous teenager who didn't have a clue about dating or being around a girl. The fact that we were in her parents' back yard only strengthened the feel of awkwardness.

She leaned her head onto my shoulder and I felt some of my anxiety dissipate.

"This may sound absolutely ridiculous, and tell me if it does." She shifted her head so she looked up at me. "I missed you today."

"It's not ridiculous at all." I shifted my arm to wrap it around Hannah's shoulders, while she covered us both with the blanket as we began to swing. I'd missed her too.

CHAPTER 25

A set of warm, soft lips on my forehead woke me. The chirp of birds, the brightness behind my eyelids, and the wonderful weight atop me made me feel as if I was dreaming.

"Wake up, sleepy head." A hand rubbed my chest.

I groaned and was damn well near blinded by the sun, but forgot all about that when I realized where I was and who I was with.

"Hannah?"

"I can't believe we slept out here." She giggled into my shoulder. "How's your neck? That couldn't have been comfortable."

I smiled. "I'm fine."

"Coffee?"

"I thought you'd never ask."

Last night, Hannah and I had stayed up talking. I had been adamant that she sleep, but she refused. The woman ended up cuddling into my side as I spoke about anything and everything in an attempt to lull her to sleep. It worked! So well, in fact, that I had fallen asleep with her in my arms.

"Good morning, Ben!" A rather chipper Adam walked out onto the patio. "You could have used the couch instead of that swing, you know."

I felt the heat rise in my face and my mouth opened to say something. Nothing came out.

"Relax." He chuckled. "I'm quite fine with it, really. She evidently sees something in you that's helping her. I'd be lying if I said I didn't see it. You two are cut from the same cloth. You're good for each other."

"I…uh…"

"Here you go–" Hannah's steps faltered when she noticed her father's presence. "Daddy, what are you doing up so early?" She looked between her father and me, color suffusing her face as embarrassment took over. She looked guilty, and her overall reaction had me chuckling at the same time, thinking that it was a good look on her.

"Well, will you look at that!" Adam harrumphed. "She blushes for you, too."

Hannah's colour deepened and began to spread from her cheeks to her face until it had reached her neckline.

I couldn't help myself, and teased. "Red is a nice color, isn't it Adam?"

"The best, Ben." He laughed along with me. "You'd think that something was going on with–"

"No…nothing." She was quick to say. "We were talking and then we fell asleep."

"I have to agree." I moved toward Hannah. With a wink, I grabbed my cup of coffee from her and took a sip. I moaned my appreciation for the hot brew. "Thank you."

Her eyes widened as she nodded her welcome, and then looked at her father as if signaling that he go away.

"What's going on out here?" Anne came to join us. "Ben? My, you're here early. Welcome to our home."

"You're a whole night late," Adam told her and she gave him an inquiring gaze. "I woke up last night and heard voices. I looked out the window and these two were on the swing."

"I guess Adam wasn't the only one who couldn't sleep, I gather?" She looked pointedly at her daughter.

"It's more like she refused to sleep," I said. "It took me a while to convince her to try."

"And before you all ask, yes, I slept, and I slept fine," Hannah said.

"Better than fine by the sound of it, you snored."

"I don't snore!"

"Of course not, sweetheart. There's just a small bear hiding in them bushes over there, isn't there?"

She elbowed me in the side. "Be careful, Carpenter, or you might regret those words."

"Really?" She nodded in response. "I'd like to see you try." I lifted my hand and flicked her nose like I knew annoyed her in an infantilizing way.

"Oh, you will. Rest assured, white knight, you will." She gave me her best mischievous grin.

"I should get going." I swallowed the last of my coffee and Anne grabbed my empty cup from me. "I'm the only one in this morning aside from some of my kitchen staff."

Hannah set down her own mug on a side table. "Walk you to your car?"

Biding goodbye to her folks, she walked past me and I followed.

When I reached her side, our hands touched and I felt her cool fingers slide on the inside of my wrist until our palms touched. I interlaced our fingers and squeezed.

We reached my car and I paused. Our hands hadn't parted as I fished for my car keys in my pocket.

I looked down at our joined hands, smirking. "Are you going to–" Her lips cut me off as they made contact with mine for a millisecond. "W-what was that for?" I'd be lying if I said I didn't want it to happen again but…

"Thank you," she whispered and let go of my hand.

She looked cute all bashful and shuffling her feet. It appeared as if she hadn't planned on her actions, taking us both off guard.

I moved toward her and brushed the strand of hair that had come loose from her ponytail. I grabbed the back of her neck with my hand and leaned in to kiss her forehead.

"You're welcome. You should drop by for lunch or dinner some time when you're up for it."

"You should drop by for dessert." She giggled nervously as soon as she realized her comment held a double-entendre.

I pulled away, releasing her to open my car door before looking at her. "I think I just got mine." Hannah's blush pinked her cheeks for the third time that morning, making me laugh. "And that right there was the cherry on top."

She laughed. "Charmer."

"Your mom seems to think so."

"She was right." She winked. "Call me?"

"You know I will."

CHAPTER 26

I saw Hannah every day since her release from the hospital. Sometimes it was for an hour, and last night we had a repeat of Sunday night where I ended up passing out on her parents' couch, which I'll say was considerably more comfortable than the swing.

Nothing beyond that one kiss ever happened again. I was disappointed, but I did get plenty of lip to cheek and forehead kisses. I milked those about as much as I doled them out. Hannah seemed to need the little bits of tenderness I was able to provide.

Later in the week, Mike and Nicole came into Fairfax for lunch.

"What can I get you two lovebirds?" I asked when I got to their table.

"Our usual," Mike said.

"Sure thing."

After serving them their drinks, I didn't go back until their orders were ready, at which point I sat down with them for some small talk.

Nicole had me laughing as she recounted how Mike had kept her in their hotel room. "My husband is such a horn-dog!" She giggled, cuddling closer into her husband's side. It was clear she was playing up her disappointment at not having seen much of Italy, what with the sparkle in her eyes.

"I never heard any complaints." Mike kissed her cheek. "How about I make it up to you with another trip?"

"Hmm–"

"You'd better take it," I heard the familiar voice say. "Italy is worth a yearly visit." I turned to face the voice and her eyes were on me. "Sitting on the job are we?"

"Hannah!" I got up to greet her with a kiss to her cheek.

She grinned. "Any chance a girl can get some service around here? I mean, there is a white knight that works here, right, or did I get the wrong place?"

Someone was feeling cheeky.

"Mike…Nicole, this is Hannah Parsons."

"Congratulations on your wedding." Hannah extended her hand, smiling.

I looked on as she shook Mike's hand first, and then he peered up at me with a nod of approval, while she moved to Nicole.

"You alone?" I asked her.

She nodded.

"No, you're not," Nicole said. "You can sit with us, if you'd like."

I jumped into host mode. "What can I get you?"

"The same as what you brought me in the hospital if you don't mind." She made a point to look around. "I can see why people keep coming back. This place is great."

"You sure it's not the owner?" Nicole blurted out. Hannah's head snapped in the woman's direction, a look was exchanged between the two and then they both turned to grin at me. "I mean, look at him!" my best friend's wife added.

Nicole and Hannah both eyed me from top to bottom like hungry cougars. "I know." Hannah licked her bottom lip. "I bet you he tastes better than any of the desserts I make."

"I'm wondering," Nicole bit her lip, "maybe I should have sampled a few extras before saying *I do*."

"Now wait a damn minute, woman!" Mike said. Nicole laughed at her husband's protest.

"I'm not sure about that, but I'll go put Hannah's order

in." I turned to Hannah. "Can you try not to stir trouble between these two while I'm gone?"

"Relax, baby, there will only ever be you," Nicole told Mike, to which the man groaned, making both women giggle as I walked off.

When I rounded the bar with Hannah's order, my best friend let out a boisterous laugh. Hannah had a smirk on her face and a look in her eyes that I'd seen only moments before. What was she up to?

I put Hannah's order down and sat down beside her.

"I like this girl," Mike said.

"I figured you would." I grinned and looked over at Hannah to find that she was looking at me. My hand found hers under the table and clasped it. She moved it to lace our fingers together.

Mike and Nicole bid us goodbye and then there was just Hannah and I.

"I like them," she said.

"They're great."

We fell silent, then I was beckoned by Derek who had come in early for his shift. I had a quick conversation with the man before returning to Hannah's table. This time I sat across from her.

The disappointment in her eyes, which was masked with a glint of something else, didn't escape my notice.

"When are you off?" she asked.

"Now, actually. I've been done for fifteen minutes, but like a bad habit, I have a tendency of sticking around and helping."

Her smile was slight, but still genuine. "How do you feel about helping somewhere else?"

"Sure, but I need to warn you, I can't be held accountable for ruining your recipes if this helping requires baking."

Her lips quirked and then her smile disappeared. "There won't be any baking."

Something wasn't right.

I reached across the table for her hand. "What's going on?"

"I'm supposed to go back to the house today," she explained. "I tried with Mom and Dad a few times yesterday, but I can't seem to be able to last more than an hour without feeling suffocated by memories. Lee's parents asked that I pack up his things for them to take."

I growled and her eyes flashed to mine. "Why in the hell are they in such a rush?" She shrugged her shoulders. "You never explained about his parents."

She sighed and looked down at the tabletop. "It's a long story."

She wasn't ready to elaborate just yet. "It's okay. I'll go with you. We'll get everything sorted."

"Thank you. I might be weak when it comes to them, but it's probably for the best that everything is out of my sight."

I nodded. "It does make it easier."

CHAPTER 27

We spent an hour sifting through Lee's desk, filing cabinets and everything in the den. Ultimately, Hannah just huffed and said, "fuck it!" and grabbed the computer and the rest of the files, with the exception of their joined legal documents and her personal papers, stuffing it all in boxes.

She clapped her hands together as if ridding them of dust and whispered, "I have to do the bedroom."

With an arm around her shoulders, I escorted her out of the den and let her lead the way to their bedroom. Hannah headed in and straight to the closet while my feet froze at the doorway. Somehow, it didn't feel right being in there.

She turned to grab a box and stopped when she saw me watching from the hall. "Ben, you okay?"

I nodded. "It's just that it's yours and Lee's bedroom. Honestly, it's awkward for me to be in here, riffling through his things."

She dropped the box she held in her hands onto the bed. "It's just clothes." She stepped closer to me. Wrapping her arms around my waist to hug me, she said, "Besides, I haven't slept in here in the last year."

My body jolted at that revelation, but when her body stiffened against mine, I gave her a squeeze that seemed to relax both of us. "Can I ask you a question?"

"You know you can," she mumbled into my chest.

"I know why your parents aren't helping you out with all of this but, why me?"

She pulled away, pressing her forehead into my chest. "I

don't know." She sighed. "Maybe it's because you've been through similar. You understand." Then she looked up at me. "I trust you."

Her bright green eyes pierced through me on that monstrous admission.

I leaned in to rest my forehead against hers. "I'm going to have to start collecting more than cheesecakes and Italian pastries as rewards for all this help I'm giving." I smiled. "If not, I'm bound to put on a few pounds."

My eyes zoned in on her slightly parted lips, causing me to lick my own.

"We shouldn't." Her hands tightened into my shirt and pulled me closer instead of pushing me away.

"No, we shouldn't." Yet, it seemed as if we were powerless to stop. "You started it a few days ago by my car." I squeezed her hip with one hand, pressing her against me, while my other tangled itself into her hair at the back of her head.

"So I suppose you'll end it, right?" Her eyes seemed to dare me to do just that.

I groaned, no longer giving a shit, and closed the distance between us.

Her lips were warm and soft. Our kiss was slow, testing…respectful. Hannah's tongue came out to tease my lower lip, but I didn't open for her. I wanted to savor the moment in case it never happened again.

Hannah let go of my shirt, wrapped her arms around my neck and feathered her fingers through my hair. Her tongue tested the waters a second time, and I caved. If the taste of her lips was that intoxicating, I could only imagine what the rest of her mouth would be like.

The instant I took charge and plundered her mouth, her knees gave way and I held her tight against my body. I pulled away with a few extra pecks and nuzzled her nose with mine.

Hannah regained her footing, the evidence of lust in her eyes. "Where the hell did you learn to kiss like that?"

My laugh was husky. "You're pretty amazing too." I

winked. "But we should finish this. What time were they supposed to drop by to pick everything up?"

Regretfully, her dazed expression dissipated. "At four, why?" Her hands came from around my neck and stopped at my chest.

"Because if that clock is right," I pointed to the device on the bedside table, "we have under half an hour left."

"Fuck!" Hannah's arms dropped and she moved away from me.

After Lee's stuff was packed up, I remained out of sight while the Parsons came in and carried everything out.

It was damn hard to obey Hannah's wishes with what I ended up hearing.

There were three voices—two male, one female—which had proceeded to verbally attack Hannah. They spouted out everything from teardowns to blame, and worse.

"It should have been you!" the woman stated. Lee's mother was a real piece of work!

It made me sick to hear them treat such a devoted and re-silient woman with so much disrespect and hate.

In the hour after they'd left, I was the one left to pick up the broken pieces of Hannah, comforting the sobbing wom-an, working to convince her that she wasn't to blame for anything that had happened.

It's not my fault. Yes, that mantra was used again.

CHAPTER 28

I didn't get to see much of Hannah over the course of the next few days. With being an employee short at Fairfax, and being called in for fire duty during the evening, I was dead on my feet.

As Saturday morning came, my latest fire call left me sitting on a hospital gurney with a nurse fussing over me as I waited for the doctor's all clear. That's not what had me frustrated, however. I hated myself for having to call Hannah, canceling our scheduled day of baking. I had been looking forward to seeing her.

The woman in question came rushing through the cubicle curtains. "Thank God you're all right!" I hadn't been expecting her, but damn, was she a sight to see.

The feel of her hands all over my bare chest filled me with warmth as Hannah looked me from head to toe, the nurse having stepped back. Hannah's hands moved from my upper torso, to my neck and settled on either side of my face. She was a real mother hen, and I found that I enjoyed it.

"I'm fine, really, just a little headache. Candace would have never worried like–" My mouth snapped shut. Shocked, I cursed my sudden bout of verbal diarrhea. "Hannah…I–"

"It's a damn good thing I'm not her then." Her lips quirked upward, worry in her gaze still present.

"You're right about that." I pulled her into me and wrapped my arms around her, taking in the scent of her hair.

"Where's your shirt?" she mumbled into my neck.

"The medics tore what was left of it to shreds before they strapped me to the backboard."

"What the hell happened?" She pulled away to see my face. "I thought you said that this volunteer business was safe."

"It is, for the most-part. I rushed into the building to get to someone who was trapped. Part of the floor above fell on me." I saw the look of horror cross her face. "Sweetheart, it's not as bad as it sounds. They were just floorboards."

"That doesn't make me feel any better."

I smoothed her hair back and away where I framed her face with my hands. "I'm okay. Anyway, I managed to get the guy and myself out. They sent me here to make sure I didn't end up with a concussion or damage my lungs."

"Didn't you have your mask?"

"I did until I got to the victim," I explained. "I was an idiot and took my mask off to share it with him."

"But I thought you guys aren't supposed to do that?"

I nodded. "You're right. We weren't too far from the exit. I thought I had time. I just didn't expect to have the building come down as fast as it did. The medics told me that had I not shared my mask with that man that he would have most likely ended up in the morgue."

Hannah's hands rubbed my arms in a soothing motion. "What happened to him?"

"He arrested as we got here, apparently. His lungs are pretty bad too, but they think that he'll make it."

"That's horrible!" I nodded. "Is there anything I can do? Do you need anything?"

Could this woman be any sweeter? "After last night, I think I need a good shower, a comfy couch, a couple of pain killers for my head, and a few movies. What do you think of that?"

"I think junk food is needed, and baking is overrated." She smiled. "I'm just happy you're okay, but you're right."

"About what?"

"You do need a good shower." Her nose scrunched up. "You smell like a piece of beef jerky." I laughed out loud. "It's a good thing I like the stuff." She winked.

"It's a good thing I like sweets, because you smell like some kind of treat." I leaned toward her, making her giggle.

"I was playing around in the kitchen when you called."

I nuzzled her nose with mine. "Mmm."

Hannah moved to stand closer between my thighs, her hands landing on them, while I gave her lips a chaste kiss. The heat from her grip made it hard to remain respectable in front of the nurse who now eyed daggers at Hannah's back.

Hannah had other ideas that superseded respectability, however. I groaned when I felt her hand rub up my thigh and she leaned closer. She nuzzled my jaw, pulled back and pecked me on the mouth before pulling away with that glint in her eyes.

"Why do I sense that you're up to something?" I asked.

"When am I not up to something?" She grinned. "So when can you get out of here?"

"Right now," the doctor said as he waltzed into the exam room. I hadn't noticed his appearance until then. Hannah moved to stand at my side, her hip brushing the outer side of my thigh with her close proximity. "You're clear to go, Mr. Carpenter. Your lung function is normal, and there's no concussion, which means you can sleep soundly tonight."

All of this was said while the doctor eyed Hannah from top to bottom with a heated gaze of appraisal.

"Do you mind?" I growled.

Hannah's head jerked to the side where she looked at me as if I was being rude, but when she realized what I was seeing, she moved closer to me and I wrapped my arm around her waist.

Doctor *Feelgood* saw this and said, "Right. Here are the papers." I took them from his hands in a brusque manner. "We signed them so all you need to do is fill out your share and submit them to your insurance. I'm sure I don't need to say this, but if you have any difficulty breathing, dizziness, loss of vision or consciousness, have someone bring you in."

With another quick glance at Hannah, he turned and walked off.

CHAPTER 29

Hannah had taken a cab from home to come and see me after I'd called her instead of driving the rental her insurance had provided her. I knew how she felt, remembering how terrified I'd been to drive after my accident. Panic attacks threatened me constantly every time I got behind the wheel, at first.

Not having my car, we cabbed it to the fire station to fetch my ride.

"Are you sure you don't want to be on your own today?" she asked. "It's okay if you do."

"Get in the car, Hannah," I said. "I'm taking you home with me."

She smirked. "Now that just sounds like you've got some sort of sexy agenda."

"Honey, if it's all I cared about, you'd be lying on the flat of your back with your legs around my waist right now." *Where the hell did that come from?*

Her cheeks pinked. "Well that was blunt! Self-assured much?"

"Nope!" I grinned. "If I were, I would have moved on ages ago and fucked every sensible bitty that I could get my hands on."

"But you're not that type of guy," she said softly as we turned into my driveway.

"No," I parked the car and turned the engine off, "I'm not. I'd rather find someone who challenges me in a good conversation, someone who can take a joke and hold her own, someone who chooses to see the best in people."

"I think I know someone like that."

"Oh yeah? Who?"

"You. But I'm pretty sure you can't date, marry, or screw yourself."

That got me laughing. "That last one is debatable, depending on how you look at it." I made to exit the car.

After giving Hannah the grand tour of my house, amazing her with the grandeur of my kitchen—which is where I left her—it was high time I did something about the smell of smoke and layer of grime that stuck to me.

An assortment of noises downstairs, followed by a shriek, then a crash of broken glass, graced my ears as I exited my bathroom.

Chucking my towel onto the floor, I slid my jeans on and did them up, slinging my t-shirt over my shoulder, and rushed downstairs. Hannah was face down on the floor.

"Holy shit!" I hurried to help her up, shards of glass scattered everywhere. "Are you okay, what happened?"

"Would you believe that I like your floor so much I wanted to kiss it?" She got to her knees, laughing.

Her giggle cut short when her eyes settled on my bare chest, then widened.

"No, but I'd believe that you have two left feet." That seemed to get her to look up at my face. "What is all this?"

"I figured that you'd be hungry so I made you something to eat."

"Are you okay?"

"I'm fine. Ego's a little bruised, but that's it."

I kissed her forehead before heading for the closet. "Stay there." I came back with the broom only to find her crouched down, picking up pieces of food, as well as some of the larger pieces of glass, and setting them on the tray she'd been using to carry everything.

She tried to take the broom from me and put a hand on my chest. "It's my mess. Let me clean it up." She paused, her fingers rubbing lightly over my skin, and just as quick, snapped her hand back, mumbling, "And put a shirt on."

I smirked down at her. "It's not my fault you scared me half to death that I never finished getting dressed."

"Here." She passed me the tray. "I'll start over when I'm done here."

She turned and started sweeping the floor with more force than necessary. I set the tray of spoils on the side table, walked up behind her, and wrapped my arms around her waist in a hug. Her surliness was endearing.

"Are you mad?" I dropped my chin onto her shoulder.

She huffed. "No!" I gave her another squeeze. "Well, yeah. Sort of. You've been taking care of me non-stop over the last few weeks, and I figured I'd take care of you for a change, but I've gone and mucked it up."

"So you wanted to take care of me?" I murmured. Had she not been paying attention? She had been doing just that without even trying since we'd met. Just having her around listening to what I had to say made everything better.

She gave me a small nod before she turned around to face me. She found herself nose to bare chest again and looked up with an arched brow.

I chuckled. "You know you like it."

"I can't say that I don't." She got up on the tips of her toes, pecked me on the cheek and relinquished the broom by shoving it in my hands.

In the end, I swept while she went back to the kitchen to fix me more food. It may have been a sandwich, but it was one of the best ones I'd ever tasted. She did me one better and I found a bowl of fruit and berries with what looked like a simple syrup poured on top.

Hannah hadn't fixed herself anything to eat, so I asked, "Aren't you hungry?" She shook her head. I picked up a few pieces of fruit from the bowl with my fork and put it in front of her mouth. "Open up."

"I made that for you."

"And I share."

The day passed by in a flash and when the last movie of the night ended, I was sandwiched between the back of the couch and a sleeping Hannah, who had an arm wrapped around my torso and her head on my shoulder. She looked so comfortable that I didn't want to wake her, but we couldn't spend the night on the couch. Well, she couldn't.

I shuffled her legs over mine and sat myself up. When I had her in my arms properly, I got up and carried her to my room. I laid her on the bed and covered her with the comforter, bending over to kiss her forehead, where she released a sigh.

I smiled as I made my way back downstairs, taking my shirt and jeans off and laying them on the armrest of the chair beside the couch, which was where I was spending the night.

I laid back, covered myself with the throw and closed my eyes, finding myself imagining what it would be like to spend a proper night in bed, cuddled with Hannah in my arms, before I drifted off.

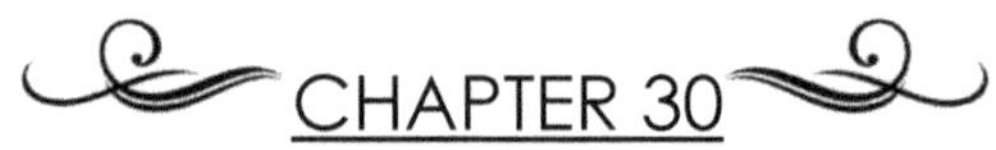

CHAPTER 30

*T*he road was dark and rough. Karen had been crying non-stop for the last hour and it didn't matter that we'd changed her diaper and fed her. She wasn't taking her soother, and it was clear that the car ride wasn't working as it normally did.

Candace was beside herself with frustration, and to be honest, so was I.

We'd been arguing, which in my opinion was why Karen was so hysterical at the moment, sensing her parents' joint frustrations.

My wife had been distant over the last month and I worried that she might be coming down with post-partum depression, despite her insisting that it wasn't an issue.

"Sue me, Candy," I said hotly. "I care. I worry. Am I not entitled to that as your husband?"

Apparently that hadn't been the right choice of words. She went off on another one of her tangents and all I wanted to do was get us home so I could put this latest squabble—this day—to rest.

After what must have been the tenth time of Candace leaning over the passenger seat to put Karen's soother back in her mouth, she unbuckled herself and flung the seatbelt to the side, its buckle hitting the passenger-side window with a loud clunk. With her rising temper, her patience was at a loss.

I peered at her from the corner of my eye in annoyance

because of her petty behavior. Sometimes she could really rattle my nerves with her tantrums.

"Would you just give it up already?" I said. *"You know she's just going to spit it out."*

"I need quiet. I need to think, Benjamin."

"What is there to think about?" I asked. *"Karen needs you at home. We're trying to get everything in order to open the damn bar! I've been working on this deal for months. I can't do that for us and carry a baby with me all day long because Chris says he needs you in New York. You agreed to take six months off and here you are, already working for the guy after two."*

"Ben—"

"No, Candace. Had he called a week ago, maybe we could have worked something out. I can't reschedule these investor meetings, you know that. Do you not want to do this anymore? You said it was your dream as much as it's mine."

"Ben..." Karen's crying grew louder. *"Dammit, Karen!"*

I took my eyes off the road and turned my fiery gaze at my wife, growling, *"Don't you dare take it out on her!"*

"I'm going to New York, Ben," she said. *"And we need to talk when I get back."* *She finished putting the soother back in Karen's mouth and turned to face forward, not bothering with her seatbelt.*

My eyes were still fused to my wife in shock at what she'd just announced, rather than anger.

"Ben..." she said. *I heard her, but I wasn't really listening.*

What the hell is going on with her? *I was trying to figure out why this supposed talk needed to wait until her return. Better yet, what could she possibly want to discuss?*

"Ben..." Her tone seemed different now, but I was too busy juggling my thoughts. I still hadn't peeled my eyes off of her either. *"Ben, watch—"*

By the time she repeated my name a third time and I registered her panic, it was too late.

"Fuck! Hold on!" I gripped the steering wheel, jerking it hard to the right.*

I managed to avoid the oncoming vehicle, but when I veered back to the left to get back onto the road, the SUV hit a rut and we were sent careening into a culvert. Candace's scream shrilled in my ears one second, then everything was dead silent the next.

"Ben," I heard as everything faded away to black. "Ben! Wake up, it's a nightmare."

I sat up abruptly and took in my surroundings. Hannah was sitting on the edge of the couch beside me, her hands cradling my face as I tried to catch my breath.

"Hannah," I choked out.

"I'm here, Ben," she said. "Look at me."

I did just that. I grabbed her forearms and squeezed to assure myself that she was really there.

Through choppy breaths, I whispered, "She was going to leave me. I remember now."

"What do you mean?"

I explained, my voice finding a bit more strength. "I remember why we were in the car. I remember the crash, the look on Candace's face, but for the life of me," I swallowed, "I haven't been able to remember what we were arguing about. I think she was going to leave me."

Hannah pulled me to her and wrapped her arms around me as I did the same with her. Her hand moved in a soothing pattern while the other massaged the nape of my neck as she cooed soothing words into my ear.

After a few minutes, I felt lulled enough to let her go. *How'd she do that?*

The sides of our faces rubbed against the other as I backed away. Her hands slid so she barely cradled my neck, but the skin-to-skin contact was still there. She pressed her forehead to mine and rubbed the pads of her thumbs in a circular motion over my temples. My eyes were fused to hers.

"Ben?" she whispered.

I kissed her. And not like all of our other friendly pecks, either. I went in hard.

Sliding my arms around her, I cradled her head with one hand, while the other pulled her into me, forcing her to straddle my waist. Hannah's purr of satisfaction fueled me further as her hands tangled themselves into my hair.

She held my head as I descended kisses onto her jaw, to her ear and down toward her collarbone.

"Don't stop," she begged in a breathless voice, and I pulled back to look at her face.

With a shy smile, she lifted her arms above her head. My fingers played with the hem of her t-shirt and she nodded to encourage me further. I lifted it over her head and groaned at the sight before me.

When my eyes were done taking her in, I looked into her eyes. I didn't see an ounce of hesitation or shyness. I saw a woman who knew exactly what she was doing, what she wanted. That was a major turn on.

"I've always known you were beautiful, but–" Before I could continue, her lips captured mine.

She kissed a trail down to my jaw and back up to my ear. I hissed when she took its lobe between her teeth and gave it a light tug. "I told you that you should have kept your shirt on."

On a husky laugh, my palms glided over her back, reaching her shoulder-blades as my lips trailed down her collarbone. When she arched back, I took advantage and began to kiss lower, toward the valley between those luscious mounds of hers. She let her hands fall from my head and trailed them down over my shoulders until they halted on my biceps.

I nipped the tender skin that edged the lace of her bra, eliciting what I will testify as being the sexiest moan I had ever heard. I pulled back and waited for her to look at me.

"Don't stop!"

"Are you sure about this?" She nodded. "Then we're doing this right."

Without another word, I picked her up, her legs wrapping

around my waist, and carefully took the stairs that led us to my bedroom.

I laid her down and covered her body with mine. She pulled away in shock when she realized that I was in nothing more than my boxers.

I shrugged my shoulders. "I can't sleep in clothes."

She cupped one of my butt cheeks as a rebuttal, and smiled up at me. "I'm not about to complain. The less, the better. Now, hurry up and take my pants off."

I laughed. "Nope." Her breath hitched. "I think I'll take my time."

"Be careful. You might be privy to the same treatment the next time around."

"Next time?"

"I'm not going anywhere." She lifted her hands to pull my head down toward hers, her eyes ensnaring me. "You need me, Ben. And I need you."

The taste of her was as sweet as her words. I couldn't get enough.

Delivering random kisses to her stomach, I peeled her jeans off.

"Don't look at my legs," she was quick to say.

I ignored her. They were still mangled from the accident, but I didn't give a shit about the scrapes, scabs and fresh scars. She could have been covered in lacerations from head to toe and she'd still be beautiful to me.

In order to maintain her ease however, I made sure to move on. I got to her underwear and ran my hand over her pelvis. She arched into my hand.

I climbed my kisses back up and she wrapped her arms around my shoulders, while arching into my chest as I kissed her neck. I took that opportunity to undo the catch to her bra, divesting her of it.

Straddling her hips, and leaning over to fetch a condom in my bedside table, Hannah thought it wise to have some fun of her own. Her mouth and hands made contact with my abs, making the muscles tense and ripple beneath the feel of her. Everywhere she touched set my skin to a slow burn.

I let her have her way for a short while, until her hands made a grab for my boxers to pull them off.

Stilling her hands, I said, "Not yet, sweetheart." I shimmied down her torso to kneel between her legs.

"Why do you call me that?"

"You don't like it?"

"I do, but–"

"It just seems fitting because it's who you are to me." I brushed the back of my fingers over her cheek. "You're sweet. You're beautiful inside and out. You're special."

My lips met hers in a long drugging kiss before I headed for her underwear. My fingers trailed over the damp spot that was there. She drew a sharp breath when my knuckle made contact with her bud through the thin material.

In one swift pull, her underwear was gone and she was exposed. I took the opportunity to push my boxers down and slide on the condom before I got down to business.

"Oh my God, Ben, no!" she said as my mouth made contact with her wet core. I gave her slit a few licks before I sucked on her clit. She moaned and writhed under me. "God, don't stop!"

I laughed internally, having given myself a new challenge. I was going to make this little spitfire beneath me find a new appreciation for what a mouth, teeth, and tongue could do.

I licked her slit with smooth long strokes, coaxing that little jewel of hers out more before wrapping my lips around it and sucking again.

"Ben!"

I added fingers to the mix, delving in one, and then adding a second digit, as I curled them to tap that sweet spot inside of her. Her hips automatically lifted off the bed and into my face.

Perfect.

"Oh God, Ben! Yes! Don't stop, please don't stop!"

In the next moment, Hannah's hands found my hair, and pulled as she screamed her release.

Without hesitation, I moved up her body, her hands locking behind my neck and bringing me straight to her mouth for a heated kiss.

I guided myself slowly inside her, plundering her mouth with my tongue, relishing the feel of her heated depth with my cock. I could feel her contract around my shaft as her velvet softness convulsed with the remnants of her orgasm.

I withdrew from her slowly with a hiss. "You're so tight."

"Deeper, Ben," she panted.

And so I gave it all to her in one swift thrust.

To my surprise, the woman broke all over again, moaning her release into my neck. I began to thrust, my balls already tightening up, making me slow my pace. It'd been so long that there was no way I was going to last much longer.

When Hannah's hips began to meet mine, I was a goner. I pulled back to watch her face. She graced me with a smile, her hands gliding up my chest as she lifted her head to kiss me. Hannah sighed into my mouth.

No longer able to hold off, I exploded, sending her into a final tailspin. Her arms clutched at my shoulders, while I brought us down from our carnal heights. Her face was flush with a look of pure bliss, and I smiled knowing I had put that look there.

"Candace wouldn't know a great lover if his dick hit her right between the eyes," Hannah mumbled into my neck.

I exploded with laughter.

In the heat of the moment, it hadn't occurred to me to dwell on the shortcomings that Candace had listed in her journals.

"Something told me you wouldn't have believed her had she been the one to tell you herself," I said. I trailed kisses from Hannah's shoulder toward her neck and enjoyed the feel of having her wrapped around me—her softness to my hardness—her fingertips running over the skin of my back, bringing forth goosebumps.

Later in the night, when Hannah had fallen asleep at my side, I knew that what happened between us hadn't been a mistake. Had it been, we wouldn't have gone for another round. Had it been, I'm sure I would be feeling some kind of regret.

My mind was going a hundred miles an hour, and it all had to do with the night of my accident—the nightmare. I'd had that dream so many times before, but why had those missing scenes played out now?

Had I been right about Candace wanting to leave me? It sure seemed like it in the dream.

I knew where I'd find the answers to my questions.

Careful not to wake Hannah, I got out of bed, and went to grab the journals. As I eased myself under the covers, she said, "What's going on?" Damn, she was cute in her sleepy daze.

"I couldn't sleep." I kissed her forehead as she came to settle against my shoulder. "Go back to sleep. I'll just read for a bit."

She looked up and met my gaze. "Read to me?"

She was wide awake now, and I really didn't mind sharing this with her. So, I opened the book that highlighted Candace's other life…

CHAPTER 31

I made a large effort tonight. It hadn't been all that hard, really. I finished reading the remainder of Candace's journals, all the way up to the very last entry, which left off a few days prior to the accident.

Upon finishing, I closed the book and rested it on my lap.

There was no other way to explain it, I was numb.

Hannah sat beside me with her head on my shoulder. Silent.

"Well," I cleared my throat, "I'm glad that's over."

Hannah sat herself up. I felt her eyes on me, studying, reading me to see what I needed next. I'd grown accustomed to her doing that. I liked her doing it. She seemed to always know what it took to soothe me, calm my frustrations, or in this case, the building rage that I felt.

Her fingers grasped my chin and turned my face toward hers. "You're better than all of this, Ben."

I looked into her eyes for any form of pity or sympathy. I found none.

I finally had my answers.

While reading, flashbacks of that night filled the small gaps that had been left from my earlier nightmare. I knew what happened down to every last word. It was clear I'd lost Candace a long time before I'd physically lost her presence on this world.

Closing that last journal was like closing the book on a never-ending chapter in my life. Despite the anger, the resentment, and the betrayal, I felt lighter. I felt free to do as I pleased, and I hadn't a clue as to where I wanted to go from there, but I knew I had time to figure it out.

In the span of a night, I'd gone from being a widower and father, who had it all, to feeling like I'd never had any of it. What I believed to have been mine over the years, I never truly possessed. And I don't mean my wife.

Karen wasn't mine as it turns out, which was another reason why Candace had begun to make plans to leave me.

Gut-wrenching sobs got the better of me when I first read those words. Hannah had simply held onto and reminded me that I'd been the only steady father that Karen had ever known, and that made me more of a father to her than her own kin. It made me feel better. Barely.

"I need to do something," I told Hannah as the sun rose behind the curtains. We still hadn't slept.

She snuggled into me. "What did you have in mind?"

"I need to go see her parents. I think it's time." *But...*

Hannah lifted her head to look at me while my gaze remained trained to the ceiling. "What is it?"

I let out a loud sigh. "I can't go there alone and I know I should."

"How about this?" She kissed my cheek. "I'll go with you for moral support, but I'll stay in the car. I doubt that they'd be thrilled to see you with a woman anyway."

I nodded. "Let's get a bit of shut-eye first." Shuffling us down, she settled into the crook of my arm.

CHAPTER 32

Later that afternoon, we jumped in my car and headed for Betty and Don's. I had called ahead to make sure that they'd be there, not wanting to turn one visit into multiples when I wasn't sure what to expect.

The drive there had been silent and anxiety-ridden. Hannah held my hand the entire time and I fed off of her strength to keep me moving forward.

I came to a stop in their driveway, turned the car off and left the keys in the ignition for my companion.

Releasing a calming breath, I said, "I'll be back as soon as I can. Knowing me, I'll be running out of there in the next five minutes."

Joking might not have been the best thing in this moment, but it was the only thing I knew to do when I felt uncomfortable prior to doing something I wholeheartedly dreaded.

"No, you won't." She rubbed the side of my arm. "You can do this, Ben. You're ready and if you need me, I'm right here." Her arms pulled me in for a hug.

I nodded into her neck and took in her scent, its soothing properties calming my erratic heartbeat. Holding her face between my palms, I kissed her forehead. "I'll be back."

The walk up to the door felt entirely too short before I was knocking. I didn't have to wait long for Betty and Don to greet me with hugs.

"I'm so glad you called," Betty said, her body stiffening as she pulled away from our hug. "Who's that?"

"A friend."

She pulled further back. Much to my disbelief, the woman was beaming. "A girlfriend?"

I chuckled. "Maybe someday."

"Well she can't stay in the car," Betty said, waving at Hannah to join us. "There's a reason she's here with you, and that makes her special."

Don put a hand on my shoulder. "We know this decision of yours to visit wasn't easy."

I hadn't heard the car door open, so I turned and motioned for Hannah to join us. I just hoped that Betty and Don were sincere about their acceptance of Hannah's presence because I knew I needed all of them in my life, regardless of circumstance, and I couldn't help but want Hannah in whatever capacity she was willing to be present.

Hannah got out of the car with the keys and locked it. She walked up to us with a shy smile. I winked at her when she looked up at me from my side.

After introductions were made, Betty and Don took us around to the back patio. Candace's mother served us some lemonade before she sat down to discuss the proverbial elephant in the room.

"I'm presuming that you're here because of what we dropped off." The pain on Don's face was obvious.

I nodded.

"You being here means–" Betty said.

"I've read them," I said.

I saw the look of relief cross their faces. They knew what their daughter had been up to.

"We tried so many times to give you her stuff," Don said.

"I know. I'm sorry I never gave you guys the opportunity, but, three years?"

"It's my fault," Betty was quick to say as she reached for Don's hand. "Her office called about a month after the funeral. Her boss had the box dropped off here. I knew that you weren't ready to deal with more of her belongings, so I got Don to put them away in the attic."

Six months ago, they'd been cleaning the space when they'd stumbled upon it and decided to take a look. It was right around the same time that their appearances grew in frequency. They wanted me to know.

"I never meant to read them, but as I leafed through the pages, it became evident that Candace had another life away from you," Betty confessed. "So I packed everything up and left it in the car until the next time we saw you, to pass it on."

"You needed to know," Don said. "We love you like you're ours, Ben."

"I know." I swallowed the lump that had formed in my throat. "And I love you both, too." The reality was heart-wrenching, but it was a fact. Betty and Don were great people and had taken me in as one of their own. "I need to ask if you've read everything?"

"We have an idea, but I felt it best that we didn't pry more than we already had," Betty said.

I nodded and took a deep breath. Hannah grabbed my hand. "She wasn't just having an affair." Both Betty and Don looked down and nodded their heads in understanding. "Chris," Betty's head snapped up, "he was her boss. And Karen," Don matched Betty's stunned gaze, "she wasn't mine." I took a deep breath. "Candace was planning to leave me."

I answered as many of their questions as I could handle, which—to my shock—ended up being all of them.

The couple was rendered to tears of sadness as I spoke. Their faces gave away the guilt they harbored for the shit their daughter had put me through.

Now that they knew about their daughter, I had one more thing to discuss.

"I never talked much about the night of the accident, and that's because I couldn't remember everything that happened."

"Oh, Ben!" Betty reached out for my hand.

I presumed that my grief and the trauma of my loss had caused me to block out certain things about that night. I explained that up until last night, I hadn't a clue as to why it was that my attention was diverted from the road, why I'd lost control of the car, what had been happening that led us down the road that led to where we were today.

"We've never blamed you, Ben." Betty squeezed my hand. "All we ever wanted was to make sure you knew that we were here for you. We want you to be happy."

I caught both her and Don eyeing Hannah and smiling at her. The woman was blushing from their attention.

Squeezing Hannah's hand, which had yet to let go of mine, I said, "I think I'm on my way there."

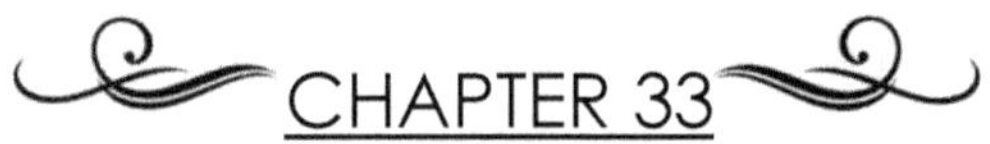

CHAPTER 33

Hannah and I left Betty and Don's a few hours later.

"Do you have somewhere you need to be?" I asked her.

"Nope, not really. What do you have in mind?"

I drove us back to her place so she could change into something more appropriate for what I had planned.

As I waited for her, I walked around the living room and found that all the framed photos of her and Lee had disappeared. Those of her and her parents, and some with who I assumed were friends of hers, had remained. Hannah was making her house her own, and those were great signs of her forward progress in moving on.

"How's this?"

I turned to see her in a tight pair of skinny jeans and a tank top that hugged her chest and flowed loosely around her waist. "Perfect!" I smiled at her. "Now let's go. I don't want to be late."

Holding my breath, I parked in the drive.

"Ben, why are we at my parents' place?"

"This is where I'm taking you to dinner." I grinned. "Your mother invited me over as a thank you, and there was no way I was coming without you being here."

"What is this? Parents' Day?" she asked. "Should I be on guard that we've got other parents to meet, for dessert perhaps? Or maybe it's for a late night tea?"

I laughed. "No, this is it. After this, you're safe from anyone's parents, including mine."

I wish I had been right about that one. As we opened the door to leave after dinner, I found myself face-to-face with two familiar faces.

"Mom…Dad," I said. "What are you–"

"Roz…Doug," Adam said. "Come in!"

"Ben?" my mother said, then looked over at Hannah who stood at my side.

"Hannah, honey…here. I meant to give this to you the other day." Anne handed her an envelope.

"Hannah?" Dad asked. "As in–"

"I knew it!" Mom clapped her hands, and that's when I clued in. Those curious looks my parents had shared during my last visit with them.

Hannah looked at me and then back to my Dad. "Roz and Doug are your parents?" I nodded and she started to laugh. "I've heard so much about you! I feel like I know you guys already. I'm Hannah." She stuck her hand out and shook my parents' hands. "Mom and Dad talk about you two all the time."

Dad grinned. "This is a small world."

"How are you feeling, dear?" Mom tucked a strand of Hannah's hair behind her ear. "Your mother told me about the accident just the other day."

"I'm getting there." Hannah looked up and smiled at me. "Thanks in large part to your son."

"Were you guys leaving?" Dad asked. Hannah and I nodded.

"I hope we see you again really soon, Hannah." Mom surprised her with a hug. It was a slightly longer-lasting one, and when I caught Hannah nodding in the embrace, I could only imagine what my mother had said to her.

They shared a look as they backed away, Mom cupping

her cheek and then turning to me. I wasn't escaping from one of her embraces. I'd missed the large punch the tiny woman generated.

"Thanks for dinner, it was delicious," I said to Hannah's parents.

"You're welcome, Benjamin," Anne said. "I hope we keep seeing you around."

"Yes, ma'am." She gave me a mocking glare, chasing it with a wink.

With a few extra hugs and kisses to her parents, I did the gentlemanly thing and helped Hannah to my car. She rolled her eyes at me, but didn't move.

"Just get in, will you." I chuckled. "They're watching."

"I know." She waggled her brows, which made me laugh loudly. Kissing me on the cheek, she then dipped into the passenger seat quickly, while our parents giggled.

After a great and very entertaining dinner at the Donners', and the unexpected run-in with my parents, I'd invited Hannah over, not wanting our time together to end just yet.

"Well, that was an interesting day," I said.

"It's hilarious, really," she said. "Like kismet."

I gave her an inquisitive look. "Kismet?"

"Like fate, chance, destiny…That kind of stuff. We've spent our lives growing up in close-by neighborhoods, own businesses that are only a few blocks from each other. We've probably gone to the same schools. And we meet in a place that couldn't have been further from where we'd normally be."

"If it's fate's fault that we're here, it's got one damn twisted sense of humor," I said as I turned the corner.

"Why are we on my street?" she asked. "I thought we were going to yours."

"We are, but I figured that you would want to pick up a few things to bring over."

Her lips tilted up. "Good. I haven't slept this great

since…Well, I don't know how long really." She proceeded almost at a whisper, her expression darkening, her eyes holding a faraway look. "I got used to sleeping in a bed alone while Lee was off on business trips or entertaining clients. I learned to sleep lightly in case something went wrong."

I cupped her cheek, which seemed to bring her back to the present. "Well, the good news is that you don't have anyone to worry about now. You can sleep soundly." I leaned forward and kissed her forehead. "Go get your stuff."

"You're wrong, you know." She proceeded to open her car door. "I worry about everyone I care for, Ben. Especially you."

Without another word, she shut the door and bounced up her front step before disappearing inside.

When Hannah didn't return after ten minutes, I went searching for her.

I found her on the living room floor, crumpled and crying, looking broken.

"Hannah!" I rushed to her side. "What's wrong?"

"I can't! I can't…*not* go!"

"Not go where, sweetheart?" I pulled her to her feet, hugging her to me.

"They don't want me at the memorial," she said, muffled into my chest.

"That's bullshit!"

She nodded. "They have no right."

You're damn right they don't!

"What do I do?" she asked.

"You go anyway." It was that simple, in my opinion. "I'll go and I'm sure your parents will come along. You won't be alone. You need this for closure, just like I needed to read those journals."

She pulled back enough to tilt her head up and look at me. She shook her head. "Why am I so weak when it comes to them?"

"You've said that a few times before. What do you mean?"

It hadn't just been his parents. She explained that it had been the same with Lee after a while of them being together.

"When we first started dating, I thought it was weird that he let them run his life. I tried to tell him to grow a pair, but after a few years, I understood him. What's worse is that he turned into them after a while, too."

"So he controlled you?"

"Yeah, but it's my fault. I allowed it to happen. The thing about Lee and his family is that they're a manipulative bunch. By the time I realized what was happening, it was too late. I was stuck, couldn't get out of the cycle."

As the years rolled on, she found herself giving more of herself to a man that ended up taking and never giving back. He controlled everything, except for Cake It Up.

I confessed to how I felt when Lee's relatives had come to fetch his stuff and I'd overheard them. "They had no right to speak to you like that, sweetheart. It took everything in me not to come down here and tell them off."

"I'm glad you didn't. It would have made everything so much worse."

"I figured as much. It's the only reason why I didn't." I rubbed her arms in an up and down motion.

"Can we go?"

"I'll understand if you want to stay."

"No!" She was adamant. "Staying here will drive me crazy. Plus, I'll enjoy making you breakfast in the morning in that kitchen of yours."

"I feel used, but a personal chef is a grand idea." That got me the desired reaction: a small laugh. "I could get used to not cooking." I bent over and picked up her bag, holding out my hand for her.

"There's only the issue of payment." I turned my head to look at her and arched my brow. "I like to be paid in advance." She chased her words with a grin, which I matched.

"I think that can be arranged."

CHAPTER 34

I brought Hannah's bag up to my bedroom for her despite her insistence that she wasn't an invalid.

"I'm just–" My words stopped dead in my mouth when I turned from dropping my wallet on my dresser and there she was, at the foot of the bed, standing over her bag, riffling away through her possessions. In nothing but some barely-there strapless lace bra and her jeans.

She turned to face me as if everything were normal. "You were just, what?"

I ogled her with a heated gaze before shaking myself out of it and arching my brow at her. "What are you doing?"

"Changing. What's it look like?"

My blubbering antics came back as I took in the see-through pink lace. "Y-you really shouldn't…" Christ on a crutch, she was gorgeous.

"Ben?" My eyes flew up to hers. "Do I make you uncomfortable?"

"No." *You make me want to lick you from top to bottom.* I cleared my throat. "It's just that after last night, *this*…It makes it hard for me to keep my hands off of you."

She stepped toward me and I backed up, my ass meeting the dresser's edge, cornering me in. The siren before me came to a stop when we stood toe-to-toe. "Ben?" she said sweetly.

"Hmm?" I stared down at the perfect view of the valley between her breasts. I licked my lips as the blood pooled in my lower anatomy. If she got any closer, I wouldn't be in control of what happened next. My hands remained at my sides, fisted tight.

She reached up and tilted my head so I could only see her face, not to mention, her humored expression. "My eyes are up here." Winking, she backed away to slip the stretched-out t-shirt she'd been holding over her head.

Phew!

"I'm going to go down there." My eyes were now glued to that firm jean-clad tush of hers. "And wait."

"And here I thought you were about to pounce."

Was that a pout? "Be careful, woman." I smirked. "If that lacy bit comes back out to play, you'll be getting more than just a pouncing white knight."

Her eyes glittered with humor. "I'll keep that in mind."

CHAPTER 35

Through the evening, we made light conversation about random things. I found myself on my back with my head on Hannah's lap. I could have fallen asleep with the way her fingers massaged my scalp.

"Tell me," I grasped her free hand and interlaced our fingers before bringing her knuckles up to my lips for a kiss, "why do you feel so compelled to help people?"

She smiled down at me. "I feel I should be asking you that same question."

"You go first."

"I've been like this for as long as I can remember," she began. "The earliest is when I brought a kid home from school. He'd confessed that his parents didn't have enough money for his school lunch. I guess my parents nurtured that in me too, since Mom didn't even bat an eyelash at the stranger in her home and fed him practically the entire contents of our fridge."

I laughed. "It does sound like something your mother would do."

She nodded. "As I got older, it was little things. I'd top up a parking meter. I'd help an old person with their groceries, a pregnant person reach for something high or low on a shelf, things like that. I think I got addicted to seeing them smile."

"And the bigger things?"

"You mean Lee?" I nodded. She took a deep breath, darkness clouding her features. "Everything was perfect from the get-go. It wasn't until about a year after we'd been together that he finally opened up about his alcoholism. He was sober back then. Maybe it's because I believed too much in him that I was disappointed when he started drinking again. I was naïve to think that a recovering alcoholic, no matter how in control they seem, was able to have a couple here and there, and that it wouldn't affect them in the long run. Maybe he never believed enough in himself to stay sober. I was taught to never give up on someone you love, but no one told me that there comes a point where you have no choice but to let them walk without a crutch. Even though I complained about his drinking, I realized too late that I had been Lee's crutch, his enabler in certain aspects of his addiction. Maybe I could have been harder on him. Maybe if I'd said or done something differently…"

"You can't know that it would have made a difference for sure."

"I know." Her eyes cast themselves downward.

Enough about Lee. "What about me?" I straightened to be closer when she answered to see her eyes clearly. To witness the emotions in those bright irises of hers.

Her smile was one of appreciation for the subtle subject change. "You, Benjamin Carpenter, are by far someone who's literally fallen into my lap." She cradled my cheek before letting her hand drop. "Like I've said before, we're connected somehow, and it showed from that very first night." I nodded. "It was never a decision when it came to helping you. That's where you're different from everyone else, including Lee. It wasn't a choice, it just was.

"Being here for you, listening, cuddling, laughing, talking…It's easy. It's natural for me. There's no effort, it's brainless. I've never had that before.

"Sometimes I think that it's too perfect, that there's a hidden agenda. That like with everyone else, you'll disappoint me, but I haven't been yet, and part of me tells me that you're different from the others. I feel that if I were to go looking for disappointment, I wouldn't find it.

Her hand cupped my cheek. "You're not a charity case, Ben, not in my eyes. You're my savior, my friend, my confidant, my lover." A blush blossomed on her cheeks and I cradled her face in my hands as our eyes remained fused to the others'. "I could go on all night, listing what I truly think of you, but they'd all mean the same thing in the end."

"And what's that?"

"The way I feel…You remember me saying kismet earlier?"

"Yeah."

"It's like you were made for me, for this particular time in my life, just like I was made to come into yours."

Her eyes left mine and she tried to angle her face away from my gaze. God how I adored her right then, but was it too quick to feel so strongly about one another?

I realized that I didn't give a damn what others thought. No one had been in our situation. It wouldn't be the first time that people heard about two traumatised people bonding rapidly and finding love.

Love?

I pondered the thought for a few seconds, waiting for the apprehension to set in, the panic to take hold. Taking another glimpse at her shy profile, I just knew. Yes, love was ultimately going to be the eventual outcome in this. I wasn't quite there yet, but I was falling, and falling fast. And I embraced the emotions.

"Hannah?"

"Hmm?"

"You forgot to mention something when you listed what I am to you."

Her eyes snapped back to mine. "Yeah?" Her voice was an octave above a whisper.

"You forgot that I'm solely, utterly, and completely yours." I grinned.

The smile that beamed back at me could have brightened up the entire house it had so much wattage. I kissed the tear that escaped, then the side of her mouth, finishing off with her soft lips.

Her hands rested on my chest as I tried to convey that what she'd just said about me mattered more than she ever thought it could.

Too quickly, Hannah pulled away. "I believe you owe me an answer," she murmured.

"I can't compete with what you just told me, but here goes."

I told her about Mom and Dad doing volunteer work since before I was born. "When I was a little kid, I always wanted to tag along, so my parents allowed it. I learned from a very young age that people came from various walks of life, and some nowhere near glamorous.

"As a teenager, the church functions grew too boring, so I began volunteering at a soup kitchen during the holidays and over summer break. I kept working there when I came home from college."

"So how does a bartender get to become a volunteer fire-fighter?" she asked.

I looked down and reached for her hand. "It was after the accident," I began. "The guilt I felt after that night was hor-rible and no amount of talk therapy worked, whether it was with family, my friends, or my therapists. I didn't want to be medicated because I didn't like the numbness the drugs caused.

"One day, I bumped into an old high-school buddy of mine. He's a full-time fireman. He mentioned that they needed guys to fill in the occasional gaps.

"I blamed myself for what happened that night, and I don't know if it'll ever go away. My eyes should have been on the road and..." I took a deep breath. "I guess I figured that if I could save one life that it would help me get back in God's good graces, even though I don't really believe in all that religious crap anymore."

Hannah nodded. "I've been thinking about that too. If God had anything to do with it, why'd he take them away?"

"Right? That's what I asked myself too. Anyway, I vol-unteered and did my training. Shortly after, I gave up on God and the church, but it seemed like a waste of time and effort to give the firefighter gig up. There's a huge sense of accomplishment after a successful call. More often than not, I help people. Sure, I put myself in danger, but it's worth something.

"What you need to know is that it's not about glory, and since the gig was on a volunteer basis, it sure as hell isn't about the money. The pay is in the form of health benefits, the conditions are less than desirable, but what does it for me is that after giving it my all, that I am able to give someone a second chance, that I helped save a family from suffering a major loss."

"And what about me?" she asked.

"I almost didn't stop that night," I confessed.

"But you did."

I nodded. "Almost didn't," I repeated. "I did because I knew I couldn't live with myself if I didn't check things out and make sure everything was okay. I remember driving up and down that winding road in my parents' car as a teenager. The faster, the better. That outlook changed the night of my accident. A few miles down from where I found you was where everything changed for me." Hannah gasped at what I'd just told her.

"When I saw your car, the past came flooding back. I could barely recognize the make and model of it. When your eyes made contact with mine that first time, it was as if I was looking at myself through you. Something about you that night shook me to my core.

"When I checked on Lee, I knew that his chances weren't good. And then…"

"…he died," she supplied.

I nodded. "As a firefighter I've had to deal with car wrecks before, but this time it was different. For one, it was my first incident on that stretch of road since my accident.

"I've always been a man of my word, so when I told you I wouldn't leave you, I lived up to it, but you…There's something about you, Hannah. You kept me coming back. I don't know what it is about you, but there was this instant connection. I cared about what happened to you before I even knew you, so I fought to be there for you."

Hannah's brows furrowed. "You fought?"

I shrugged my shoulders. "I didn't know how your family would react, but I came anyway. Then, I was willing to fight the doctor to let me through to see you. Hannah, I've never gone after someone I've saved before. I've always been curious, but I've never just shown up." Hannah squeezed my hand. "Most importantly, I was worried that your trauma would have caused you to forget who I was, and what had happened. Kind of like what happened to me. I worried that your family would have kept me from you, so I tried to convince myself to leave, to not bother…so I fought with myself too."

"Yet there you were." She smiled. "I guess you won the fight, huh?"

"Yeah." I returned her smile. "You calm me more than anyone I've ever known. For the first time in three long years, I can actually sleep without nightmares. You make it easier to smile, to laugh, to joke around. You make me happy, Hannah, and I haven't been happy in far too long.

"I can't say that I ever expected anything like this to happen, especially with the circumstances, because I don't think anyone anticipates happiness to shine through after what we've been through."

"I know what you mean."

"Over the last few weeks, you've become more than just some victim I saved. Truth is, you were never a victim in my eyes. You were my savior, my friend, my confidant and yes, now my lover." Hannah's brows arched. "Okay, so I stole your line, but it says all I need to say." She laughed. "I'm yours like I said, but at the risk of chasing you away, I need to know that you'll be mine too. I don't expect an 'I love you' because Lord knows everything's happening so fast. I want us to be happy, to live life without regret, without guilt, without ever having to look back. If it could only happen to one of us, I'd want it for you. Your mother told me something while you were still asleep…"

"You deserve so much more than what you've been handed," we said together and I smiled at her.

"That's right," I said. "It's the truth. I have no clue what the future holds, only that right now, you're all I need, and I don't see it changing any time soon."

"So let me get this straight," she said. "I'm not the only one who's crazy enough to think that there's something more going on here? I'm not the only one who's falling? God, it sounds ridiculous, despite my knowing my own mind."

"I know. But it feels right. I know we have a lot to work through, and some people will say that it's–"

Her hand came up to stop me from speaking. "I don't care what anyone else thinks. You're mine."

"All yours."

She kissed me hard and pulled back. "And you have me…Just me."

"Not just you, sweetheart. All of you."

"In that case, *boyfriend*…"

Despite feeling too old to be labelled as such, my heart warmed at the title.

CHAPTER 36

Hannah got up, stepped out of my reach and pulled her shirt up and over her head. That pink lacy bra taunted me again and I groaned, all the while appreciating the sight.

"I hope you know that you can't say all that you have to a woman like me and not expect anything in return," she said.

"Get back here you little minx." I leaned forward, swiping a hand out in an attempt to grab and bring her to me, but she was quicker.

Jumping out of reach, she waved her index in a teasing gesture. "Nuh-uh-uh! No touching."

"What?"

"This is about me, pleasing you."

"You'd please me a hell of a lot if you'd let me touch you, baby."

Lust darkened her eyes with my endearment. "If you promise to not touch until I tell you to, I'll come closer." She made to step forward.

Her lips formed into a wide grin when I nodded.

Having always been the one in control with every woman I've been with, this was one hell of a surprise. The women of my past had always been so demure, a little traditional, we'll say.

"Relax, baby, I won't bite. Much." Damn, but her biting her lower lip only made me want to pounce.

Still, I forced my back to melt into the couch as I watched her every move. "I have a feeling that you might be one of those closet kinksters." *God, I hope so.*

She straddled my thighs and ran her fingernail down the side of my jaw. "And what if I am?"

"I'd have to ask you to prove it." I made myself comfier by extending my arms up across the back of the couch and grinned. "Show me what you've got, sweet cheeks."

She leaned down and flicked the tip of my earlobe with her tongue. "Gladly." The sexy breathy tone to her voice sent a jolt through me. "Just remember that you asked for it." Her tongue trailed my jaw and nipped it before she straightened.

"Don't leave me hanging, sweetheart."

"I don't plan on it." Her nimble fingers made haste of her jeans as she turned so her ass faced me, revealing a matching pink lace thong. "I'm just making myself more comfortable for your surprise."

I quickly readjusted my hardening shaft in my pants. "S-surprise?"

"Yes." She turned to lean forward, putting weight on her hands on either side of my thighs. She peered down and grinned at the sight of the bulge in my pants. "Remember…" Her eyes met mine. "Hands. Off. But feel free to use your lips at any time." She turned to peer over her shoulder at me. "That's if you're not too busy enjoying the show."

Next thing I knew her ass was positioned strategically over my crotch. Her head lay back on my shoulder where I could peer down and see everything.

Hannah began to move her hands, tantalizing the skin of her collarbone, trailing a path over the supple skin of her breasts. She grabbed her tits and squeezed them, letting out a light moan and arching her butt further into me. She continued, skimming the skin of her stomach.

I nipped the spot just below her ear. "You're going to kill me doing what I think you're about to do." Oh, but what a way to die!

Hannah laughed, but never said a word.

*H*oly *fuck!* Hannah's hips were grinding into me—into her hand.

Any mental pictures I could possibly conjure of her masturbating for me sure as hell would never hold a candle to the real thing!

My cock was steel, and if she kept this up, there's no way I wouldn't humiliate myself before we even got to the part where I got inside her. I needed her desperately.

"I'm going to come." She ground herself aggressively on my dick, which I'm pretty sure now held a permanent imprint of my zipper. "God, Ben! I-I wish…I wish these were your fingers."

My voice came out hoarse. "Just say the words." Fuck, but this was the sweetest form of torture, but I no longer knew how much more of it that I could take.

"I'm so wet, Ben. Oh! Oh fuck! I'm coming! I'm coming!" She panted over me.

Her words, combined with her moans made me snap. "Fuck this!"

Before her orgasm had the chance to taper off, I was scooping her up into my arms, and rushing us toward my bedroom where I unceremoniously dropped her to the mattress. Looking down at the front of my pants, I grinned at the large wet spot on my crotch and proceeded to rid myself of them.

I grabbed the condom, rolled the thing on, pulled her panties to the side and rammed into her as far as I could go.

The cry she emitted made my balls clench.

I looked down at her and tisked. "That was pure evil, Hannah." I pulled back, then slammed myself back to the hilt, eliciting another cry of passion from her. "Fuck, you're hot."

"You feel so good." She arched further into me. Her nails digging into my shoulders as I pulled back to slam into her again, making me grunt. "Fuck me, Ben!"

I lost it. There was no holding back.

I buried my face in her neck, scraped my teeth on the tendon there as I pumped my hips into her with an almost violent fervor. It was pure carnal, voracious in nature. Something we both needed in that moment.

At a pace like that, it's safe to say that we didn't last long. Hell, Hannah had me already at a boiling point before we even got off the couch!

I rolled off of her and collapsed at her side as we both breathed hard and tried to calm our bodies, the sweat cooling on our skin.

I turned my head to the side to find that Hannah had done the same and was looking back. "Well," she said, "that was…"

"…fucking amazing!" I finished for her. "Where the hell have you been all my life?"

She laughed, then rolled onto her stomach to hover over me. Brushing a strand of my hair from my forehead, she said, "In hiding, apparently. It felt good to let loose."

"Well, feel free to let loose any time." I lifted my head to capture her lips in a hungry kiss. "Damn, baby, that was hot." She giggled and buried her face in my chest. "You're being shy now?" I harrumphed.

"I was just thinking about it all. I might be sore tomorrow."

I flipped her to her back and hovered above her. Junior had begun to rise for a repeat session. Then again, he had never fully gone down. "Want me to kiss it better?" My lips left a trail of wet kisses down her neck and over her collarbone, making their way down toward her heat.

"Mmm."

"I'll take that as a 'yes'." Our gazes locked on each other. "This time, I'm taking my time."

Hannah had wanted a shower first, and dragged me along with her. My admission that I'd never taken one with a partner before shocked her. It was something I had always wanted to try, but Candace had never held a sexually adventurous bone. It wasn't until I watched Hannah through the glass enclosure, the steam rolling off her skin as the water cascaded around her shoulders and down her back, that I concluded that she was the sexiest thing to ever grace my presence.

Hannah turned to look at me and smiled with her hair slicked back. "Aren't you going to join me?"

She didn't have to ask me twice. When I got to her, I wrapped an arm around her waist, bringing her snug against my body as the water rained down on us.

"I could get used to showers like these." I nuzzled her nose.

Hannah tilted her head up and gave me a sweet kiss. "Glad I could oblige."

It may have been a simple shower, but the tenderness that was exchanged as we lathered each other's bodies, the kisses to the scars on my chest, the intimate discovery of every inch of skin that was exposed, sent my emotions reeling.

She made me feel like the most important person in her world. I tried to reciprocate in hopes that she would know that she was the most important in mine.

In that shower stall, actions began to speak much louder than words…

CHAPTER 37

When my alarm went off the next morning, Hannah was sleeping soundly on her back. My robe had fallen away from her body revealing so much delectable flesh that begged for my attention. Her lashes feathered at the tops of her cheeks, fluttering about as she dreamt. Her auburn hair spilled across her pillow with soft waves.

Slowly, I reached out to her. The tips of my fingers running over the lushness of her firm breasts, each nipple stiffening. Her breath caught as her body wakened for me, despite the slumber that still had her within its grip.

My fingers headed down the middle of her stomach, following an imaginary line to her belly button, causing her back to arch. She let out a low moan. "Ben," came out on a sigh.

With a flattened palm, I continued my feathery light touch to that treasure between her legs, licking my lips as soon as I felt the humid heat radiating. I cupped her bare sex, thankful that we hadn't redressed last night, and she arched her pelvis into my hand.

A quick swipe of a finger through her folds confirmed that she was ready for me. Still unconscious, her legs parted further.

I knew I should get up and get ready for work, but those glistening folds begged me to finish what I'd started, and there was no way I'd leave her hanging.

Hannah let out a soft snore as I made my way between

her thighs, inching them further and further apart gently so as not to wake her.

When my mouth connected with her heat, her body jolted. I continued my ministrations, keeping them light and feathery, alternating between my fingers and my mouth. She tasted like heaven. I don't think I'd ever grow tired of her sweetness.

"Mmm…Ben."

As I grew desperate to find myself buried inside her, I peered up to find Hannah wearing a devilish smile. She crooked her index at me in a come-hither gesture.

With a quick flick of the tongue to her nub, I pulled away from her haven and slowly kissed up her body, coming to a stop as I hovered above her.

"You!" She grabbed on to my throbbing length, and began to pump, making me groan. "That was quite the wakeup call." I laughed and pecked her on the mouth. "But you need to finish what you started," she squeezed my girth, "with this."

After sheathing myself, I slid nice and slow into her depths. Where last night had been animalistic, this morning, it was sensual, lazy, and far from quick. I wanted to enjoy my time with Hannah, wanted her to enjoy it too. By the way her body molded to mine, matching each thrust, giving me as much as she received, it was the perfect way to start the day. To hell with getting to work on time, we only opened at lunch anyway.

When Hannah exploded, she clenched down on me so hard that I had no choice but to follow her over the edge.

Exchanging lazy kisses, Hannah's hands stroked my back, her legs hugging my hips. "You should get ready," she whispered into a chaste kiss. "I'll go make you breakfast."

As she tried to make her way out of bed, I pulled her back to me. "I don't have time, sweetheart. I should have been out of here half an hour ago."

"Then take me with you. You can drop me off at the shop and grab something there."

Who was I to decline an offer that kept me in her company longer, not to mention, that would have me sampling her tasty treats?

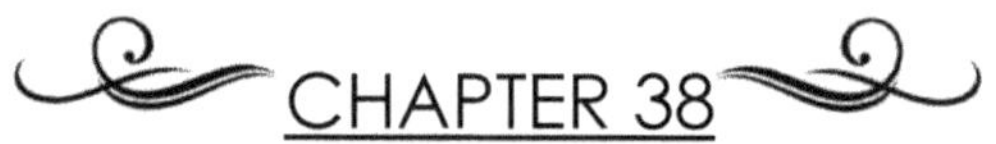

CHAPTER 38

I parked the car and was about to get out when I paused to look at Hannah. She'd been so excited to see her shop again after nearly three weeks of being away from it. So why is it that her face had fallen?

"Hannah?" I shut my door and stayed in the car with her. She seemed stuck in her thoughts. I reached out for her hand. She turned to face me, her smile forced. "Ready?"

"Yeah. I just got carried away with my thoughts, it's all."

"You're worried about what you'll have to deal with when you walk in there, aren't you?"

"How'd–" She cut herself off. "You've been through it. How'd it go for you?"

"You'd be surprised, but most treated me the same as before. I'm not saying that people won't look at you when you walk in there but–"

"They're not going to judge."

I nodded. "The best part is that you're the boss, so if they want to treat you like shit, you fire their asses." This made her laugh. "There it is."

"There's what?"

"The best sound in the world." I reached up to tuck her hair behind her ear. "Well, next to–"

She smacked my chest, still laughing. "Behave! Now, come on."

I walked in behind Hannah who was greeted by her workers with hugs and kisses on the cheek and the slew of welcome backs. I recognized a few of her employees from the times I'd been in, one of them eyeing me like I was one of their desserts.

Hannah noticed right away. "He's taken," she said over the girl's shoulder and I couldn't help the smile.

"Lucky lady," the woman muttered.

I'd like to think so.

Hannah went to the other side of the counter and grabbed a few things from the display cases, stuffing them in a small takeout box. She walked back around and leaned onto the counter before presenting me with the goodies. "The breakfast rush seems like it was a little earlier than usual this morning, but I think what I put in there will do the trick." She winked.

I took the box from her and kissed her forehead. She groaned. "If I kissed you the way I want to right now it wouldn't look good."

On a sigh, she said, "True, but you didn't have to make it feel so damn brotherly."

This made me laugh. "I promise I'll make it up to you later," I whispered.

"I'll hold you to that. See you later?"

"You got it, sweetheart."

I turned for the door.

Hannah's, "Will you all quit it with your shenanigans and get back to work already?" had me smiling all the while shaking my head at the women's comments about the sexy looks I'd been giving her.

CHAPTER 39

I'd been tending to reservation bookings for the last hour since my arrival when I heard the door to Fairfax open and shut.

"We're closed until eleven," I said without raising my head and continued to work, keeping an ear out for the door to open and shut once again. A little annoyed at the fact that whoever had come in hadn't left, I repeated myself. "I'm sorry, we're closed right now."

"And what makes you think I care? I'm not here for service."

My back straightened, and my feet reversed a few feet from the man who stood on the other side of the bar from me. Crossing my arms at my chest, I said, "Can I help you?"

His disgruntled demeanor was clear. "No, you can't."

"Then why are you still here?" I asked, sick of this guy's hostility toward me when I was pretty damn sure I had never seen him before.

"I just wanted to see what my sister-in-law left my brother for."

"Excuse me?"

"You heard me." His gaze was assessing. "Yeah, I know you two are fucking."

"What the hell is your problem?"

He snorted with evident disgust. "She couldn't be rid of Lee fast enough."

"Not that I owe you or anyone in your family an explanation, but I tried to save your brother." The man had the decency to look surprised. "I have no clue what kind of deranged sense of thinking you and your family have, but had I not been there, none of them would have lived, and you would have been planning a double funeral. Now, I suggest that you get the hell out of my establishment before I throw you out. Unless you're willing to apologize to Hannah for the way your family's treated her, I don't want to hear another word."

"So she's been crying to you about it, huh?" The man seemed delighted. "Good. She deserves a lifetime of tears for the shit she's put us through. I'm not shocked that Lee turned to drinking again. It's that damn woman's fault."

I was glad that the solid oak bar was between us because I was about two insults away from jumping the countertop and defending Hannah's honor by tearing this man a new one.

"There's nothing wrong with Hannah. It's you people who make me sick, preying on her when she can't do much but try and heal, and you've taken away all of her options. What's next? Do you not realize that she's left with nothing? You have no clue do you? You've never been through what she's been through. Well I have! I know! I was there with both of them that night!"

I took a moment to gather my wits. "And about tomorrow's memorial," I began. "We'll be seeing you there. For the record, Hannah loved Lee, but I guess you're too dense to get that. Just like you and your family, she needs closure, whether you like it or not, and I'll be there making sure she gets it."

"If she loved my brother then what the hell is she doing with you?"

"What's it matter?" I asked. "You wouldn't believe me if I told you. You're not worth my breath. Get the fuck out!"

The man stood there and eyed me from top to bottom, his gaze softening. "I won't say anything to my folks about tomorrow, but I'll warn you…Don't let her come alone."

"Don't worry. She won't be."

Once Lee's brother left, I grabbed the phone to finish off my last reservation call when the door opened once more.

"Look, if you–"

"Whoa!" Mike said, and my head snapped up to see him standing with his arms in a defensive position. "I'm assuming that this has everything to do with that bulldozer of a dude that just stormed out of here?"

"Yeah." I sighed. "What's up?"

"I have a wife who's looking for a girls' night out, and since she loves Hannah so much, she wondered if she'd want to join in," he said.

"So your wife's got you over here doing her bidding?"

"Not quite," he said. "Things are crazy at the office. It got me out. And there's the fact that Nic's birthday is coming up and I wanted to see if you had some availability. Maybe we can use their girls' night as a diversion?"

I worked out the kinks with Mike for Nicole's surprise bash, finding myself looking forward to spending time with the gang again, more than I ever could have imagined.

Somehow, Hannah had gifted me with the ability to look forward to future events instead of dreading them like I had been for the last three years. Mike's and Nicole's wedding had been a vast improvement, but those pangs of jealousy of mine had put a damper on my enjoyment.

"So, Hannah?" My best friend snapped me out of my reverie. "How are things going with you two?"

As my employees trickled in, Mike and I took a seat at the back of the pub, and I filled him in on where she and I stood.

"Do you think she's ready?" he asked.

"I wouldn't have taken the chance I have if I didn't think so. It's hard to explain how strong I feel. It's fast, but it feels–"

"Right?" Mike's gaze was assessing.

"Yeah."

"She's a keeper, Ben."

"Why thank you, Mike," Hannah said, standing right behind him, making him jump. I couldn't hold my laughter in any longer.

I had watched her creep up on him with that mischievous glint in her eyes, urging me to stay quiet with a finger held to her lips.

She bent over and kissed him on the cheek to which he blushed, making me laugh harder. "What are you doing here?" I asked her.

"I've got to eat lunch, right?"

"I have yet to eat the breakfast my girlfriend gave me." I pulled her so she sat on my lap before giving her a quick peck.

"Hold on, girlfriend?" Hannah smiled proudly and nodded. "You said things were phenomenal, but you left that little tidbit of information out, Benny-boy."

"Mike's got something to ask you," I told Hannah in an effort to take the heat off of me.

"Since when have you been his girlfriend?" The man winked at me.

"Last night."

"Answer me this then."

"Go for it, hot shot." She crossed her arms, pecking me on the cheek with a sure-of-herself look on her face. That confidence of hers was sexy as hell. "If this is a best friend test, I'll ace it."

"When's his birthday?"

"June twelfth."

"Who are his parents?"

"Roz and Doug have a game night with my parents every couple of weeks."

Mike's eyes met mine in inquiry.

I shook my head. "We had no idea."

"How many sisters does he have?"

"Trick question…he's an only child."

"What's his favorite sport?"

She pondered this for a few seconds. "To play or watch?"

Mike paused, grinned, and said, "Both."

"Football to play, but to watch…hockey."

"What does he like to bring when he goes out to someone's house for dinner?"

"Strawberry cheesecake with a chocolate crust." Mike looked at her in shock. "The one I make," she finished.

My best friend looked at me, his thumb pointing in Hannah's direction. "She owns that place?" I nodded. "Wow! Okay…Uh…Oh, right! If a woman walked up to him and made a move, what would you do?"

"I'd watch as she walked off on the verge of tears, rejected because he's amazing and a one-woman-man that I trust with my life."

"You know that's happened right?"

"I don't doubt it for a second."

"Final question." He paused for effect. "In the bedroom, what does he like best?" He smirked. I knew he was only going the mile to see if he'd stump her. The damn man sure loved a good sparring session. I'd have to let his wife know that she wasn't challenging him enough.

"Mike," I warned.

Hannah looked at me and then back to Mike. "Seriously?"

The man nodded.

Hannah looked my way again, and shrugged her shoulders. "You asked for it." She turned to him with a grin. "Ben likes taking the lead, but loves it when a woman surprises him and takes control over things once in a while. The kinkier, the better." She had me stiffening in my seat when she ground her apple bottom in my crotch adding a, "Right, baby?"

I grabbed her hips to stop her movements and groaned. "Hannah."

There my woman sat on my lap where she'd rendered Mike into a shocked and speechless fool, while I was a turned on mass that wouldn't be able to get up and walk around until my junk had relaxed some.

"Fuck," Mike finally said, meeting my gaze. "You're screwed."

Hannah harrumphed. "Quite literally."

"I definitely agree with him." Mike pointed at me. "You and Nicole in the same room are going to be definite trouble, forget adding Dani to the mix."

I hooted. "And you wanted her number for Nikki and her girls' night."

"What girls' night?"

CHAPTER 40

The rest of the workday flew by, leaving me to meet up with Hannah at Cake It Up.

Aside from the habitual smell of sugar and vanilla, the next thing that struck my notice was the fact that there was no one around. I made to the back of the shop, finding the one and only open door.

"You're here by yourself with the front door unlocked," I scolded.

"You just missed Cara. She's the one who I disappointed this morning by telling her you were off the market." She got up and came around the desk to face me. I walked toward her and backed her up so her legs hit the side of her desk. "Are you ready to go?"

"Since that stunt of yours at lunch, I've been ready to *go* all afternoon." I leaned in to kiss her neck. "The only question I have for you, baby, is your place or mine?"

She pushed herself up onto her desk, hiking her flowing skirt up to her hips and pulled me in between her thighs by my waist. Her hands began to unbuckle my belt and she smirked. "How about right here?"

I stopped her hands' progression. "We don't have–"

"Take your pants off, sit in my chair, and look in the bottom left-hand drawer." So I did. I took out a box of condoms and gave her an inquiring look as she began to shed her clothes. "You didn't think that you were the only one left horny after Mike's little game earlier, did you? I stopped at the drugstore on the way back here and picked some up because I knew that you were running low at home too."

"Damn!" My hand released my cock from my unzipped pants. "That desk is going to need to be cleared." I watched as she turned that lacy-briefed-butt of hers toward me and after slipping on the condom, I pounced.

I bent her forward onto her desk, the desk clearing simply being a diversion, just so her back was facing me for what I had planned.

My hand reached around her, two fingers dipping into her core, settling to rub her bud with their slickness. "You're not getting away with your earlier teasing, and I do believe that I owe you after being so reserved with that kiss this morning that it made you think of me as a brother." I removed my hand to grab her underwear, and pulled them to the side. I grabbed my length and rubbed against the crease of her heat.

"Oh, God! Let me turn around, Ben. Please! I want to see you. I need–"

Her words left the second my shaft sank into her moist core. Her body stiffened as she pushed herself up onto her hands and my arms wrapped around her waist, pressing my front to her back as I began to thrust. She leaned her head back on my shoulder and let me take her along for the ride.

Her arms cradled the back of my head, the slight stinging as she tugged on my hair added to the sensation of pleasure.

We were well on our way to bliss when, "Hello...Hannah?" came from the front of the store, making my woman stiffen.

"Who's that?" I whispered against the side of her neck, scraping my teeth along its length.

"My mom."

"What?" I pulled myself out of her, immediately missing our connection.

"Quick, get your clothes on!" she hissed and I rushed. "Hold on, Mom, I'll be right out!"

"If you're busy, I can come back, honey."

Yes! Please!

"It's fine, Mom." She was grumbling as she left me in her office.

I tried to listen in on their conversation, wondering if we'd been found out, but I couldn't make sense of the bits that I was able to hear. I heard a squeal of delight and clapping hands.

"We'll see you tomorrow, Benjamin!" the older woman said as I heard her footsteps retreat. "Just a quick pointer guys…lock the door."

Busted!

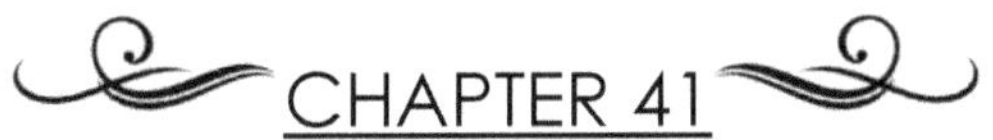# CHAPTER 41

The sexual tension had reached a boiling point by the time Hannah and I got to her home.

As her front door opened, I wasted no time, rushing us through the threshold, slamming the door shut behind us and securing the deadbolt. I was done with interruptions.

Turning Hannah so she faced me, I grabbed her head and crashed my lips to hers, hungrier than I'd ever been for a woman in all of my life. She jumped up, wrapped her legs around my hips. "Upstairs," she said into my mouth as I took in her taste.

No longer caring about the bed she'd barely shared with her husband, I carefully made for her bedroom.

Unceremoniously dropping her to the mattress, my hands got to work on my pants, then threw my shirt to the floor as she shimmied out of her skirt.

I growled at the sight before me as she sat up, took her shirt off, undid her bra, and threw them to the side before she kneeled in the middle of the bed, fully bare for my taking.

Crawling up the mattress to her, my hands grabbed her roughly around her hips and pulled her so my sheathed shaft rubbed up against her core. Her arms wrapped themselves around my shoulders as she whimpered the moment I probed the entrance to her folds. My length slid slowly inside her heat, throbbing with the tension of unreleased passion as she straddled my thighs.

Buried deep inside her, Hannah pulled my face in for a searing kiss and began grinding against me. She felt as soft as silk and tasted as sweet as sugar. I needed more.

Hannah rode me until she exploded first, at which point I laid her down and covered her body with mine without disconnecting us. I thrust long and deep, powerful yet with enough gentleness so as not to bruise her. Once wouldn't be enough. Not today.

Her core gripped me like a vice, initiating my release. I can't recall a time where my climax had been that explosive. Every time Hannah and I came together was better than the last.

As the night wore on, I could feel Hannah's apprehension about tomorrow's memorial growing. It left me debating if I should tell her about Lee's brother's visit.

We were cuddled on the couch, watching the evening news when I decided to open up about it, only realizing then that I should have said something when she had mentioned the memorial earlier.

"You never mentioned that Lee had a brother."

Hannah stiffened in my arms. I ran my fingers over her arm so as to calm her. "What about Luke?"

"He paid me a visit earlier today."

She pushed me back so she could sit up. "I'm so sorry." Her eyes welled up. "I shouldn't go. I'll find another way. Maybe–"

"Hannah, it's okay. We're going. Your parents are coming, and I don't give a shit what anyone thinks, and neither should you, but you're going to be there."

"What'd he say?"

"He suspects something." I shook my head. "I've never met anyone so damn bitter. What's the history with you two?"

She shrugged her shoulders and looked down at her hands. "He blames me for Lee's drinking."

I snorted. "He said as much."

"What do you mean by 'he suspects something'?"

"He knows that you left Lee. I don't know how, and I never told him that I knew you had. In fact, I never told him that you'd been pregnant. It's none of his business. He knows that I was there on the road that night. I think he's been following you. He accused you of being with me and claimed that's why you left his brother."

"What'd you say?" Her eyes were wide. "Oh, God! I can't go now!"

"I told him that I didn't owe him any answers. It wasn't his business and I never gave him any indication that I was anything more than a friend of yours."

She nodded. "Anything else?"

"The way he spoke about that night struck me as odd. It's like they don't seem to have the full story on what happened…or maybe they've only heard what they wanted to hear." I grabbed Hannah's hand and squeezed it. "And I don't think they're ready to listen, but Luke had no choice but to hear me out. I think I might have hit a nerve with him, and he walked away with something to think about.

"I asked him to put himself in your shoes. Told him that I understood that they were hurting, but that their grief clouded their perception. They never took the time to realize that you were dealing with your own demons along with their bullshit." I grabbed her hand. "For Christ's sake, Hannah, they never even called you, or sent flowers! They never bothered to check on you when you were in the hospital. What kind of family are they?"

Hannah was crying silent tears by the time I was finished. I pulled her into me, holding onto her tight. She gripped me hard and I knew that there was no way that these tears would be done until at least after the memorial.

"You shouldn't have had to do that," she whispered.

"But I did and it needed to be done."

"I need to learn to stand on my own two feet where they're concerned."

She did, but all in good time. "I didn't mind." I pulled on her hair, tilting her head so I could look into her eyes. "I would do it again if I knew it would make a difference. It's not a matter about who's hurting more, it's a matter of respect. They didn't respect you and I have a feeling they never have. I can't have that, Hannah. You're—"

Her fingers covered my lips. "Thank you," she muttered, then pressed her lips to mine in a tender show of appreciation.

"You're welcome, but I don't think it's all done and dealt with, sweetheart." I tucked a stray strand of her hair behind her ears.

She sighed. "I know. Did he say anything about the memorial?"

"He was adamant that you not go." I sighed. "I told him it wasn't an option. He understood and said he wasn't going to say anything to his folks, but to make sure you weren't there alone. I think he expects fireworks."

"I'm having a hard time thinking that it's a good idea to keep them in the dark."

"How about you don't think on it right now. We can deal with it all when the time comes."

She nodded and I kissed her forehead.

"Can you stay the night?" she asked.

"I didn't know I had the option to leave."

"You always have the option, Ben. I don't ever want you to feel obligated to stay."

"I stay because I want to." I cupped her cheek in my hand. "Not because you're someone I feel like I need to coddle or protect. You're stronger than you give yourself credit for. I know that you'd be well on your way even if I weren't here."

She smiled. "You always know what to say, don't you?"

My shoulders shrugged. "I've been there. I forced everyone away. I learned to deal with things on my own even though it never worked out like I'd planned."

"You seem all right to me."

"You didn't know me three years ago." My laugh lacked any humor. "I was a right bastard to anyone that approached me with what I felt was pity. It was easier to be alone and bitter than to deal with not knowing what I'd see and hear from my surroundings."

"And now you have to grieve all over again." She was speaking about Candace's secret life.

"True, but it's a bit easier when you find out that the person you chose to spend your life with had been betraying you for years."

It was true.

The lack of respect I found myself having toward Candace, the anger, the bitterness…it all helped me in some way to move forward and seek out something better. The sadness had been there, but with Hannah in my life, I was moving on pretty quick. Hell, I was falling in love with one woman, while falling out of love with another!

❧ CHAPTER 42 ❧

I woke refreshed and ready to take the day by its proverbial balls.

The smell in the air told me that if I turned to my side, I would find the bed beside me empty. Whatever it was Hannah was concocting in that kitchen of hers, it smelled amazing.

I got up, put my pants on, and headed downstairs.

Pausing on the bottom step, my ears picked up on Hannah's singing. She might not have been up to par with Nicole where talent was concerned, but she had a beautiful voice.

My feet began to lead me in the kitchen's direction, curious about what Hannah looked like when she sounded so fancy-free.

The instant I caught sight of her, my smile turned into a grin. Before me was a beautiful woman who simply felt like stealing a moment of normalcy—of peace—before what I knew would be a day of pure hell. She was relaxed, enjoying herself, and completely comfortable. In her element.

When the song ended and the next one came on with more of an upbeat feel to it, Hannah's hips began to sway to the tune as she continued to stir the contents of the bowl in her arms.

I took in the short shorts, the wool socks on her feet and the overstretched t-shirt that fell to the side, exposing a shoulder. She reminded me of some hot co-ed that I'd had the pleasure of spending the night with, only better, because she was all mine.

Checking the oven for whatever it was she was baking, Hannah dipped her finger in the bowl and turned to see me staring at her with her pinky sticking out of her mouth.

She smiled shyly around the digit.

"By all means continue." I laughed. "I'm enjoying the show."

"Good morning," she said as I dropped a kiss on her forehead.

"Good morning indeed." I looked at the counters and the small roll-away tabletop that surrounded us. "What's all this?"

"Inspiration at its best!" She smiled brightly at me. "Here, taste."

Before I knew it, I had the tip of her finger at my lips, leaving a blob of batter on my bottom one before she stuck her finger in her mouth to lick the residue off. I instinctively licked whatever it was off of my lip, and the pop of flavor that hit my taste buds made me want to steal that bowl away from her, hide in some dark corner, and devour it like some starving child.

"What the hell is that, and how the hell do I get more of it?" I asked.

"It's a loaf."

My stomach rumbled, making her laugh. "I hope it's breakfast, or part of it, at least."

"That was the plan." She turned and began to pour the contents into a bread pan.

I walked to stand behind her, wrapping my arms around her torso, pressing my lips to her cheek. "Do you often do this, bake without a set knowledge of the final outcome?"

"It's the best part about it." She turned her head to the side and pecked my chin. "If you're asking if I play mad scientist in my kitchen constantly…" Once empty, she put the bowl down and turned to face me. "I haven't done anything like this in nearly a year." Her face took a somber look. "I haven't had a lick of inspiration in so long that when it hit the other day, I didn't know what to do with it, so I decided to dabble around this morning while you slept in."

I smiled down at her. "Wherever the inspiration came from, I can't wait to see more of it."

Hannah didn't move as I made my way for the pot of coffee. She stood beside me, a hip leaning against the counter and set her mug beside mine. "It came from you." She turned from me after she'd grabbed her mug and went back to her creation, hiding behind the steam of her coffee. "At least, I'm pretty sure that's where it's from."

My heart leapt and began to beat at a staccato pace. *Me?*

I wasn't going to dismiss her statement like she had. Maybe Hannah saw more good in me than I had ever been able to see in myself. I knew there were far worse men than me in the world, but to be responsible for someone's inspiration…that was…what was the word? Deep? Heavy? Yeah. Heavy.

I took a sip of the fragrant coffee and my eyes widened. "How is it that coffee is always better when you make it?"

She turned to face me and smiled. "It's a secret."

"I like it. It seems to always go with what I'm eating."

"I'm good like that." She smirked.

I set my cup down and grabbed her hand to pull her toward me. "Yes." I cupped her cheek with my hand. "You are. But I have to ask…" I dropped my hand so I could circle my arms around her.

"Ask what?"

Giving her my most angelic grin, I said, "When are we eating?"

Hannah gasped, then delivered a playful slap to my chest. "Be careful mister, you might have to make your bacon and eggs yourself if you keep pushing."

"Bacon and eggs? But I thought we were having that." I nodded toward the oven.

"That's for after." She pecked my lips. "Now let me go so I can make you a proper breakfast."

Much to my reluctance, I dropped my arms from her.

"Can I help?" Hannah turned with a look of shock strewn across her face. It made me chuckle. "What?"

"You want to help?"

"You're surprised?" I took the carton of eggs from her.

"Well, yeah. It's just–" Her mouth snapped shut.

"Tell me." I took the eggs we'd need and set them on the counter before handing Hannah the carton back.

"I've always been the one to make everything." Her voice was soft, almost inaudible. "I'm not used to having someone in the kitchen cooking with me, unless it's Mom or Dad, or the workers at the shop."

"Get used to it, sweetheart, because I plan on being around, and that includes helping my woman in the kitchen."

The grin she sported told me she approved my statement. "Is there anything you don't do?" she asked.

"Stick around long enough and you'll find out. How did you want your eggs?"

CHAPTER 43

The wrought iron fencing and its arched gateway were all too familiar as we arrived at the cemetery for Lee's memorial.

We waited in the car until we caught sight of Anne and Adam before making a move to exit the car.

"Hannah?" I put a hand on her knee. "It's time, sweetheart."

She nodded. With a deep breath she composed herself into the strong woman I knew she was, and opened her car door. I breathed in a deep one myself and got out to stand at her side. Today was about Hannah putting her past to rest, not about me or my ghosts. And so I ignored the plots that loomed a mere ten rows away from where we were headed.

I greeted Anne with a hug and shook Adam's hand, keeping words to a minimum.

Hannah walked between her parents, as I followed a step behind them, making our way toward the small crowd of people surrounding a coffin and preacher.

The sight was all too reminiscent of three years past. My heartstrings tugged tight. *Keep it together, she needs you.*

The pastor's words were interrupted by a gasp from a woman that stood between an older gentleman and who I knew to be Lee's brother.

"What the hell are you doing here?" she asked, effectively putting an end to a dead man's tribute. "You're not welcome here."

"Mom," Luke said.

"Did you…" She turned to her son. "How could you?"

"We have every right to be here, Lois," Adam spoke up. "Lee was a son to us too. It's only fair for us to pay our respects."

The woman snorted in disgust. "I don't care about you two. It's her I want gone."

Everyone's gaze shifted to Hannah who looked as if she were ready to bolt.

I moved from behind Anne and grabbed her hand, shocking her back to reality. "You can do this," I whispered in her ear.

Anne moved so I could stand at her daughter's side. Hannah's grip on my hand first tightened, then she let go. "I'm not going anywhere. For ten years I've let you dictate what went on in Lee's and my life. I'm done, Lois. Lee is…*was* my husband, and by that fact alone, I've earned my place, *my* right to be here."

Lois snorted. "Some job you did caring for him."

"Do you really want to do this in front of these people?" she asked.

"They deserve to know the person that's driven him to ruin his life." Lee's mother's tone was venomous. "The one that killed him."

There were hushed murmurs in the crowd, but most had held their silence.

Hannah took a few steps toward her husband's mother. "Lee was an alcoholic long before I met him, Lois. You can't blame me for that."

Not able to trust that Lee's mother wouldn't try anything physical, I remained close at Hannah's back. My girlfriend's fortitude had me bursting with pride.

Hannah paused with a gasp when Lee's coffin came into full view. After clearing her throat, I watched as she lifted her head with more confidence. "I've done all I could have done for that man. Your son sure as hell wasn't without his faults, but I loved him. And that love wasn't enough to keep him from giving in to his demons.

"You say I never did anything to make him stop, but neither did any of you. I'm not solely at fault here. He chose to drink. He chose to ruin his life. He chose to push me away. I was nothing to you people, and it became apparent that I meant very little to him as well, if he was willing to sacrifice us for the bottle." Hannah's tone had grown bitter.

"That night…" She sniffled. "I was pregnant." Cue the crowd's murmurs and gasps. "Lee wasn't the only one that died, Lois. Our baby died with him too, and so did a part of me." Hannah's voice faltered with an abundance of emotion.

Except for Lois, her husband's and Luke's faces had softened at Hannah's declaration.

"You left him and you were pregnant?" Incredulity laced the woman's tone.

The lack of reaction from Hannah's parents confirmed that she had confided the truth about her relationship with Lee.

"I left him because I had to. We were trying to work things out. That's why we were out that night. You want to know what he said when I told him we were having a baby?" Hannah didn't wait for a response. "He told me that he didn't want our son or daughter, that I should just, and I quote 'get rid of it'. All that after my promising him that I would be there for him when he chose to get help. He didn't want to stop drinking. He didn't think it was a problem. He told me so, that night. My decision to make our separation permanent was made the night of the accident, *not* before that. I suggest that when you start pointing fingers, you get your facts straight. I was loyal to Lee to the very end." I knew that she was eyeing Lee's brother with that statement. "Lee's drinking killed us all that night. It was *him* who caused me to lose control! It was *him* who rejected me, who refused our child! It wasn't me. It's not my fault!"

Hannah's body began to shake violently and I rushed to her side, wrapping an arm around her waist for added support.

"How dare you!" Lois said, but when her husband let her go, Lee's brother jumped in to stop his mother.

"Mom, she's right." Luke met my gaze, and gave me a curt nod. "I saw the police report. What she's saying is true."

"No!" She turned to face her son, collapsing into his chest, tiny balled fists hitting him between sobs. "No, no, no!"

"Lee was a kind man when he wanted to be, Lois." Hannah's voice was soft. "There's a reason why I loved him, why I stuck by him all these years. Out of the bad, I saw the good. I believed in him, in *us*. I couldn't help him unless he was willing to ask for it. I'm not sorry for what I've just said. And I'm not sorry for being here either. I have just as much of a right to say goodbye. What I am sorry about is that it all had to come out in front of all of these people; that I hadn't, up until now, stood up to your incessant bullying and your constant judging."

"Please go," Lee's father finally spoke.

Hannah walked forward, grabbed a handful of dirt and deposited it on top of her husband's coffin. "I hope you're finally at peace." Her hand paused on top of the dark oak finish. "Goodbye."

She took a look at Lee's closest relatives, bowed her head in a sign of respect, turned around, and when she looked up at me, I could see that she was holding on to the last bit of strength she could muster. The woman was pale and shaking. Her knees made to buckle after two more steps.

To hell with propriety! I picked Hannah up bridal style and walked us away from the gathering, while she clung to me. The further we got, the louder her sobs grew and her shaking intensified.

"I'm here," I cooed into her hair, taking a seat on one of the visitors' benches. "You did great. You're so strong, sweetheart. I'm so proud of you." Was there really anything I could say that would soothe her, though?

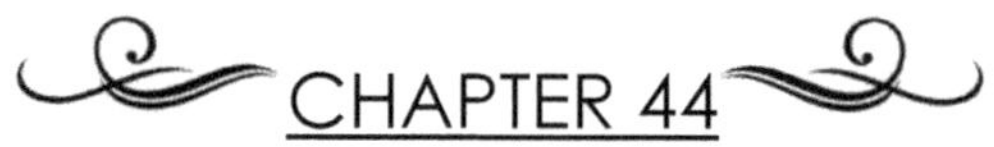

CHAPTER 44

Hannah wanted a moment with her parents, so I walked off to give them their privacy. Anne and Adam both looked thankful, not to mention relieved, that their daughter was reaching out to them.

Instead of heading to my car, my feet carried me toward a spot that held so much grief for me—one I hadn't visited in over a week.

My fingers only ran over one name when I'd reached the double headstones. Karen's.

"Hey, baby girl." I cleared my throat. "I'm so sorry." I fought the tremors of sobs that wanted to burst, but it was a losing battle. I broke down.

"How could you! Dammit, Candace! I'm so angry with you. I'm not one to use the word hate, but I think I hate you just a little right now." I wiped at one wet cheek with the back of my hand. "I loved you…so much. And Karen. Fuck! She's not even mine," I whispered the last bit. "I can't keep doing this anymore. Coming back to see two people that never belonged to me in the first place. I can't do it. I can't be miserable for the rest of my life, so girls, this is my last visit."

I couldn't bring myself to leave just yet, so I sat on the grass and listened to the stillness of the day.

Hannah's hand landed on my shoulder. "Is everything okay?"

"Yeah." I wiped the last few stray tears with the back of my hand before getting up and grabbing her hand.

Hannah turned to face the headstones. She crouched down, running her fingers over the names briefly, then looked over her shoulder at me. "Do you mind if I say something?"

"Go ahead."

"I'm sorry that you're both gone," she started. "Karen, I'm sure you would have given your Daddy a run for his money. He loves you so much, and you would have made him a very great Daddy too." She paused to wipe at her cheeks, her shoulders straightening as she took a deep breath and continued. "Candace, I feel I owe you a world of thanks for being so blind to the greatness that was in front of you all this time. I promise to take care of him. Thank you for letting go of your love so I could give him mine."

Stunned at her words, I couldn't move. I couldn't speak.

Hannah stood from her haunches and faced me. My eyes met hers when her hand cupped my cheek. "Ready to go?" she asked as if her words hadn't just tilted my world on its axis.

My smile was strained. "Y-yeah." Taking one last look at my past in the form of a double plot, I uttered that final word. "Goodbye."

CHAPTER 45

By the time we reached my car, I realized something was absent from all of my other visits. My usual dark cloud of grief had disappeared. I felt lighter, albeit still slightly drained by emotions.

Is that how it felt to know that you'd moved on?

We drove to my place in silence, exchanging glances here and there whenever we stopped at a light. Hannah's hand held mine, her thumb rubbing the top of it in a soothing manner.

When we arrived, I let her precede me.

I dropped her bag of clothing she'd packed up this morning to the floor before closing the door.

Hannah slid her heels off of her feet and I walked up to her. Grabbing her roughly around the waist with one hand, she dropped her shoes as I cradled the back of her head with my other. "I'm so proud of you," I said before crushing my lips to hers.

"I embarrassed myself, is what I did," she said when I pulled away.

"Oh, sweetheart, you didn't. You kept your cool. You were calm, polite, composed and graceful. You made Lois look like The Wicked Witch of the West. You're amazing! How can you not see what I see?"

"Funny." She gave me a small smile, her hands coming up to caress the sides of my face. "I wonder the same thing about you, Ben. I meant what I said by their graves. You

would have been a fantastic father, and I'm sure you will be some day."

"And what about the other stuff?" I smirked down at her.

"I…" Her face went from nervous to mischievous. "I do think you're amazing. In every way." I pressed my lips to hers lightly and pulled back to let her continue. "I plan on taking care of you for as long as you'll let me."

I kissed her again. "And what about–"

"Shut up and make love to me, Ben."

"I can't do that," I deadpanned. "You don't love me back."

"But you never…" Her voice trailed off. "Hold on." Her eyebrows knitted together before they rose up toward her hairline. "Y-you love me?"

I nodded. "Wholly. Irrevocably. There's not a doubt in my heart and mind, Hannah. I swore that if life ever led me to a moment where I felt this way again, that I wouldn't hold back, that I'd say something. I don't want you to–"

Her lips crashed to mine feverishly before she pulled away too soon. "Don't even finish that sentence, you crazy man." Her eyes were glistening with unshed tears, her lips quirking up with a subtle tremble. "I'm completely, whole-heartedly, and without a doubt in love with you too, Benjamin."

"I knew, but I didn't know how I felt until you were standing there in front of Candace's plot. I couldn't help but think I had a new lease on life and found myself wondering what I'd do if you were in Candace's place right now, if I'd lost you that night before finding what we have."

"Kind of morbid don't you think?"

"Let me finish." She nodded for me to continue. "I thought about it, and as broken as I've been over Candace, I know I was on my way to finding myself again. The journals sped things up, thankfully. Hannah, the thought of you being in her place makes it hard for me to breathe. If it were you, I don't think–"

Her fingertips feathered over my lips. "I'm not going anywhere, Ben."

I'd taken Hannah to my bed and made love to her, turning my cell off because of its incessant ringing. We spent the entirety of that afternoon lounging in bed until dinnertime.

In the midst of cooking dinner, the doorbell rang.

One look at Hannah, who was leaning back against the counter wearing my dress shirt, gave answer as to who was presentable enough to greet our unannounced guest.

"You stay here." I zipped my pants before making for the door, our sexy interlude to dinner-making now delayed.

Hannah grabbed hold of my belt loops quicker than I could get away, and pulled me back to her.

"You're not answering that, baby." She bit my bottom lip before sucking it into her mouth, then released it. "You started something and you're going to finish it."

I growled as I crushed my lips to hers. "You're right." My lips trailed a combination of nips and kisses along her collarbone. "If it's that important, they'll come back."

"Probably some door-to-door salesman anyway." She panted, her fingers releasing the button and lowering the zip on my trousers.

My pants pooled at my feet as I sat her up on my kitchen island. She hissed at the coolness of the granite.

In one swift thrust, I was inside her, her legs pulling me closer while wrapped around my waist. Her lips were trapped by mine, my hands fisting her hair, keeping her where I wanted her, while her fingernails scraped at my back, digging into my flesh at an almost painful intensity. The bite of her nails only fed me with more lust.

I tilted Hannah's head back with a tug of her tresses and began to ravage the sensitive skin of her neck.

"Fuck that's hot!"

Hannah jumped in my arms, clinging to me so tight that she'd buried my face in her breasts.

"Nikki?" Hannah squeaked.

"You might want to let him up for air there, sweetie." I could tell that our guest was amused.

Hannah did just that, and I turned to face Nicole, heat suffusing my face.

"I never knew that a surprise like that awaited me when I rang," Nicole said. "Seeing something like that definitely gets the juices flowing, doesn't it, Ben?"

I groaned at the memory and Hannah tilted my head so my eyes met hers, and she gave me an inquiring look.

"Long story." I gave her a quick peck. "I'll tell you later."

"It's not a long story at all, Benny-boy," Nicole cajoled. "Ben walked in on Mike and me one night. The end."

"If what you saw got you so hot and bothered, why aren't you trying to get home to your husband?" I asked. *I can't believe I forgot to lock the fucking door.*

"Relax, Casanova," Nicole said. "I was in the neighborhood so I figured I'd stop by to give Hannah the details to our girls' night on Friday since you haven't been picking up the phone. We're still on, right?"

"Y-yeah," Hannah said. "Is Mike still driving us?"

"Yeah." She smiled mischievously. "I'm thinking some dancing somewhere and I like your idea of stopping in at Fairfax for a nightcap before our men hunt us down."

"Sounds good."

"Good! By the way, I think you need to take care of big guy here," Nicole said. "Seeing as you two are busy, I'll call later with the rest of the details and the decision on the club."

"And leave a message next time!" I grumbled.

Nicole rolled her eyes. "I'm out of here, lovers! And you're right, Hannah, he does have a tight ass." The damn woman had the audacity to wink at me before she turned and strolled out of my kitchen, the front door slamming shut in her wake.

After a moment of silence, I turned to my woman and smirked. "You talk about my ass?"

Hannah shrugged her shoulders. "She just asked me if it looked as good naked as it did in your jeans."

"And what did you tell her?"

Her mischievous grin said enough. "I told her it was way better naked."

CHAPTER 46

Good thing Derek was at Fairfax to greet everyone and that the place had been closed to the public. Friday had arrived and I should have been back at the pub fifteen minutes ago, but I wanted to see Hannah before her night of wild fun with the girls. And 'wild' was a fitting descriptor when Nicole and Danica were concerned.

When Hannah came downstairs decked out in a sexy strapless black dress that hugged her curves in all the right places, showing off some leg where her knee-high stiletto boots didn't cover, I wanted to beg off our prior engagements.

"You're killing me." I pulled on my shirt collar for added effect.

She laughed. "You're looking pretty damn sexy yourself." Leaning against me, her lips met mine in a sensual dance.

The doorbell interrupted our kiss and Mike helped himself in with an impressively dressed Nicole at his side.

"Damn," he said as he eyed Hannah from top to bottom. "Honey, we need to get you some boots like those."

"I think we need to impose a curfew," was my rebuttal as I held Hannah's back against my front.

"And I think it's time to get going," Hannah turned to face me. "I'll see you later."

"Yeah." I kissed her chastely. "Have fun."

The party was well under way, the whole gang having shown up with a few sets of parents and family members added to the mix. My phone signaled an incoming text and when I looked at it, my heart leapt in my chest.

We're on our way. I read.

Why so early? I texted back.

Allie's friend Mia got caught up with some creep, and we got kicked out since said creep is the owner's brother.

How far out are you ladies? I asked.

Five minutes. We're walking.

"Guys," I shouted to the room. "Get ready, they're here in five!"

To say Nicole was floored with her surprise would be an understatement. I never thought a woman could jump that high in heels.

Hannah had gone off to the bar to get herself a drink with a few of the ladies, while I mixed and mingled.

I turned to find a few men surrounding her and Alissa's friend Mia.

Maybe it was the fact that I hadn't had my dose of Hannah for the day, but I headed toward them and wrapped my arms around her from behind, effectively erasing the sudden pang of neglect I felt.

"Hey, baby," Hannah said and squeezed her arms over mine.

I looked up at the guys surrounding us and my eyes widened when they landed on a familiar face that made me growl. "You've got real nerve showing up here, asshole." Hannah stiffened. "This is a private party."

"One I've been invited to," he said.

"Hannah, let's go," I said and pulled her away by her hand.

"Save me a dance there, Hannah."

"Her card's filled up," I snapped without giving him a backward glance.

I pulled Hannah to my office, slammed the door and locked it.

"What the hell was that all about?" she asked, hands fisted on her hips.

I leaned on the ledge of my desk, pinching the bridge of my nose with my thumb and forefinger, trying to get my breathing under control. All I had to say was one word, and I watched as her face fell with what I'd implied.

"Chris? As in…" I nodded. "What the hell is he doing here?"

"He said he was invited."

"I heard that, but why the hell would he show when he knows this is your place of business?"

That was a really good question.

My fists clenched and my body shook with anger. I had wanted to wipe that smug look off the man's face, but it wasn't worth ruining the evening.

A soft hand on my cheek brought me back to reality, but it was already too late. The memories of what I'd read were all too fresh. All I could see in my mind's eye were pictures of Candace and him together. Intimate ones. I shuddered before pulling Hannah into my arms.

The door vibrated with a knock. "Buddy, it's not the time to get it on with your woman."

"Shut up, Mike." I nuzzled Hannah's nose, seeking the comfort she offered.

"All right, man, but you're missing one hell of a show out here."

The sound of breaking glass—and not just a small amount—had my brows knitting together. *What the hell?*

"Do your friends always get this rowdy?" Hannah asked before something else crashed, entirely different from glass. If it were my guess, it had to be wood.

Images of my pub being torn to shreds invaded my mind. Holding her upper arms, I pushed her away from me. "I don't know what's going on, but I need to get out there, Chris or no Chris."

She grabbed my hand and I proceeded to pull her along.

Two men were on the floor, tumbling. I saw a broken table and a few broken chairs and stools, along with lots of glass. I couldn't make out who was on the floor as the fists that swung blurred my sight.

"You fucking left!" one of them shouted, and I heard the sickening sound of skin against skin accompanied by a groan. "Do you have any idea what that did to Mom?" Another hit. "We thought you were dead!"

"We can't pull them apart," Mike said at my side with Nicole at his other, wincing with every hit.

I turned to find Danica holding on to a crying Alissa.

My brows furrowed. "Where's Pax, and why is Allie crying?"

Jake's gaze went straight to the two that were pummelling each other on the floor. My eyes widened. *What the fuck?*

We waited it out until they seemed to have lost some energy, and that's when Jake, Mike, and I jumped in to put a stop to it all.

"Get the fuck out of here!" Paxton yelled to the other man.

My eyes took in Paxton's opponent as I held on to his arms and my breath caught. *It can't be!*

"I just got back and that's all you have to say?" he asked. "The least I deserve is a chance to explain."

"For what? So you can leave again? We thought we buried you!" he yelled. "Theo, we thought…"

Oh fuck! It is him!

"I'm sorry," Theo said and looked down, shaking my hands off of him before meeting my eyes with a double-take of recognition. "I'm cool." I let the man go as he turned back to his brother. "I couldn't do anything about it. It was work."

Hushed whispers could be heard all around about people wondering who Theo was, and what was going on.

I've known Theo since my high school days. He was a trouble maker, but Paxton and he were the best at throwing parties back then, the closest of brothers I ever knew, too.

When Theo got a drunk driving charge, his parents had put him in military school. They just never expected him to like it so much that the man would make a career out of the armed forces.

I remembered the day we all found out that Theo had gone missing and was presumed dead.

Seeing the man standing before us filled me with relief that he was safe but I couldn't begin to wonder how Paxton felt about his brother's sudden return from the dead.

"What happened to you, man?" Those words were out of my mouth long before I could stop them.

He gave me a quick glance and then aimed his eyes back to his brother. Then he set off to give us the Cliff's notes version, leaving any sensitive information out of where he'd been, what had happened to him.

"And you couldn't be bothered to let us know you were okay?" Paxton asked, his breathing still ragged once his older brother was done explaining.

"It would have been too risky for you, Mom, and Dad. You have no–"

"Don't tell me I have no idea. *You* have no idea of the shit we've been through."

"Pax?" Alissa approached her husband.

"Don't! His own nephew nearly died and he wasn't here. He hasn't even met his niece. He knows nothing of our lives and he expects us to welcome him back with open arms?" Paxton lifted his head, and his eyes bore into his brother's, the look of betrayal hard to miss. "You deserted me!"

Theo wore a tortured expression. "I knew."

Paxton froze. "What?"

"I knew that you and Julie didn't work out, and about the divorce. I know what happened with Jasper, and when that beautiful little princess of yours was born. Just because I didn't stay in touch doesn't mean I don't care. I've kept tabs on my family the entire time I was away because that's the only thing they allowed me to do. I don't think I would have survived if they hadn't given me that much."

"I believe you." Paxton sighed, pinching the bridge of his nose between his thumb and forefinger as if trying to rid himself of a sudden headache. "I need a drink." He headed toward the bar and paused mid-step. "Want one? It's the least I can do for that busted lip. When did your face get so hard?"

Theo laughed as he walked at his brother's side. "Training. By the way, your left hook could use some practise."

"Are these two for real?" Hannah asked, her arms surrounding my waist.

I slung an arm over her shoulders and hugged her to me on a chuckle.

Jake was the one to answer. "They fought like that over girls back in the day. I sure as hell didn't think I'd see Pax swinging like that again."

After watching the two men sit at the bar and have Derek pour them a few shots, I looked over at Hannah, who was busy making Alissa laugh the remainder of the stress of the latest Lowell squabble away. I smiled as I approached her.

"Looks like someone's looking for a good time," Alissa said, which made Hannah turn to face me.

"Dance with me," I said to my girlfriend.

"Ladies, I will see you later. My man is in need of my services."

"I'd like to know what services those entail." Nicole giggled with Danica.

"Believe me, Nikki," Hannah said, "what you walked in on the other day was nothing."

"You dirty minx!" Danica harrumphed. "I'm sure Ben won't complain about what you have planned."

I watched as Hannah put her index over her lips to hush the hens up before turning to me, setting a hand on my chest. She pushed me back toward the space I'd cleared for a dance floor. "I believe I owe you a dance."

"What was that about?"

She bit her bottom lip, and shrugged her shoulders. "That's for me to know and you to find out."

CHAPTER 47

By the end of the night, everyone was having a good time. Much to some guests' amazement, Paxton and Theo behaved like they hadn't swung punches at each other only an hour before. Those two would have a lot to sit and discuss in the upcoming hours, days, weeks, well, you get it.

Chris had disappeared prior to the fight. It seems that Mike had noticed him and had given the man the boot.

The crowd had considerably thinned as the night grew late, but the sound of laughter and enjoyment gave me a sense of peace. It eased the remainder of the tension in my body from earlier, and I found myself enjoying myself a hell of a lot more than I had in years.

The ladies were sitting in a corner talking amongst themselves and I couldn't help but wonder what they were up to since every few minutes, one of them would lift their heads, their gazes aimed at our group of men.

I excused myself from the guys and headed off to relieve myself. With a hand against the men's room door, my movements halted as I heard a feminine giggle through the metal panel.

"Allie." Paxton groaned. "Baby, let's just go home, then you can have your way with me."

"Oh, I'll have my way, baby, but I want it now. Just shut up and let me…"

"Fuck, Allie!" He moaned.

I shook my head, turning to the ladies' room to take my leak instead.

Those two and their tendencies to lose their heads when the mood struck had me smiling this time instead of feeling envious. They're little foray in the barn at Nicole and Mike's wedding had become somewhat of a legend in our circle. After a year of marriage, the two still ran hot. It filled me with hope that maybe the flame didn't extinguish itself through time, provided one was with the right person.

Leaving the stall door open, I was relieving myself when I heard the door open and shut. It wasn't until I had zipped my jeans up and turned to wash my hands that I saw Hannah leaning against the restroom's door with a smirk.

"Quite an interesting show next door. I think Allie has the right idea."

My brow arched. "Does she now?" I approached her after drying my hands. I was right thinking that the girls were up to no good. "Turn around," I ordered her. When she didn't move fast enough, I turned her myself so her back was against my front. "Do you want to hear about *my* idea?" I slid my hand down from the bottom of her ribcage to fan my fingers over her abdomen.

"Please," she said, a little breathless.

I grabbed a fistful of her hair in my hand and pulled back so she looked at me. She gasped but it was out of enjoyment, the lust in her eyes having given her away.

"I plan on hearing a lot of those noises when we get home."

"Ben—"

"But I think I need to make it clear about who's in charge tonight." I nipped the tendon in her neck.

She braced her hands on the bathroom's door as my hands went down to hike her dress up to her hips. I was in the shock of my life when I saw that her underwear was missing.

"Baby." I groaned. "That's got to be the best sight ever." I unbuckled my pants and dropped trou. "Now spread 'em."

Hannah shivered under my touch as she conformed. My hand ran down to her pussy, feeling her juices start to leak out of her with a fingertip. She arched her ass into my crotch.

"Please, Ben." She moaned. "I need you in me now."

I thrust into her hard, eliciting a loud cry from both of us, which also served as a reminder of where we were. And for the first time in my life, the idea of being heard made me keep my pace instead of slowing down.

"Fuck, how I love the way you feel without the rubbers." I pulled out and slammed back in.

"Baby!" she cried out.

"Be quiet, or I'll fuck you harder and really give you a reason to be heard." She moaned.

I plowed into her and she kept our agreement. Somewhat. Well, at least until she came all over my aching cock, crying my name and a series of profanities, causing me to follow her over the edge.

"Hey, man," Jake said through the door. "I don't know if this is a competition, but next time, leave one of the restrooms available. By the way, that was better than porn!"

My head hit Hannah's shoulder as I fought for breath. The woman's body was racked with silent giggles. "Blame the women," I called through our barrier.

"Fucking right!" Paxton shouted out and I could hear Danica, Nicole and Mia cheering.

I was never one for exhibitionism, but I can honestly say that my first bout of it with Hannah had been far more than enjoyable.

CHAPTER 48

To say we avoided embarrassment upon exiting the women's washroom would have been a dream come true, but then again, Hannah and I weren't alone in our humiliation.

As I pulled my girlfriend behind me and exited, a beet red Paxton and smug-looking Alissa were already poised outside of the men's room.

The men held their silence, but their smirks said more than enough. When I looked down at Hannah, to gauge her level of embarrassment, I found her and Alissa grinning, Paxton's wife nodding her approval.

"I think we need to put a stop to this," Jake said as Alissa and Hannah both went to join the circle of women who were now throwing appreciative glances at each of their men.

"I agree," I said.

"I told you they'd be trouble together," Mike added.

"I'm not complaining after that," Paxton said.

"I can't say I didn't enjoy it either." I patted the man on the back. *But payback will be sweet later.*

If Hannah was in the mood for frisky she was bound to get a good dose of it when we got home.

Satisfied with my plan, I smiled, my eyes glued to Hannah's ass. The knowledge of her parading around without underwear had me aching for more already. My eyes rose to find Danica and Nicole eying me, their cheeks flushed.

Huh!

When Hannah turned to see what had the two women's attention, she winked at me.

Grinning, I called the boys up to the bar for another round. "Men," I began, "do me a favor and whoop your woman's ass a little extra tonight. I think they've been feeding each other ideas."

Mike laughed. "What makes you think I wasn't planning on it?" Jake nodded, Paxton smirked, and Theo groaned.

CHAPTER 49

Morning came, and despite last night's exhaustion and our inebriated states, I barely managed to sleep a wink thanks to too much silence after Hannah had fallen asleep in my arms.

The fact that Chris had been at the party bothered me, but I could overlook that fact, if it weren't that he had come off a little too interested in Hannah for my liking.

Being left alone with those thoughts for too long had insecurity warring within me. After all, the man had already succeeded in winning one of my women's hearts. What if Hannah saw the same appeal in him that my wife had?

Disgusted with my train of thoughts, I got up, letting Hannah sleep in. Pulling my boxer briefs and jeans on, I headed toward the kitchen to get a start on breakfast.

Fifteen minutes later, a set of arms surrounded me and hands palmed my chest, while lips pressed against the skin between my shoulder blades.

"I missed you up there," she said with a sleep-roughened voice. "I thought we were cooking breakfast together this morning. Why are you out of bed?"

"I figured…" I sighed. "I figured I'd handle it."

Her arms instantly fell away from me and I felt her body retract. "What's going on? Is it because of what we did last night?"

"No. It's nothing." I set the knife on the cutting board and wiped the fruit juices off of my hands. Instead of turning to face her, I walked further away and poured us each a cup of coffee. I opted to leave mine black and took a sip. I spat it out in the sink, my temper flaring. "Fucking shit tastes like tar!" I dumped my cup in the sink and went back to chopping the fruit, albeit a little violently.

"If it's not me and last night," I could feel her eyes boring into my back, "then what's going on, Ben?" Her warm hand landed on my bicep. I shocked myself when I pulled my arm away from her as if she'd burned me. "Right…" her voice cracked. "It's not me at all." Hannah set her cup in the sink and walked away, her bare feet marching up the stairs.

Was she going to leave? Panic overwhelmed me at the possibility and I found myself rushing for my bedroom.

Something about the shower running in my en suite relaxed me as I entered the room. I knocked on the en suite's door.

"Go away!" Those words conveyed Hannah's bitterness. God, how I wished I'd reacted differently to her last approach.

I peeled away my clothes, letting them drop to the floor and was glad I found the door unlocked as I slid quietly into the room. Her back was to me and it was evident that she wasn't doing much but standing under the showerhead. My feet landed in front of the shower door and I let myself in. I wrapped my arms around Hannah's waist, making her jump in fright.

"Son of a bitch! Are you trying to give me a coronary?"

"It's not what I meant," I said into, then kissed her shoulder. "I'm trying to apologize. I woke up on the wrong side of the bed and I took it out on the one person who didn't deserve it."

"Mind telling me what that was all about?"

I turned her to face me. "Am I forgiven?"

"I think I can let it slide only because I love you," she said on a small smile. "Now, out with it."

I kissed her hard and it wasn't as if I'd planned for her to forget her question—and I doubt that it was the case—but judging at how she pulled me to her, and how much her body seemed to cling to mine, it was as if she was postponing the inquisition for the time being.

Her lips were soft but demanding. Her fingernails dug wherever they touched: back, shoulders, scalp. It was an erotic punishment of sorts for my crass behavior, but what a great way to be taught a lesson!

Before I knew it, the shower was cut and I was carrying a dripping Hannah to my bed. I covered her body with mine and gazed into her fiery eyes.

"Say you love me."

"I love you, Ben."

"How much?"

"Ben…"

"How much do you love me, Hannah?"

She grabbed the sides of my face. "Where's this coming from?"

I sighed and instead of pushing for her answer, I went in for her lips. I didn't count on her holding me back, though. "Ben," she said with sternness, "what the fuck is going on? What's gotten into you?"

I leaned my forehead on her shoulder and closed my eyes.

All I could see was Chris' smug look from last night, re-plays of graphic sex scenes between Candace and him where sickeningly, Candace morphed into Hannah. It was an utter waking nightmare.

"Ben, you need to talk to me." Hannah's hands went around my head and she cradled me to her bosom. "You're scaring me, baby. What's wrong?"

The room filled with silence and after a few minutes, I tried to pull away, but Hannah wouldn't let me.

"Let go, Hannah."

"No. I love you and I'm not letting this go until you tell me what's bothering you. You say that it isn't me, yet you won't talk. How am I supposed to take that?"

Hannah did let me go, but only after a long moment,

where I maintained my silence. She scurried off the bed and tried to make her way past me to get to her clothes.

I grabbed her wrist with a firm hand and she paused to look at me with wounded eyes. In essence, me not saying anything implied that I didn't trust her, and if I didn't trust her, was my love for her real?

Fuck me!

I knew what I had to do, but she already had me figured out. "This has something to do with Chris, doesn't it?" My silence was answer enough for her. "I'm not her, Ben, and I won't let you think of me that way." She ripped her wrist from my hand and proceeded to put on the change of clothes she had left behind on her last visit. "I will never be her, and if that's what you're looking for, then I can't compete with the image of your dead wife. I'm not a replacement. I think this might have been a mistake. I love you, but I can't let you do this to me. I've been hurt too many times."

I stood there gobsmacked as she walked out of my bedroom. How could I have fucked up twice within the few hours of starting the day?

I caught up to her as her hand was on the doorknob, in nothing but my underwear. "I know you're not Candace, and thank God for that." She froze but didn't turn to face me, so I made to approach her like I would a skittish animal. "I love *you*, Hannah. I need you. *Only* you."

By the time I finished, I was a few feet from her. She behaved almost as if she hadn't heard me. When I reached out for the hand that sat on the knob and turned her so she faced me, tears were running down her face. "Then why won't you trust me? How can you say you love me when you can't trust–"

I shut her up with my mouth, and clicked the deadbolt into the locked position again. Her hands wrapped themselves on either side of my neck.

"Why didn't I just tell you?" My lips brushed hers again. "I love you so much, Hannah. So fucking much that it terrifies the living daylights out of me."

"Then tell me, Ben. What's got you so terrified that you can't tell me?"

"It's pathetic, really." *A moment of temporary insanity is more like it.*

"It's not if it's got you this bent out of shape. What about that asshole?"

The weight that had settled in my gut since last night lifted. "Thank you for calling him that." A small smile made its way onto my lips. "There's just something about the way he behaved last night. I can't quite pinpoint it."

"Like he was after me?"

My eyes widened. "So I wasn't imagining that?"

"No, I picked up on it too. He gave me the creeps before I knew who he was."

"It's just–"

Her hands moved from my neck to either side of my face. "You've been burned bad. And I'm going to answer your earlier question; not because you asked me to, but because I know you need to hear it. I'll paint you a picture so you can't doubt where my heart is, where my loyalty lies, or where I want to be."

After making me put a shirt on and refusing to come back to the bedroom to talk, she made me sit on the living room sofa.

"You're putting up walls, sweetheart," I said.

"I'm not. I can't think clearly with you being half naked. This is already going to be hard to tell you without wanting to show you."

"Show me?" My brow arched and my grin made an appearance. "I'd like to sign up for the show and tell if it's up for grabs."

"Benjamin." She sighed. "I'm being serious."

"All right, sweetheart."

I was shocked when instead of sitting next to me, she straddled my thighs, and then I realized why that was—we were at perfect eye level. I went to wrap my arms around her but she lifted her hands to halt me.

"No funny business. I need you to keep your hands to yourself until I'm done talking. I need this closeness as much as you do, but I can't get what I need to get out if you're–"

"Distracting you?" She nodded. It amazed me how much I could affect the woman.

"So you wanted to know how much I love you. What I'll tell you next will help answer that question." She paused long enough to take a deep breath. "When I think of being yours and you being mine, this is what I see…I see happiness, laughter and peace. I see myself free to be exactly who I am, and I know that you'll love me for it, even my insecurities and quirks, and yes, I have insecurities, Ben.

"When I think about our future, I can promise you that I would be in it for the long-haul. I don't believe in the whole love them and leave them bullshit. I see kids, marriage, the big house with the white picket fence, the pool and the trampoline out back. I see vacations and large gatherings with our friends and family, celebrating each birthday, each milestone…everything.

"I've never been able to see all of that with Lee," she said with chagrin. "I think we were so wrapped up in dealing with his alcoholism that we never had a chance to really look that far ahead. With you, the past is in the present for both of us, yet I can still see the future, and it's what I've always wanted.

"I would never betray you because your heart is the other half of mine. Without you, I can't fully be me," she said. "You told me a few days ago that you wouldn't want to live if I wasn't around. I believed you. I still do. What I never mentioned was that I felt the same.

"I would never leave you for another because you and I run deeper than any physical connection. I love you, Benjamin Carpenter, and it's not something I can just turn on and off like a light switch. It just *is*. Candace might have been able to do that, and if that's the case, then she never loved you. She loved the idea of you because from where I'm sitting, you're perfect; insecurities, idiosyncrasies, and all."

When Hannah finished her diatribe, she sat there in silence, her gaze averted from mine. *You're such a schmuck, Carpenter.*

I didn't ask if I could touch her, somehow knowing that I could, more importantly, that I should. My hand clasped one of hers. "You've thought that far ahead?" Hannah didn't look at me, but she nodded. "I'm such an idiot."

"Yes, you are." Her eyes snapped to mine. "But you're my idiot. I should have known that I'd have to set you straight at some point. You were too perfect."

"Still..."

"Never mind." She freed one of her hands to cup my cheek. "As much as you want to admit that you're done with the grief and everything, I know you're not, and you won't be for a while. Loving you is not all about sharing the good, Ben, it's about being able to share the bad and get each other through it like we have since we've met."

"You're right."

"I know I'm right." She smirked. "I'm right about other things too."

My brows arched. "Oh, really?"

Hannah was right about being right about a lot of things, as it turns out. She began proving it to me within seconds of her statement and continued to do so throughout the day.

"How am I not boring you to death?" I asked. "I mean, it's been four weeks and you already know me so well that you can tell me what I'll do next."

"I may have said I'm right about a lot of things, but for all your predictability, I enjoy your unpredictability even more." She rested her head on my shoulder.

"Unpredictable, huh?" I asked. "You mean like what you pulled on me last night?"

"Oh!" Her body quivered. "I love it when you get all bossy like that."

I laughed. "I gathered as much. Maybe it's also time for

me to let you know that I'm right about a lot of things too."

Her head lifted, the side of her mouth quirking up. "Oh, yeah?"

I nodded. It was time to have a little fun with this one. "For instance," I began, "I know that you're about to roll onto your back, spread your legs wide, and beg me to take you nice and slow, even though I know you really want it hard."

She giggled and did exactly what I told her she'd do, minus the verbal request.

"What will I do next?" she asked as I rolled over her and slid inside her heated folds. I watched as her eyes glazed over and my name came out in a breathless plea.

"You'll tell me how much you love me." I pulled back slowly.

Her lips parted, her breathing growing heavier. "I do that a lot, don't I?"

"Well, since we've been saying it, yes, you do." I smirked down at her, sliding back into her again. "And now you'll roll…Ah, there it is." She rolled her eyes as I said it and threw in a head shake to boot.

"Baby?" she said.

"Yes, sweet cheeks?"

"Shut up and kiss me." She pulled my head down to hers as I laughed, crushing my lips to hers hard before pulling away. "And Ben?" My eyes glued themselves to hers. "If you ever doubt me again, I'll literally paint you that picture and bash you over the head with the canvas."

My slow thrusts halted, then I pecked her lips. "So there is a violent streak in you."

"Very." She gave me a mischievous smile before going serious again. "But if you ever doubt, promise you'll talk to me, and I'll promise to listen, and make sure you're smiling again."

"I like the sound of that." I ground my pelvis into hers, her breath catching. "Now, where were we?"

CHAPTER 50

Over the next month, Hannah and I fell into a routine of sleeping at each other's homes—mine more often than hers—and spending most of our free time together, enjoying each other's company.

I didn't think I could love anyone so damn much—it surpassed the love I had for Candace by miles. Hannah made me happier than I'd ever been, and those battles of wits we got into always ended with a tumble between the sheets.

On another note, Chris became a thorn in my side. The man was now using Fairfax as his new turf to conduct his business.

I managed to avoid the man by having someone else serve him, while I disappeared into my office. Suffice to say, if the man wasn't aware of my hostility toward him, I'd have to say he was blind.

Although I've spoken to my parents during this time, I hadn't made the time to go over and visit them. It took Hannah overhearing one of my mother's messages to finally light a fire under my ass to set something up with them. I suppose the fear of hearing their speech about us moving too quickly was why I'd distanced myself. To be honest, Hannah was doing the same with her parents, seeing as every time I asked her how her folks were doing, she'd give me the runaround. I, for one, knew how they were since I had made a point to keep in touch, but she didn't know this.

I was bringing in the last case of beer, and had set it behind the bar, when Adam walked into the pub. I knew it was only a matter of time before he tracked me down. His showing up confirmed my suspicions. Hannah was still avoiding them.

I greeted the man with a handshake. "How are you guys holding up?"

"Anne's worried," Adam said.

"And so are you." I gave him an all-knowing look.

"What's going on with her?"

I sighed. "Same old. She seems perfectly fine. I mean, we've been busy."

The man's eyebrows rose. "*We*?"

Damn those loose lips.

My stomach twisted in knots with what I was about to let the man know. I took a deep breath in an attempt to settle my nerves. "Adam…"

Adam's lips formed a thin line, but the twinkle in his eyes was more prominent. "You're falling for her."

I nodded. "It's more than that."

"Can I just say something?" I nodded. "This isn't just for Hannah, but it's for you too. You've both been hurt before and–"

Oh no! Here we go! My annoyance got the better of me and I cut the man off. "I know, don't rush things," I finished for him. "Look–"

"That wasn't what I was going to say." Adam looked at me pointedly. At that moment, I regretted letting my mouth run away with me. "I've been there since the night of the accident. I know your parents, the kind of family you're from. Most importantly, I know *you*. I knew that this day would come."

My eyes widened. "What do you mean?"

"You think it's too soon?" he asked.

"Some would say that." *My parents sure as hell had their concerns.*

"You've known each other for a couple of months now," he began and I nodded. "A lot has happened between now and then, big things that have brought you both closer." I gave him another nod. "The way I see it, my daughter was already moving on before that accident, and you've been lonely for far too long." The man's eyes held some sadness, but he shook it off and grinned like a loon. "Frankly, Anne bet me that you two were going to announce that you were dating within weeks of Hannah being back on her feet."

I laughed. "What did you bet?"

"I told her that it'd be a few months."

I guffawed. "Tell your wife she was right."

CHAPTER 51

Having Adam's support and Anne's obvious blessing, what with that bet of hers, I knew that I owed them so much for having blessed me with someone like Hannah. So, I put in a call. One that could possibly land me in the doghouse later, but if Hannah could run interference, why couldn't I?

Hannah took my hand as I led us to Mom and Dad's front door.

"Honey, I'm home!" I called out.

Hannah looked confused by the ruckus coming from the back of the house.

Before she could ask questions, I escorted her down the hallway toward the kitchen, only to find ourselves swarmed by parents. Mine and hers.

"Mom." I hugged the woman tight, then shook my father's hand.

"What's going on here?" Hannah asked as she greeted my parents.

"We figured that with you two being together, that we could all celebrate," Mom said.

"Mom…Dad," she said and walked over to her parents for quick hugs and pecks on the cheek. "You know?"

"You're doing a poor job at keeping in touch," Adam said. "If it weren't for–"

"Weren't for who?" My girlfriend's eyes narrowed on me. "What did you do?"

"I may or may not have kept in touch with them, but–"

When I expected her to be mad, she surprised me by giving me an endearing smile.

"We would have gone crazy had Ben not called us every week," Anne said, "but I'm so glad that you guys are official now."

"I'm sorry, Mom." Hannah came to stand at my side, where I wrapped an arm around her shoulders. "I just didn't know how everyone would take knowing Ben and I were together so soon after…I thought I didn't care what everyone would think, but I did."

The ladies were busy talking and, despite my protest, Mom was showing Hannah some old photos of my childhood. It was like reliving my high school days all over again.

The men, on the other hand, were discussing the latest sport statistics, while indulging in a glass of brandy.

My eyes snagged on Hannah who was looking my way with a beaming smile, which I returned with one of my own, and winked. It was nice seeing her so relaxed around her parents, not to mention mine. It looked like my meddling had worked.

"So how's it going with you two?" Adam asked.

My eyes snapped from my girlfriend to her father. His eyes were humored and his smile widened at the sight of the grin that spread across my face. "Great," I said.

"Why do I sense that there's more you're not saying?" Dad asked.

My gaze fused to Adam's. "I love her."

"Can't say I didn't notice with the way you look at her." Hannah's father patted me on the back. "You could have told me earlier, you know."

"That's it?" I asked. "No warnings, no threats, no–"

"Ben, what's there to say? You're two adults. You know

what's at stake here." Dad nodded in agreement. "You were a stranger that chose to look after our little girl. If we trusted you then, we sure as hell will trust you now."

"Thank you, sir." I cleared the ball of nerves from my throat. "Dad, what do you think?"

"I couldn't be happier," he said with conviction. "That woman brought you back to us. If anything, I'd propose on your behalf right now."

"Well let's not get carried away." I chuckled. "But don't be surprised if it happens."

"Oh, it'll happen." Adam crossed his arms, wearing a sure expression. "And I want grandchildren before I can't move."

"I'm with you on that one," Dad said, tipping the rest of his drink back.

I smirked. "You two sound more like old maids than grown men. Does old age make you go soft over the years?"

The men looked at each other, then burst out laughing.

The three women lifted their heads at the commotion, and as our eyes met and locked, I mouthed those three little words to Hannah without thinking.

"You what?" Anne got up to her feet and looked about ten years younger with the beaming smile on her face.

"Mom!" Hannah got up to stand beside her mother.

She looked at her daughter. "He just said he loves you."

"Well, I didn't say it as so much as mouth it, Anne, but I guess the secret's out now. I love Hannah."

"You're not going to start yelling it from the rooftops are you?" Hannah asked, walking over to me.

I pulled her onto my lap, my arms surrounding her waist, and she wrapped hers around my neck.

"I could if it would make things even better, but they're pretty damn perfect enough as they are." My lips met her temple.

"Hot damn!" Mom said. "Did you hear that, Doug?"

"Hear it? I can't believe we knew about it a whole two minutes before you two hens," he said, and I laughed along with Adam. Hannah shook her head at our fathers.

"Thank you," Hannah said after a moment.

"For what?" Our surroundings had grown quiet.

"For having my parents be here tonight."

"You're welcome, sweetheart."

While she pulled my head down for a soft kiss, our fathers snickered about young love and our mothers giggled like schoolgirls.

At that point, everything felt right. Everyone who needed to know about us knew.

Everyone but Candace's parents, but something told me that they'd be fine, what with them already having warmed to Hannah.

CHAPTER 52

By the time we'd reached Hannah's house, I was bursting at the seams and trying hard not to curse the woman that sat next to me.

Getting head while driving hadn't been what I'd imagined it to be. Talk about the mother of all driving distractions!

I rushed around the car, grabbed Hannah, and set her over my shoulder in a fireman's hold. Giving that firm ass of hers a good smack, I hurried us to the door and made sure the damn thing was locked before I took us up to her bedroom.

"Baby, you're evil," I said to which she giggled.

"What'd I do?"

Lifting the hem of her dress up to her waist, I made sure nothing would come between my hand and those cheeks of hers. I smacked her ass for good measure. Her legs tightened together, and she squirmed over my shoulder.

I growled. "You know very well what you were doing."

"It was only a little sexy gratitude." I let her slide down the front of my body. "Can I make it up to you?"

Sexy gratitude? I liked the sound of that. Hannah's eyes glittered in the dim lighting, pleased as punch that I was considering her latest pitch. "What do you have in mind?"

"Well," she grinned lasciviously, "I have me a fireman here, and his hose still needs clearing since I was interrupted earlier."

Her hands made haste at divesting me of my pants rather quickly before her silky fingers grabbed hold of my length and pumped it once.

She nipped my chin before dropping to her knees, my jaw dropping along with her.

"Han-na-nah," was all I managed as her tongue traced the rim of my head. And then those sensuous lips wrapped themselves around me, taking me to the hilt. "Fuck!" The woman had clearly held out in the car. If she kept this up, she'd render me to my knees.

My hand fisted her hair and pulled back. "Baby, you have to stop."

The slight shake of her head and her refusing moan around me sent tremors down my spine. She continued to slide my length in and out of that criminal mouth of hers.

Overwhelmed by the sensations, I couldn't bring myself to release her tresses. Hannah's throat muscles worked around my length, my release imminent. Blood pounded in my ears, white spots filled my vision, and my hips jerked forward as she broke me, swallowing all I had to offer.

When Hannah released me from her mouth and stood up, I pulled her against me, my hand tightening around her hair to tilt her head back. Her eyes widened with lust.

"I'm going to make you come so many times you'll be climbing the walls backwards in an attempt to get away from me for that stunt, baby." I growled and captured her mouth with mine in an aggressive kiss.

Pulling away, much to Hannah's protest, I retreated enough to remove my shirt, as well as to kick away my pants, which were pooled at my ankles.

"Take off your clothes," I commanded. She started as if it was a race. "Slowly. And stop after each item so I can admire you." *This is going to be good.*

I sat down in the armless lounge chair that took up a corner of her bedroom and proceeded to enjoy the show.

To my delight, Hannah twirled after she removed her dress, exposing her thong and the pink mark of my hand on her left cheek.

Her bra and underwear were next.

Hannah reached to remove her shoes. "The heels stay."

Her posture straightened. I held out my hand to her. "Come here."

When Hannah's fingers laced with mine, I pulled her closer so she stood in front of me in naked perfection, her hands connecting with my chest. I ran mine over her back, up to her shoulders, barely touching her heated skin.

"You're beautiful, sweetheart." She blushed at my heated appraisal. "Now, I need you to sit on my face."

Getting up, I positioned myself so I straddled the back of the chair and laid back, my head at its foot. Without argument, Hannah straddled my head, facing my feet, her feet tucked under my armpits as I pulled her closer to my mouth.

"Have I ever told you that your pussy was the best I've ever had?" My tongue traced the length of Hannah's lower lips, where she graced me with a whimper.

My mouth worked her, as I nipped with my teeth, sucked with my lips, and probed her with my tongue. Her moans turned guttural and mixed with the occasional shriek as my fingers joined the mix.

Hannah was so into it that she hadn't even realized that she was attempting to ride my face.

At some point, her body began to shift forward and she gripped my shaft. My hand connected hard with her ass, making her hiss. The clenching of her hot channel on my inserted fingers told me she loved it.

"You don't touch until I tell you to. You got me once already, this is my time."

"B-but…" I slapped her again and this time, she moaned and pressed her bottom closer to my face in a submissive offering.

Hannah came twice before I allowed her sweet pussy away from my face.

"Get on your knees on the lounge," I told her.

She moved into position, gasping loud when I breached her entrance hard and without warning, from behind.

"Play with yourself while I fuck you, baby. I want to hear you scream."

Boy did she indulge me! Lowering a leg to the floor for added leverage, Hannah pistoned backward onto my shaft. My hands gripped her hips and pulled her into me until she came again, her screams making my ears ring.

Her body was a limp mass, but my cock sure wasn't.

Pulling out, I picked her up and set her down on the bed where I opened her legs, lifted her hips and plunged right back in, eliciting a grunt from her.

My thumb tweaked her clit as I thrust balls deep into her and after a few hard flicks over her nub, I could feel her hips and legs start to work as she tried to get away from me.

"Ben, I can't…I can't come anymore."

"Just one more, baby, one more." I gritted my teeth, picked up the tempo and added more pressure to her already hyper-sensitive jewel.

A vice-like contraction took hold of my cock and that was my undoing.

Hannah's screams became silent, her breathing remained heavy and her eyes were closed.

"Baby?" I asked.

"Hmm?"

I lay back and pulled Hannah's limp form into me. It took a minute for her to respond, but she eventually wrapped her arms around me, while I rubbed her back.

"Baby, are you okay?"

"You're a maniac," she mumbled. "Call me crazy, but I want to do that again some time."

The tremendous relief I felt at her words surprised me. For once, I didn't have to hide that part of me that loved control with an aggression that all of my partners over the years had gone running from. It only solidified the fact that Hannah was made for me.

I chuckled and kissed her forehead. "Sleep, sweetheart." I pulled the covers over us, kissing her forehead. "I love you."

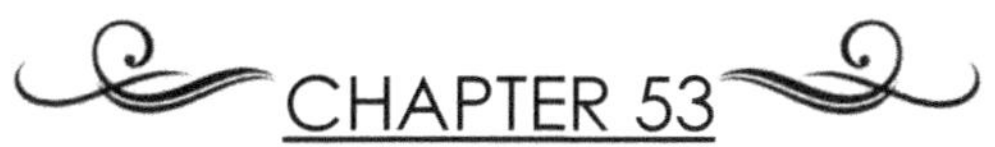

CHAPTER 53

A few weeks came and went in a flash.

Work was a pain in the ass today with some hot-shot businessman's wife having a fit about one of my servers checking her out over breakfast.

By the time lunch rolled around, Hannah had called me to cancel our daily lunch date because of a last minute order.

My day had gone from bad to worse when Chris walked in and made a beeline for me. There was no escaping the man this time.

"What do you want?" I growled out.

"We need to talk."

My eyes narrowed on him. "You fucked my wife, what's there to talk about?"

The heads of the few remaining lunch patrons turned toward us.

Chris stepped back, his voice cracking when he spoke next. "You know."

"Oh boy, do I ever." My blood boiled. "What other reason could I have for being pissed off at you?" *Now this I have to hear.*

He looked around and saw that some people were still looking our way. "Can we speak somewhere a little more private?"

"Are you sure you want to do this right now?" I could be liable for a hell of a lot more than just yelling at the man if he pushed me over the edge.

"I'm done tiptoeing," the man said.

Give the man what he wants and move on.

Derek took over as I led Chris to my office.

He refused the seat I offered him, and I shut the door with a little more force than necessary.

"So what do you know?" he asked.

"Does it really matter? Let me ask you a question, Chris. Did you ever love her? I mean, for a married man, there had to have been something about Candace that made you want her more than your own wife." At least the man had the decency to look guilty. "Tell me…What did you do when you found out that Karen was yours and was being raised by another man?"

The man's face grew red with fury. "Leave my baby girl out of this!"

"That's right, Chris, *your* baby girl." I walked toward my desk. "I have something for you. You had your assistant drop them off at her parents' house and they finally came my way a few months ago." Opening the drawer, I pulled out all five journals, letting them drop to my desk with a loud thud. "They make for great, kinky reading. I'm sure you'll enjoy them since they're all about you two."

"Ben–"

"Don't Ben me. We're not old friends. You were an ex-boyfriend of my dead wife's, her boss, her lover. Were you ever really out of her life?"

The man shook his head. "I should have never left her to begin with." The man's eyes teared up. "I loved her, Ben, so much. I–"

"I don't want to hear your apologies or excuses. You've had three years to come clean and you haven't. Fuck, you had a hell of a lot longer than that if we're being honest here." I took a deep breath, giving him a hard look. "Take them, read them, they're yours. They don't belong to me just like Candace and Karen never did. It's too bad I wasted so much of my life thinking I was happy when

I was clearly about to suffer the biggest heartbreak of all."

"I know you don't want to hear this, but–"

"What?"

"She did love you," he said. "She loved us both."

A snort escaped. Was he for real? "You must be delusional. You don't love someone and fuck around on them. Get your head out of your ass for one second and take a look around."

The man remained silent.

After a long minute, he picked up the journals, tucked them under his arm.

"I have one request of you." I sighed. "I know that you haven't changed and the fact that you're standing here in front of me with no wedding band around your finger tells me that life hasn't been all that kind to you over the last few years. I need you to move on. As for your business meetings, you need to take them elsewhere. You're not welcome in my establishment."

The man nodded. "Is that all?"

"No. I saw the way you honed in on Hannah."

"I didn't know she was taken."

"Fair enough. But what you said after knowing she was mine indicates that you're still an ass."

"I'm sorry. I know it doesn't mean anything to you, but I need to say it. Candace's parents were the ones that said I needed to talk to you."

"You talked to them?"

"I bumped into them about a month ago. Her old man looked as if he was ready to throttle me. They told me that they knew what their daughter had done and urged me to be a man for once."

"So that's why you've been in here," I said, piecing the puzzle together. The man nodded. "Fine."

"I've seen you visit them," he said. "I can't bring myself to walk up to their graves."

"What is this?" I turned away from him, irritated. "For all intents and purposes, we've cleared the air, Chris. Be a man, go see them, cry your eyes out for all I care. Lord knows I've done more than enough of that when I shouldn't have." I headed toward the door and held it open. "If you'll excuse me, I've got a business to run."

"Ben–"

"I said get out!"

CHAPTER 54

By the time my shift was done, I sped home like the Hounds of Hell were on my ass. I walked through the threshold and slammed the door behind me, ignoring the unfamiliar car that was parked in my driveway.

"Well that wasn't the kind of 'glad to see you' I was expecting." My head snapped in Hannah's direction.

Much like the vehicle, I hadn't noticed her standing there until she'd spoken.

Marching past her to the liquor cabinet in the den, I poured myself a generous amount of scotch, downing it and enjoying the numbing burn as it slid down my throat.

Hannah's arms surrounded my torso as I tilted the glass down from my lips. "Bad day?" she asked into my back.

I groaned my response. After a few seconds, my eyes widened. "Who's car is in the driveway, and why are you here? I thought I was picking you up later."

"Mine, and I took an early day because I was desperate to see you, why?"

"You got a car?" I put my glass down on the cabinet and turned to face her. "When?"

"Today. I can't expect you to drive me around all the time. Let's face it, I needed to get back behind the wheel."

"I wish you would have told me." I grabbed her face in my hands, trying to gauge where her head was at. This had been a big step for her, what with the anxiety that riddled her every time she tried to get in the driver's seat. "We'd decided that I'd go with you."

"I wanted to do this on my own." She gave me an apologetic look before it was chased away with a look of excitement. "What do you think of it?"

Aside from it being a black SUV, I hadn't really paid that much attention. "Let me go look at it."

A hand grasping the back of my shirt stopped me before I could move away. "Hold on, mister. You're not getting away without my kiss first."

My lips met hers for a quick peck. "Like magic. You can always make my day better with one of your kisses."

"And you look like you could do with a good one with this mood you're in." She wrapped her arms around my neck. "Come here."

The moment her lips captured mine hungrily, the world faded away. Chris? Gone! My problems? Gone! It was just Hannah and those luscious lips of hers that brought me more than pleasure. They brought me comfort, brought me home.

She pulled away first and I leaned my forehead against hers. "Hi, sweetheart," I said huskily, then grinned. "Let's go check out your new ride."

"I gave you a kiss like that, and all you want to do is check out the car?" She huffed melodramatically. "Men! You may be a sweetheart, a sex God, and one hell of a boyfriend, but you men are all the same aren't you, all for the toys?"

I stepped out onto the front step and realized a Range Rover Sport sat in my driveway. "Oh, baby…" I looked at her. "We'll do more than just check out the car. I'll help you christen the back seat."

Hannah's face took on a beautiful shade of pink before she gave my side a slight shove and jumped off the front step, then turned to face me.

"Baby, the only thing that back seat will be seeing is cracker crumbs and spit-up. This is a no-sex zone." She gestured toward the car as if she were Vanna White.

"Awe, come on!"

She leaned up against the driver side door as I stepped toward her.

It wasn't until I looked into the vehicle and saw a car seat that her words hit home. My heart pounded a tattoo, my head started spinning, my legs felt like jelly, and then, my ass hit the pavement.

CHAPTER 55

I could hear Hannah crying hysterically as my senses came back.

Cracking my eyes open, reality came crashing down on me. A smile spread over my lips and my hand reached up to cup her cheek. Hannah's head shot up and her eyes connected with mine. In that moment, I lost it, and not with the reaction either of us was expecting.

What started off as a small chuckle quickly turned into a full out belly laugh. My girlfriend's brows furrowed and when my giggles continued, she knocked my hand away from her, sat back on her knees and crossed her arms over her chest. "I don't think any of this is funny."

"Sweetheart." I stifled another giggle and reached up to cup her cheek once more. She let me. "I'm sorry."

"Sorry for what?" Her agitation was building. "For fainting? For damn well near giving me a heart attack? Or is it the fact that your child has some superpower that can ratchet up someone's nausea a notch or a hundred in point-two seconds?"

"Baby?" My smile was still firmly in place. "Calm down."

"Don't you 'baby' me, Benjamin Carpenter."

My fists twisted into the front of her shirt, stitches tore, and she landed on top of me with an "oomph" escaping her lips.

"Now listen here, woman." I rolled us so I lay over her. My hand found its way beneath her shirt and stopped over her stomach. "The fact that you're pregnant is amazing, and I can't be more thrilled. Fuck, Hannah, you caught me off-guard and I passed out. I'm sorry I scared you." I leaned in and kissed her hard, feeling her body lose some of its tension. "Move in with me." I pecked the corner of her mouth. "This weekend." I pecked the other. "I don't care whose house we take, sweetheart, my home is wherever you are."

My lips caressed hers in an all too short tender kiss before I pulled back to watch her gaze soften. "Now that's a reaction I've always wanted." She nuzzled my nose.

"Yeah?"

She nodded, her smile brilliant. "Baby?"

"Hmm?"

"You think we can get up now? This asphalt isn't exactly comfortable on the back."

"Shit!" I hurried to my feet and pulled her up, crushing her into my chest before taking her hand to steer her toward the house.

"Didn't you want to look at the car?" she asked.

"Not now. I have something more important to do."

She giggled at my urgency to get us inside. "Oh yeah, what's that?"

"Make love to my beautiful pregnant girlfriend. Nice and slow." I opened the door and let us in.

"Make it dirty and hard and we have a deal." She groped my manhood through my pants as I turned to latch the door. "Knock this nausea back a notch and pound it out of me, will you? We can have it your way all night long."

Grabbing her shoulders, I turned us so her back hit the door and my body crowded hers. "I love it when you talk dirty." I crushed my mouth to hers in desperation. She jumped up and wrapped her legs around my waist, shocking me with the hard, quasi-painful bite to my lower lip. I growled and pulled back, licking where her teeth had snagged.

"Hurry up, Daddy! Mommy's hungry and she'd like for you to fill her up with your—"

My hand connected with her ass as I pulled us away from

the door. "Sweetheart, we're not getting up those stairs right now," I announced, walking us backward until she was against the wall at the bottom of said stairs.

Her legs loosened and I lowered her so she could stand.

Pants undone, my knees met the floor where I pushed Hannah's small sundress up over her waist. My hands roamed the sides of her hips and stopped at her tiny waist, my thumbs rubbing her belly. I spread tender kisses over her stomach just as the front door opened.

"We just dropped by to–" Mike's words froze. "Whoa!"

My hands removed themselves from Hannah and set her dress to rights as I groaned out a "Seriously, guys, don't you ever knock?"

Mike's sarcasm was potent. "Seriously, a Range Rover is nice but it's nothing to get that excited about."

I got up to my feet with a grin and pulled Hannah into my side. "It's what's in the back seat that's got me all fired up. Go ahead, look."

The couple ran off while my girlfriend and I waited.

Here it comes.

Mike came barrelling through the door, white as a ghost, with Nicole latched to his back. "You're fucking kidding me, right?" Nicole jumped off of him and tackled my woman to the wall with a large hug, squealing with excitement.

I shook my head and grinned at the spectacle that was my woman and Mike's.

My best friend's color came back and the man grinned. "I'm going to be an uncle?" For some reason, his reaction was even better this time around than when I had told him that Candace and I were expecting. The man took two large steps and crushed me in a hug. "I'm so happy for you guys. You are happy, right?" He pulled back.

Hannah made her way back to my side. I had yet to answer my best friend. "You are happy, right, Ben?" Hannah asked with hesitance.

I turned her to face me. "I'm happier than I could have ever hoped to be." I wrapped my hand around the back of her neck and took my time kissing her with slow languorous strokes of my tongue.

"And that, ladies and gentlemen, is how he got her knocked up in the first place," Nicole said, and Mike laughed. "And I thought my husband was insatiable."

Hannah and I pulled away from each other and looked at the both of them. Mike's arms were wrapped around his wife. "I'll show you insatiable when we get home, woman."

After a quiet dinner with Mike and Nicole, Hannah and I had called it an early night. That's when I realized that Hannah hadn't answered my earlier question about us moving in together. Cuddled into my side, my fingers combing through her hair, I said, "Sweetheart?"

She sighed peacefully. "Hmm?"

"Will you move in with me?"

She lifted her head, the look in her eyes was one of concern. "Are you sure?"

I nodded. "We can live here…or your place." My hand found its way to her stomach. "I'm even up to buying something new for the three of us."

Hannah's features darkened. "I can't live in that house, Ben."

"You still haven't answered my question."

"Yes, I want us to move in together." She kissed me softly. "But we have to tell our parents."

"Fuck!" My palm connected with my forehead. "Your dad is going to kill me."

She laughed. "He's always wanted grand-babies."

"Yeah, I know that."

"So, why the worry?"

"I always thought I'd be married before that happened."

"Good thing we were both married before, then." She winked at me.

My eyes rolled. "It's not funny."

"It is, a little bit," she said. "And Daddy would never beat on a woman, let alone a pregnant one, so just stand behind me and stay real close when we tell them."

"Shouldn't we wait?" I asked. "I mean, how far along are you? God, I'm already off to a bad start. Instead of grinning like a fool, I pass out. Instead of asking how you were feeling and how you found out, I jumped your bones like a caveman–"

"Baby," she grabbed my face, "passing out aside, you reacted just the way I wanted you to. I love you, Benjamin."

God, did I love her!

CHAPTER 56

Hannah had been in her seventh week of pregnancy when she'd broken the news to me.

In the following week, things moved along pretty quickly. Hannah had put her house up for sale and moved in with me, we'd had our first doctor's appointment, and things couldn't have been greater between us.

Overcome with bliss, the recollection of Hannah's vision for our future hit me—the one with the white picket fence. So, I built it as a gesture to prove to her that I would do anything to make her happy.

Mike, Jake, Paxton and Theo joined me in the sweltering heat to make my woman's vision a reality. Suffice to say, Hannah was in quite a shock to find five men greeting her with swinging hammers and an abundance of lumber. The tears were immediate, and it took me a good ten minutes to get her calmed down, after which she then rushed out the front door to hug each guy out of gratitude.

I stood and watched it all with my arms crossed at my chest, my smile frozen in place, and then she finally turned to me, making her approach.

"You okay?" My arms wrapped themselves around her.

She kissed my chin and then pecked my lips. "I couldn't be happier." Her smile and the brilliance of her eyes confirmed it.

"Good."

I bent my head to kiss her and she met me half way, pausing to say, "You're so getting lucky tonight," before she continued louder so the rest of the men could hear her. "I need to make a few calls. Seems a few girlfriends of mine would enjoy scoping out the hot construction men that are hard at work in my front yard."

With a searing kiss, Hannah made a mad dash for the house.

Within an hour, women began arriving. And yes, they sure did enjoy watching their men at work, if the giggling, the whispering, and the hot looks were anything to go by. Hell, even some new little blonde shorty I hadn't met yet, had joined the fray, her gaze intent on Theo.

CHAPTER 57

Hannah's morning sickness began to wane by her thirteenth week of pregnancy. The woman seemed to glow, and the slight bulge in her belly caught my attention often. Knowing, without a doubt, that Hannah was growing round with my child made me crave our physical connection more than ever before.

"Baby!" Hannah called out. "They'll be here soon and I need your help down here. You know everything will be fine, so please stop wearing out the carpet with your pacing."

Mike and Nicole had been sworn to secrecy about our baby news since Hannah and I had decided that it was for the best to wait until we were over the riskier part before making a formal announcement. Today was the day. Under the guise of a semi-housewarming barbecue to celebrate Hannah's moving in, we invited everyone over.

As the crowd settled with their plates and drinks, I got up to my feet and held my hand out so Hannah could join me.

"Thanks for being here," Hannah began. "It's been a wild and fast-paced series of months since I met this handsome and sweet man." She looked up at me, her smile beaming.

"We have something to say to all of you." I stood behind Hannah, putting my arms around her waist and leaving my hands on her belly. She covered my hands with hers.

"Ready?" she asked so only I could hear her.

I nodded.

"We're pregnant!"

We didn't have to wait long for a reaction. Hell, as soon as the words were out, the commotion was instantaneous. Two mothers got up, barrelling toward us. Our fathers seemed a bit too pleased with our news, which helped me relax a bit.

The tension never really left me, because I had to worry about the two additional people who were seated at the back of the crowd.

The moment Hannah and I approached Betty and Don, I knew they didn't object, what with the teary smiles we received.

With her arms around me, Betty whispered in my ear. "You deserve this and so much more, Benjamin. Promise me you'll call the minute the baby is born."

"You'll get a call about the baby shower before then," Mom told her. Betty let me go to hug my mother.

Don shook my hand. "This baby might not be our grand-child but–"

"Don, you two will always be family," I said.

"He's right," Hannah said, standing beside me.

Don let go of my hand to take her in his arms. "Sweetheart, you're a godsend."

I couldn't agree more.

W ith the folks having left for the night, Hannah and I were surrounded by friends reminiscing about the last few months.

My girlfriend had fallen asleep on my lap, while I held her in front of the fire pit as the gang chatted quietly. I looked down and studied her face. There was a slight smile there, and I couldn't help but be fixated.

"So when's the wedding?" Jake asked as he fed one of the twins.

Mike chuckled. "He'd have to pop the question first."

"You two are worse than women." Paxton nodded his

agreement. "I'm curious though. No one's mentioned how quick this all has been."

I watched as every couple turned to one another and smiled and then looked back at me.

"Have you seen yourself lately?" Danica asked. "You haven't been the same since Nikki and Mike's wedding. The old Ben is back."

"Dani's right, bro," Mike said. "After getting to know her, seeing the way she looks at you, she's what you've been missing."

My lips stretched into a grin. "I think so too."

Hannah woke not too long after the proposal conversation ended, at which point the gang decided that it was time to take their leave.

After locking the front door behind the last of our visitors, I grabbed Hannah's hand and led her toward the staircase.

She pulled back on our interlocked fingers. "No."

"But you're tired, sweetheart. You should be in bed."

"I should be in your arms."

"Well since you put it that way," I kissed her forehead, "let me make sure we're locked up tight, I'll wash the rest of the dishes, and then I'll come and join you?"

"How about you lock up, we leave the dishes until tomorrow and you come and shower with me?" she countered. "The smell of barbecued food is making me nauseous."

"I'd definitely rather wash you than those dishes." I pecked her lips. "I love you."

"We love you too, Daddy," she said and looked down as she rubbed her belly, and then I saw her stiffen and her hand stopped its movement. She jumped and gasped, and then her eyes snapped to mine, tears present, but judging by the grin on her face, they were happy ones.

"What is it?"

"Butterfly flutters," she whispered and then broke out in a giggle.

"The baby kicked?" She nodded, then grabbed my hand, placing it firmly on where she was feeling it. "I don't feel a thing." Hannah seemed more disappointed about it than me, but I knew it was still too early.

Okay, so I've been reading the books too. Sue me. I'd done the same when Candace was pregnant with Karen.

"This is amazing," she said, breathless and consumed with emotion.

You would have thought I was used to a woman sharing this stuff with me after having been through it once already, but no.

Candace had had a miserable pregnancy. She'd barely wanted me to touch her. Hell, things like wrapping my arms around her, kissing on my woman's belly never happened more than once. When it did, my wife had pulled away. What woman wouldn't want to share that with her man, despite how shitty she felt? What's more, what husband doesn't get to feel his child kick? It was safe to say that Hannah was entirely different. It was as clear as glass that the woman loved me unconditionally, faults and all, and that she wanted me to be part of every little step in this journey of ours.

"I wish you could feel this." Her bottom lip quivered.

"Hey!" I grabbed her face, tilting it up toward mine. "Don't be sad. I will soon enough. That flutter bug in there still has loads of time to dazzle me until she comes out."

"*She?*"

"Yes." I smiled sheepishly. "I think it'll be a girl, and she'll be a spitting image of her beautiful mother."

"I wouldn't mind a mini-Benjamin running around."

I groaned. "We'd be in trouble, then." I laughed. "Now, go warm up the shower and I'll make sure all is closed up."

"Hurry up." She kissed my nose before heading up the stairs.

Keeping my eyes on her retreating form, I couldn't help but wonder how I'd gotten so damn lucky.

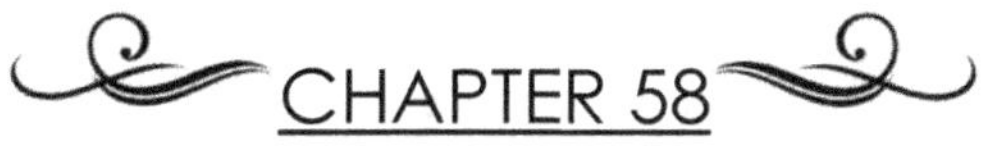

"**B**aby!" Hannah called out.

"Yeah, sweetheart?"

"What do you think of this?" she asked.

Nearly two months had gone by since our house-warming-slash-baby-news get-together with the gang. Hannah's pregnancy had been going beautifully and she was growing rounder by the day at her twenty-one weeks. Truth be told, she'd never looked sexier to me, and I made a point to tell her that every day before, during, and after loving on her.

I walked around the aisle and came face-to-face with my girlfriend who was smiling while running her hands over a beautiful dark oak crib. I was too busy looking at my woman to be bothered with bedroom layettes, clothing, and nursery items. I was going to be a father—to a boy!

The ultrasound from this morning had confirmed it. Seeing as this was Hannah's first full-term baby, I argued that we should keep the gender as a surprise, but she refused, stating that she didn't want yellows and greens to dominate the baby's quarters. She wanted us to build a room for our little prince or princess that everyone would envy. I think it's safe to say that our child was going to be loved, yet spoiled just the same.

"So?" Hannah snapped me out of my daze. My hands were on her belly as I kissed her forehead.

"So what, baby?"

"You're still on cloud nine about the fact that I was right

and it's a boy, huh?" She giggled before kissing my cheek. "What do you think about this crib?"

"I think–" I felt the slight twitch beneath the palm of one of my hands. "Was that a kick?" My eyes shot down to her belly and then back up to her face.

She nodded with a wide grin.

"Oh, God!" I got down to my knees and kissed her belly through her shirt. Hannah's hand feathered through the hair at the back of my head as she whispered "Do it again, slugger, do it for Daddy."

"Daddy?" I heard coming from behind me, Hannah jumping with a gasp. "You're pregnant?"

I got up, turned around and saw a tiny woman with a massive belly and a man standing behind her where they'd both had yet to introduce themselves.

"Dee!" Hannah exclaimed. I moved to stand behind Hannah, wrapping my arms around her waist, covering her small bulge with my hands in a gesture of protection.

"Well you haven't wasted time, have you," the woman said, but even though her words could have sounded judgemental, this Dee woman wore a beaming smile on her lips. And where in the hell had I heard that name before?

One look at Hannah, to gauge her reaction, and I found her returning Dee's smile. As soon as I released her, she rushed to hug the woman.

"I'm so sorry I haven't called," Hannah said and the man that stood behind Dee walked around the two of them and stuck out his hand, smiling. "Blake."

I took the man's hand. "Ben."

We ended up spending the next few hours in a nearby coffee shop talking with Dee and Blake.

Deidra or Dee—as she likes to be called by her friends—is Hannah's best friend. Because of Lee, the women hadn't spoken since before the accident. Hannah had voiced at one point that she wasn't quite ready to re-enter the world of her past just yet.

Watching the two women interact as if they'd never missed a beat put a smile on my face. Hannah needed this. It's not that she was without friends, but they were from my bunch of people. She needed people that knew her past and that were willing to stand by her side well into her future, people that weren't her parents.

"So how'd you two meet?" Dee finally asked as Blake kissed the side of his wife's temple before leaning in to listen to the story.

By the time Hannah and I told them the entire tale, Deidra was rendered to a complete blubbering mass of tears consoled by her husband whose gaze was soft toward my girlfriend.

"I'm so relieved." Deidra made a grab for Hannah's hand. "I would have come to visit. I tried to go into the shop once, but I couldn't do it. I couldn't walk through those doors and see how broken you were. Not with these hormones. I was terrified of how'd you react if you saw me after I found out from your mom that you had lost the baby."

"You talked to my parents?" Dee wiped at her cheeks and nodded. "I love you, you know that Dee? I should have reached out. Why–"

I rubbed Hannah's back. "Because you're still worried about what those who are close to you will think," I told her. "Lee's parents ensured that with the way they treated you, sweetheart. And let's face it, it's not like you told everyone that you and Lee were separated, even though you guys tried to make another go at it." I looked at the couple across the table from us and both their faces darkened.

"I'm sorry about you losing the baby, honey," Deidra whispered, voice shaking with another bout of emotion.

"I'm sorry I ignored you for the last five months." Hannah squeezed the woman's hand.

"You're happy now, right?" her friend asked, and Blake's as well as his wife's gazes were fixed on Hannah in assessment.

Hannah looked at me and said with utmost confidence, "Blissfully."

"Oh, thank God!" I dramatically clutched at my chest, then dropped the hand to Hannah's belly. "I thought that we had only shacked up because of this little guy." Hannah rolled her eyes at me while the other two laughed. "I love you," I threw in and kissed her temple.

"I like this guy," Deidra pointed her thumb in my direction.

"Thanks." Hannah dropped her head on my shoulder, releasing a peaceful sigh. "I think I'll keep him. I kind of like him too."

"You're stuck with me whether you like it or not." This made Blake chuckle.

When Deidra and Blake left us, Hannah and I headed toward the car to get home.

"I love seeing you like this." I stopped to open her door for her. "I have to say that I've been seeing a lot more of those smiles lately."

"It's because you make me so happy."

"You're sure it's not the foot rubs or the sex?"

"I'm sure both have a great deal to do with it, but I loved you before we ever slept together, baby," she said. "Now, hurry up! You mentioning sex only reminded me of a few little things I've been meaning to do to you."

"Fuck me," I mumbled under my breath as my body went taut.

Nudging my jaw to shut my mouth, she smirked up at me and said, "That's the idea," before taking her seat, and buckling herself in.

CHAPTER 59

As Hannah's twenty-fifth week arrived, so did the day of her baby shower.

And I was anxious.

I hadn't told Hannah why it was that I was so tired by the time the sun set on each day over the last week. She assumed that it was because work was hectic. I never told her any different.

A week after meeting Blake and Deidra, Hannah and I had invited them over for dinner. As per their usual fashion, Mike and Nicole came and crashed our small get-together.

Needless to say—after a few group events—Deidra, Nicole and Danica hit things off so well that they got together to organize Hannah's baby shower with help from Mom and Anne.

I think our mothers loved being part of the whole process just as much as I enjoyed not having to deal with any of it this past week, since I had my own workload to deal with.

You see, there's a reason I was exhausted. And like you may have guessed, it wasn't because I'd been working at the pub. Despite a week off from Fairfax, I hadn't stopped, and stress was definitely a contributing factor to my exhaustion, not to mention my climbing anxiety.

"Ben!" Hannah called after I'd heard the doorbell. "Nikki and Dee are here." I knew it was my cue to take the men out back and get the beer flowing.

Showers weren't a coed kind of thing, but since none of the men had plans, Hannah mentioned that we should have a barbecue afterward so I'd have some guy time. I agreed, seeing as it was a great way to stay away from a bunch of squealing ladies that would most definitely be fawning over cute outfits, booties, loads of diapers, and gift baskets that we were bound to receive. Hannah might not know it yet, but the get-together would end up serving a dual purpose.

"Coming!" I called out.

With one assessing look that told me everything was perfect, I shut the door and headed downstairs.

The gifts were opened and my entire living room looked like a baby store had exploded in it. I think we were ready for a set of triplets by the amount that had taken over the room, but I could deal with the surplus, having loved how Hannah had been doted upon. The beaming smile the mother of my son wore on her face throughout the day was testament to her joy and proof that she was loved by everyone around her.

"Hey there, handsome." Hannah hugged me from behind as I was putting the last of the food on the grill.

I set the flipper to the side and turned to wrap my arms around her. "Hey there, sweetheart, having fun?"

She nodded vigorously. "The best time, only..." Her brows furrowed.

"What is it?"

"I just heard from Derek's girlfriend that you haven't been at work this week."

Fuck!

I looked around at all of our family, the friends, the kids, the joy that surrounded us, and realized that despite my original plan to do what I'd planned once we were alone, there was no better time than the present.

I held out my hand to her. "I have something to show you. It'll explain everything, I promise."

Hannah took my hand and I turned to see Mike giving me an inquiring look. I headed toward the house and nodded in the barbecue's direction and mouthed "turn it off and follow" while I made a circular motion with my free hand meaning he should get everyone to tag along.

I brought Hannah upstairs and down the hall from our bedroom.

"You know those clippings from those baby magazines you've been keeping with the rest of the ideas of what you wanted for the nursery?" I asked her.

She nodded and after a fraction of a second, her eyes widened. "You didn't."

Grinning, I said, "I did," and turned the knob, pushing the door inward.

Hannah gasped and her hands flew up to her mouth as she took in the sight around her.

I'd painted, changed the carpet, assembled the furniture and set up the room in the way I knew Hannah had envisioned.

With a bit of help from the girls, I got the decorations, some story books, even the lounging chair where I was sure mother, father, and baby would surely be bonding in the dead of the night during feeding times.

Hannah walked further into the room, running her hands over the furniture and I heard her sniffle. "This is beautiful, Ben," she said on an emotionally drawn breath. She reached for the stuffed toy I had set in the middle of the crib: the miniature blanket-looking bear that had scripture on its chest that read *Little Angel.* "It's pink."

"It was Karen's," I said as I approached Hannah and stopped right behind her. "I figured that even though she wasn't mine by blood that she was still mine in my heart, and she would look out for our little guy when he gets here."

Hannah squeezed the plush toy to her chest and set it back down. "It still smells like baby," she whispered and my breath caught in my throat.

I heard some rustling behind me, followed by a few gasps and I knew everyone was there for this moment.

"Hannah," I said since she was still so taken with the room that she had yet to turn to face me.

"Hmm?" She wiped a tear from her cheek.

"Sweetheart?" I moved to take a knee at her side and pulled out the ring.

Her hand came to settle on my shoulder, but she still hadn't looked my way. Instead, she said, "What are you doing, Benjamin, get up."

Giggles funnelled through the doorway and she turned to those instead of me.

"Look at me, woman! I'm trying to do this right, but you're too distracted." A few of our onlookers snickered.

Hannah's eyes flew down to mine and her eyes welled up with more tears.

"I love you, Hannah." I was having a hell of a time pushing away the ball of emotion clogging my throat. "So much. You've brought me back to life with your smiles, your words, your presence, your…well, let's not go there with kids here." I winked, bringing forth a teary giggle. "You said that it was fate…kismet. It's true. I've never been this happy in my entire life, sweetheart." And then I went in for the kill. "Marry me, Hannah. Marry me because I want that same dream with the white picket fence that you do."

"You've already built me one of those." Everyone laughed, while the boys groaned.

"Marry me because I want babies with you," I persisted.

"We got a head start on that now haven't we?" I tried not to laugh. Instead, I shook my head at her smart-assed comment. The woman had an answer for everything.

"Marry me because without the house, the fence, the friends, the babies, you're all I need to survive in this world. Hannah, you're my life, my world, my home, my everything."

"Are you shitting me right now?" she blurted and lifted her head and looked toward the door. "What do you think, Mike?"

"Put the man out of his misery, Hannah," he said.

I grinned at his words.

"For goodness sakes, Hannah, stop teasing the man and

give him the answer I know you've been dying to give him for a while now," Anne threw in.

"You're right, Mom." She looked down to me before getting to her knees. "I wouldn't want to be punished for toying with your head now would I?" She smirked at her double-entendre. "Mrs. Benjamin Carpenter, it has a nice ring to it."

"It does. So what's your answer?" I knew what it was, but it seemed as if our little show was keeping our family and friends on pins and needles, and toying with them was almost as much fun as toying with each other. Almost.

"Did you really have to ask?" She grabbed my face. "Yes, Ben, my answer is 'yes'. I would have married you a month ago, yesterday, today, tomorrow, ten years, even a hundred years from now. So, Benjamin Carpenter, yes, I will marry you."

With that, I grabbed the back of Hannah's head with one hand and went in slow, fusing my lips to hers. I wanted to savor this moment, the feeling of completeness, of joy, of peace that came with it.

I pulled back, grabbed her hand to slide the diamond in-lay white gold band with the large three diamonds at its top onto her left-hand ring finger. "What do you think?" I pecked the top of her hand before holding it so she could admire the band.

Her breath caught in her throat. "It's really beautiful, but I would have been happy with a twist-tie if it's all you had. I already knew you were mine for life; this only solidifies it. I love you so much." She kissed me but this time, I wrapped my arms around her and held her tight as she returned the gesture.

"Break it up, kids," Dad said. "We have minors here."

"And I'm hungry," Mike added.

"When are we eating, Daddy?" Jasper asked Paxton, and as I got up and helped Hannah to her feet, I turned and crouched down to face the little guy.

"Tell you what, buddy," I said, "we'll go downstairs after all these hugs and kisses and you can help me flip the last few burgers once I get the grill fired up again."

Jasper turned to his father, bouncing on the tip of his toes. "Can I, Daddy?"

"If Ben says it's okay, then go for it, but be careful."

"Let's do this!" he shouted his excitement as he rubbed his little hands together and licked his lips. He gave me a quick hug and jumped at Hannah with the same treatment before running straight for the stairs, making us all laugh. "Hurry up guys, Mike's starving!"

CHAPTER 60

I finished cleaning up after everyone had left and decided to go check on Hannah. I found her where I suspected she would be. What surprised me was that everything we had received had already been neatly stowed away, and my fiancée was sitting in the chair I envisioned us spending some long nights in. She had a book in her hand and was reading it aloud to herself. It was Robert Munsch's *I'll love you forever*. I remembered reading it to Karen every night since the day she was brought home. I planned on doing the same when our little guy graced us with his presence.

Leaning against the doorway, I was mesmerized by the woman who had only hours before agreed to be my wife. The thought of it made my stomach flutter with excitement.

When she finished reading, she set the book on the side table, stuck out her left hand and admired her ring. She sighed and leaned her head back, smiling in pure contentment as she rubbed her belly.

"I have to say the sight of you like this makes me want to do it all over again." I moved from the doorway and crouched down in front of her.

Her palm cupped my cheek. "You're amazing."

Grinning, I said, "Funny, I think so too." Her hand withdrew and she smacked my shoulder. "But I think it's time for bed, beautiful."

She yawned. "I think you may be right." As I helped her to her feet, she wrapped her arms around my neck and kissed me softly. "I can't believe you did all this."

"I had a bit of help from the girls," I confessed.

"Still…"

"I'd do anything for you, Hannah." I rubbed her back.

"I see that." She gave me a drowsy but sweet smile. "Can I add one more thing to today's list of honey-do's?"

"I think I can be persuaded to oblige." I kissed her nose before smiling down at her.

I'd stripped Hannah to nothing and made her lay down before taking my own clothes off. Crawling over her, my hands slid over her heated skin. "You're so beautiful." I kissed around her baby bump.

Her internal walls clenched and released in a slow rhythm as I eased into her depths, settling her over my lap, while I kneeled in the middle of our bed.

The heightened sex drive was one thing about Hannah's pregnancy that was great. I hadn't counted on the fact that she'd make me feel like a god, but her increased sensitivity was outstanding, and worked to my advantage at every turn. Hell, I'd even managed to set her off with her still wearing multiple layers of clothing. It was sexy as hell, and I enjoyed giving her release whenever and wherever I saw fit, knowing that I would get mine at some point down the line, usually never having to wait too long.

"God, baby," I mumbled into her neck.

Hannah's nails raked up my back, then her hands fisted themselves in my hair. She pulled back, tilting my head and began to nip, lick, and suckle on my skin.

Her rhythm picked up with a sudden urgency that sent my balls tightening ready for total release.

My hands grabbed her hips and helped her on the up-stroke while she'd let herself drop over my shaft.

She pulled back so she could capture my lips with hers and moaned into my mouth as I felt the spasms that brought me to completion with her.

Our kisses grew from frantic and needful to tender, passion-filled, and relaxing. Hannah's arms were still around my neck as she massaged the back of my head. My hands rubbed up and down her back, bringing forth those goosebumps I loved so much.

And then I felt it.

After our shopping trip, I hadn't felt our little guy kick again. This time, it was different. Our stomachs were pressed against each other's, and I felt it through my own belly. My hands went straight for the sides of her bump, feeling this highly and quite suddenly energized bundle of joy of ours.

"I think we woke him," Hannah said.

"Does that mean you won't be able to sleep?"

"It'll be a bit difficult until he calms down since I'm not used to this, but I love it when he's active."

I shifted us slowly and laid her onto her back. I pulled the covers over us as I slid out of her heat, and lay down beside her.

"He moves a lot when he hears men's voices."

I grinned and then scurried down the bed, wrapping my hands around her belly. I spent the better part of the next half hour talking to our son. When I finished with a lullaby my mother had come up with for me when I was a baby, I looked up to find Hannah with watery eyes. "Sweetheart, what's wrong?" I moved back up so I lay on my pillow and cradled her into my side.

"Nothing," she said and started to laugh. "I…"

I tilted her chin up so she could see my face. "Is this one of those times your hormones take over?"

She giggled through her tears, nodding. "I'm just so happy." She moved to straddle my waist, then leaned forward onto my chest. "This," she placed my hand on her belly, "you and me, our baby, the three of us…*everything*…it's all I ever wanted, and then some."

I smiled. "And then some, huh?"

She nodded. "I never once asked for mind-blowing sex, or a handsome firefighting bartender, or the fact that I could love someone again so much that it hurts."

"But it's all yours, I'm all yours." I lifted my head to kiss her chastely.

"And I'm yours." She shifted, grabbing onto my length and began to rub it against her bud, making it harden instantly. "I want you again, baby, and I want you hard and fast."

She dropped herself onto my cock with a loud moan.

"Then let's get one thing straight." My hands braced themselves on her hips, halting her movements. "I'm in control here, and as much as I could get off on your sounds, I think I want you to be quiet until I tell you to let loose, which would be about the same time I tell you to come for me."

Hannah's eyes went wide. "You wouldn't." I smacked her ass and flipped us so she lay on her back with my dick still buried balls deep in her slick heat.

"I would and I am," I told her, pulling myself back slowly and then plowing into her. She bit down on her bottom lip.

I continued the slow pull-back and fast slamming for a short while before I could see the tension in her face build, feel the tremors beginning in her core, and the worried look that she would possibly fail at not coming flashing in her eyes.

I stilled.

I stopped until I could barely feel her walls spasm at which point I gave short thrusts while I used my thumb on her clit, circling but never truly hitting that spot that would push her over the edge.

"Baby?" She panted. "I don't think I can take much more of this."

"It's not your choice, sweetheart." My stern voice made her clench my length. "It seems like someone really enjoys not being in control."

"Only with you."

Her words warmed me, but she shouldn't have been talking regardless. "I hear something more out of you, and I'll have to figure out some kind of punishment."

Her bright green eyes darkened further, and then I saw her smirk. "Fuck. Me."

"You pushing me?"

"You bet your sexy ass I am."

I pulled out and flipped her onto her knees so she could use the headboard for stability. I had an inkling that if we kept up this kinky hard fucking habit of ours, we'd be in need of a new headboard every couple of years, if not sooner. The thing was already rattling against the wall.

I grabbed my steal shaft and ran its tip up and down her slit. Her juices were running down her thighs and I loved it when she got this wet for me. I ran my tip from the front of her slit to the back, and every time I passed the spot where I'd normally thrust into her, she'd arch and try and follow me to get me inside her. I smacked her ass hard twice, and smoothed my hand over the redness that was already appearing.

I leaned forward, grabbed her hair, and pulled her head back before nipping the side of her chin. At the same time, I ran my cock and nestled myself at her entrance, pushing in slightly to tease her. "Fuck yourself on my dick, baby."

There was no hesitation as she did just that.

My balls were killing me with how much they ached to explode, but I was adamant to keep this going for as long as possible.

"Stop," I ordered, and she froze. I allowed my hands to skim her back and my lips kissed her shoulders.

A single hand of mine made its way between her legs, playing with her nub with a sole purpose; to render her shattered at the hand of one massive explosion.

"Fuck me," I said into her ear. She shivered against my chest.

I feathered my fingers over her hips to help guide her since her legs were quivering so much. I could feel her clenching on me and damn did I ever want to give in. I almost did too.

"Stop!" She released a throaty growl. "Easy tiger, I'm not done with you yet."

Hannah whimpered as I pulled out of her and felt the bucking of her hips when I pulled her knees further away from the headboard so she was leaning forward more, and her ass stuck out.

My how I loved those cheeks, and even better when they had my hand print on them.

I stuck two fingers inside of her and felt her clamp down on me.

"Not yet, sweetheart." I began to slightly tap my fingers on that sweet spot of hers, observing the look of carnal desperation that made its way onto her face as she tried to peer at me over her shoulder, and enjoying the panting sounds she made.

I ran my slickened fingers backwards, bringing her juices around to that tiny little puckered hole at her rear. Instead of hesitance, Hannah jutted her ass out in presentation. I'd just about had enough when she did that. I moved my knees behind hers and repositioned my cock at her entrance.

"Push back, honey." I thrust up as she powered backward. I was amazed she'd remained silent and even more, impressed that she hadn't come undone.

I held onto her hips as I allowed my thumb to inch its way into her ass, massaging that little rosette of hers as it followed her thrusts.

"Baby, grind on me," I told her. "I want to be buried as deep as possible."

She did just as I said and with every hip rotation, I pushed harder on that forbidden hole until it gave way. She stilled.

"I-I can't. If I move, I'll come."

"Did I tell you to speak or stop?"

She started to say no, but stopped herself.

"Then come with me, baby," I told her and pulled back slightly to give her a bit of friction.

I slowly increased my thrust length and speed and within minutes, we were flying apart.

The sounds that came out of my woman's mouth were

ethereal. I didn't know windows could actually shake like that, or that my dick could feel as if it could possibly be bruised from being clenched so damn hard.

I eased out of Hannah, pulling her back onto my chest as her head lulled back onto my shoulder, her breathing erratic. My fiancée's eyes were shut, and it seemed like every subtle move, every touch of mine, made her entire body quake.

Once she was lying down, I hurried to wash my hands and return to her with a moistened washcloth.

I wiped her down, cleaning our mixed juices off the insides of her thighs and chucking the cloth toward the hamper. That's when her green eyes opened, her lips gracing me with what looked like a drunken smile. Pure satisfaction.

Damn, but that look on her face simply undid me.

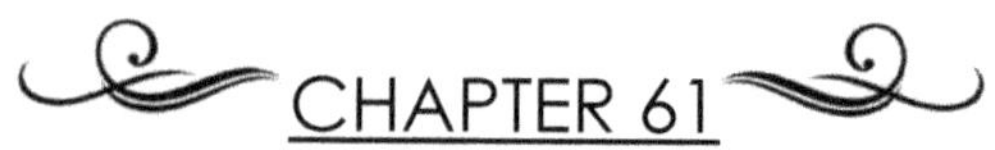

CHAPTER 61

It was the morning after proposing to Hannah that I realized something monumental.

Gone were the questions, the anger, the resentment, the guilt, the sadness and misery. What I held in my arms was all I ever needed, all I should have had all along.

"Good morning, baby," Hannah said, and snuggled closer.

I kissed her forehead. "Good morning, beautiful. Sleep well?"

"Mmm…very."

After breakfast, Hannah wanted to take a walk.

We'd pretty much spent our entire morning outside, lazing about in the park, watching cyclists, runners, parents with their kids coming and going.

Leaning up against a large willow's trunk with Hannah leaning into my chest, I said, "It's hard to believe that'll be you and me in a few months," and kissed the top of her head.

"I can't wait."

I was busy taking in more of our surroundings when Hannah's body stiffened in my arms.

"Well, well," I heard an all too familiar voice.

"Luke," Hannah said breathlessly.

"Lost the baby, huh?" His tone was accusatory.

"Luke–"

"Hannah, you don't have to explain yourself," I said.

"I think she does."

With a growl, Hannah ripped herself out of my arms and got up to her feet. "Enough! Luke, if you've stopped by to pester the fuck out of me, then get lost, otherwise say what you need to say and leave us alone. I'll say this and say it once." Her hands covered her belly with tenderness. "This isn't Lee's baby. I would have been showing at the memorial had I still been pregnant, you idiot. I would have been near fifteen weeks along. Do the math. If this were your brother's, I would have gone into labor by now."

The man looked away, shoved his hands in his pockets and took a deep breath. Then came a nod of understanding, accompanied by a look of embarrassment lacing his features.

"Why are you still here?" I got to my feet and wrapped myself around Hannah's back.

"I saw you two and I vowed to myself, after Lee's memorial, that if I ever saw you both again, that I owed you guys an apology."

"Forgiven," Hannah snapped. "Now, go."

"Can you just wait a damn minute?" Luke said.

"For what? For your far-from-sincere apologies?" she asked.

"Just give me five minutes, that's all I ask."

And being the person that she was, Hannah did give him that time.

Five minutes turned into ten, and then twenty.

Once I got past the fact that Luke had sided with his parents because of a sense of loyalty and grief, I'd have to say that Lee's brother was a good man. It was clear that Hannah was seeing the same thing, because in the end, her forgiveness was neither faked nor forced.

"Just so you know, I never agreed with the way Mom and Dad treated you," Luke told Hannah and then turned to me. "I wanted to thank you for giving me something to think about that day I walked into your pub. If it weren't for what you said, I'd probably be as bitter as my mother is right now."

I nodded my response.

"I'd better go," he said and moved in to give Hannah a kiss on the cheek. She took him by surprise if the look on his face was anything to go by when she hugged him.

"Take care of yourself, Luke," she said.

"You too." Luke gave her one last squeeze and released her.

Hannah and I watched as Luke walked away, arms wrapped around each other's backs, and somehow, I felt like I needed to add to this meeting so he knew that everything was okay with not just his former sister-in-law but with me as well.

"Hey, Luke." He turned his head our way. "Stop by for a beer next time you're around the pub. At least we'll have happier things to talk about."

The man smiled. "Sure thing. Make sure you have a few photos of the new babe. I'll want to see."

And with that, a day that could have clouded over with grief only got brighter.

CHAPTER 62

With four weeks left to go, Hannah was far from happy with her doctor's most recent orders. Blood pressure too high, fainting spells, early contractions that weren't Braxton-Hicks, were the bane of our existence. So, in an effort to cheer her up from her newly forced boredom, I urged her to start planning our wedding.

What I hadn't expected was that I'd actually enjoy planning it alongside her.

So, on a Saturday morning, at the table over breakfast, that's what we were doing before we were interrupted by the doorbell.

I answered the door only to have my visitor force her way through the threshold. "Where is she?" she growled.

"You're not welcome here," I told the bewildered woman. It was clear that the blow from the loss of her son hadn't ebbed at all, despite Hannah's funeral diatribe.

"What's going on?" Hannah asked as I knew she was heading our way.

"Sweetheart, call Luke."

"Why?" My fiancée rounded the corner from the kitchen and gasped. "Lois, what are you doing here?"

"So it's true. You are pregnant, and by the looks of it, due any day now."

Mrs. Parsons made to walk up to a pale looking Hannah and I put a quick stop to the woman's advance.

"Lois!" Lee's father appeared in the doorway, sucking in air as if he'd been running. "Honey, what are you doing in here?"

"I told you I wanted to see." She gave him an accusatory glance. "I needed to see for myself."

"Now that you have, let's go." He tried to make a grab for her elbow, but the woman fought his grip and won. "I'm really sorry about this, Hannah."

"Why don't you guys come in for a bit," Hannah's voice was soft, compassion-filled. My head snapped in her direction. She looked at me and nodded to indicate that she'd be okay, but I wasn't so sure of that. Not with the slight sheen of sweat on her forehead, or the paleness to her skin. "Have them sit in the living room, Ben. I'll be in with drinks in a minute."

I settled the Parsons in the living room and quickly excused myself, finding Hannah with her head in her hands, crying by the sink. Stopping behind her, my hands reached to rub her arms in a soothing motion. "You don't have to do this, you know," I whispered. "You've already said your piece."

"And that's fine with me," she began, "but have you seen her? She's broken, Ben."

"She's also out of control, sweetheart. I'm worried for you and our son."

"I know that, but just because the woman wreaked havoc on my life doesn't mean I get to just walk away from that."

"Baby, it does."

Her turn to face me was abrupt. "What happened to 'family sticks together'?"

"I believe in it, Hannah, but that woman isn't family. She would have never treated you like she has if she was."

"I don't care!" She brushed my hands away from her, fire consuming her eyes. That look told me that she was deter mined to see this through, and there was no talking her out of it. "It's got to stop now."

"And how do you think you're going to stop it?"

"She'll just have to listen this time." She turned toward the hallway entrance and paused. "What was said at the memorial might have been enough for most, but it clearly made things worse for her. It's time she knew all of the facts, Ben. Maybe then she can put it all to rest and begin to heal."

Fuck, but she was right.

So I followed Hannah to the living room, grabbing the tray of drinks my fiancée had forgotten, and brought it along.

Lois hadn't said much the entire two hours they'd been in the house, but Daniel, her husband, sure had a slew of questions which Hannah or myself answered. I could only help Hannah out with explaining what had transpired after the crash, since the before wasn't my story to tell.

The more we spoke, the more vivid the picture became for them.

Daniel listened with a look of horror on his face for most of it as his wife switched from looking dejected one minute to broken the next.

As the story reached its climax, Lois broke down in her husband's arms.

By the time we finished, Lee's mother's tears had calmed and her eyes seemed clearer.

That's when Hannah excused herself for a few moments and came back with a small piece of paper I knew she kept in her bedside table, as well as a photo frame.

"Here." Hannah handed the slip to the woman who took it with shaking hands. "That's the only photo of baby Parsons I have, but it's yours if you want it. And this," she handed the frame to Daniel, "is baby Carpenter. I'm not lying. I'm moving on. It may not be to your liking, and yes, I'll admit that it's quick, but what Ben and I have been through in our lives brought us closer in ways no one could have seen coming."

"I get it." Daniel cleared his throat before adding, "And I'm sorry for everything, Hannah."

Lois shocked us by whispering, "It was easier to shift the blame onto you instead of looking in the mirror." She lifted her head to look at Hannah and I. "You were right about what you said at the memorial."

"I shouldn't have said it," Hannah said, and my jaw dropped as I took in the sight of Lois' hand reaching out to Hannah's, more so, the fact that Hannah accepted that hand.

"You had every right to say those things. I just hope that you can forgive me."

"I can." Hannah reached for my hand with her free one, squeezing it.

My guess is that the baby moved because Lois' eyes grew and narrowed onto her stomach. "Can I?"

Hannah giggled and nodded. "Of course!" She guided the older woman's hand to her belly.

Daniel looked at me and nodded in silent appreciation for allowing his wife to be granted her request. "Gosh that's wonderful," the woman whispered, then looked at her husband. "Daniel, come feel this."

"No, it's okay, honey."

"Don't be ridiculous," Hannah said, dropping my hand. She reached over, grabbed Lee's father's hand and pulled him so he had to stand bent over the coffee table to connect with her belly.

Immediately, the man grinned. What made me smile more was the look on Hannah's face when she met my gaze: pure joy, mixed with one heck of a dose of relief. She seemed younger, and—as if it were possible—she glowed even more than usual.

After profuse apologies, we watched the Parsons drive off.

Hannah leaned into me after I'd closed and locked the

door. She took in a large breath and I felt the residual tension leave her taut body.

I brought my arms around her and hugged her to me. "You never cease to amaze me," I murmured into her hair, then kissed the top of her head.

"I think I amaze myself sometimes. I never saw that coming."

Neither had I.

Hannah flinched, then released a small hiss, prompting me to ask, "How are you feeling?"

"I think I'll go lie down for a bit."

Smart girl.

She knew that I would have carried her up those stairs and put her in our bed if she'd said otherwise.

CHAPTER 63

When I went up to wake Hannah for lunch, I was surprised to see what awaited me.

There she was, sprawled out on the bed, naked as the day she was born, smiling. "Hey there, handsome, care to give me a hand?"

In the right frame of mind, a man would have yelled a 'hell yes' and jumped to it, but me being the idiot I can be at times—and this was one of those times—I said, "Shouldn't you be sleeping?"

Hannah laughed. "I'd rather be sleeping with you, baby," she said, and stuck out her hand. "Come here."

I went to her. I mean, why the hell wouldn't I? "We shouldn't, sweetheart. You've been through enough today, and I'm worried about those contractions."

I hadn't made love to Hannah except for the one time since the doctor had told her to take it easy. And the pregnancy books I've read so far said that sex was a great labor inducer. Call me crazy, but I sure as hell wasn't looking for a pre-term baby.

Hannah's eyes welled up. "Baby, you haven't touched me in two weeks."

Her words felt like a sucker punch to the gut.

She pulled me to her by my shirt and started kissing me as I leaned over her. Damn, I missed those kisses. They were the best. You know the kind…the bring-a-man-to-his-knees-and-make-him-do-everything-you-please kind. Yeah, she was a pro at those.

Her hand snuck into my track pants and cupped my arousal. I was failing at restraint, and fast.

When her lips pulled away, mine continued to trail down her cheek, to her neck and toward those enlarged breasts of hers.

"Nice and slow, please, baby," she begged in my ear. "I need you so much right now."

"Lie on your side, sweetheart."

I pulled down my pants and got into bed behind her. I lifted her leg and positioned myself at her entrance. It was a painfully slow entrance that I revelled in and clearly, Hannah did too.

"I've missed this. I miss being this close."

"I missed you too, sexy." I turned her head to capture her mouth, slowly beginning to thrust.

Two weeks of nothing clearly put a dent in both our stamina, and as quick as it began, it ended.

"Thank you." Hannah rolled over to cuddle against my chest. "I know you're worried and so am I, but the doctor said that it was fine. You were there when he said so, and I missed you." Her voice cracked. "And I thought you weren't attracted to me now that I'm this fat cow and…" She broke down into tears.

My heart shattered at her revelation. I cradled her head in my chest and spoke into the top of her head. "Is that what you thought?" She nodded. I sighed and tilted her head up so she could see my face. "You are by far the most gorgeous creature to ever walk the planet. Do you have any idea how many times I've had to think of wrinkly old ladies and road-kill just to get rid of a stiffy over the last couple of weeks?" She wrinkled her nose at the imagery I projected and emitted a watery chuckle. "You're right, I'm worried. But I swear it's the only reason why I haven't initiated or taken you up on your advances, sweetheart. Seeing you this round with my boy makes me want to bend you over and fuck you until you don't even remember your name."

Her eyes widened. "Seriously?"

"Seriously, baby." I kissed her forehead. "I love you

more because of this." I rubbed her belly. "I love you so much, Hannah."

"I love you too."

Nuzzling her nose, I asked, "Do you feel up to coming down and having some lunch?"

"I thought you'd never ask."

CHAPTER 64

We spent the rest of the day lazing about.

Deidra stopped by with the baby. She and Blake had a girl. Mary Jane. She was a beautiful little angel with a head of whitish blond hair and obsidian eyes. At two months old, I could already tell that the new parents would have their hands full chasing the boys away in later years.

A moment of embarrassment hit Hannah when MJ started rooting at her breast while she held her. Her milk had let up with the stimulation and soaked through her shirt, causing Deidra and I to laugh. To say my woman was annoyed at me would have been an understatement.

I tried to apologize to her, but I ended up feeding MJ a bottle as the two women went upstairs. The fact that Hannah preferred her best friend to me stung. I should have known better than to have found humor in a humiliating situation.

I was stuck on MJ and watching her facials change as she slept in my arms when I finally looked up and saw my woman dressed in one of the pregnancy dresses I had bought her a few weeks back. She'd called them tents and told me to return them, but I hung them up in the closet instead. Could you blame me for wanting to see more of my woman's legs instead of her wearing my t-shirts? She'd even begun to highjack my boxers because, and I quote, "They're comfier than all my other clothes".

The dress Hannah wore was white and ended above the knee. It was one of those baby-doll type numbers with spaghetti straps. Perfect for the late spring heat wave we were having. It was snug at the bust and flared the rest of the way down. Deidra had even done her hair, pining half of it up and out of her face.

On an exhale, I said, "You look beautiful." I didn't even realize that Deidra had taken her newborn daughter away, but when I did, I shot up to my feet.

Hannah blushed at my breathless statement. When I was halfway to her, I froze. A tremendous amount of fluid gushed out from between her legs and onto the hardwood floor.

Holy fuck!

Apparently my vulgar thought had been verbalized time and again for the next five minutes. To be honest, I can't quite remember the words, but what I do recall is Hannah's eyes meeting mine in a wide and frightened gaze.

After that look, I was useless, frozen in panic, until the lights went out.

It could have been seconds like it could have been minutes when I heard Deidra make the call to 911. Darkness kept creeping in and the last I heard was my fiancée's best friend asking her a series of questions while Hannah answered and followed each one with a "Please tell me I just peed myself and I'm not in labor."

Consciousness came with a sting to my cheek.

When I opened my eyes, Mom was crouched down in front of me.

"Mom?"

"Get up off your lazy ass and tend to your woman, you fool," she scolded. "You need to get to the hospital and fast."

"The ambulance is coming," I said, my mind still hazy, but recalling Deidra being on the phone before I lost my faculties.

The moment I heard Hannah crying out in pain, I jumped to my feet and rushed toward her. She had her arms braced on Dad's shoulders while Dad held her hips, urging her to swing them from side to side, coaching her on her breathing.

If I had time to think about the comical look of it all, I'd say they looked like awkward teenagers dancing at a school function.

"Her parents will meet us at the hospital," Deidra said. "I have to go, but I'll be there when Blake gets home to take care of MJ. Take care of her, Ben."

I nodded.

"Oh fucking sweet baby Jesus this fucking hurts!" Hannah yelled out. "Christ! I'm sorry Roz…Doug."

Mom looked at Hannah with a humoured look. "It's okay, sweetie. I've heard worse from these two."

Enough! I snapped to action. "Mom, I need her bag packed upstairs. We started but never finished, do you think you could do that? Oh! And can you grab the baby's bag from the nursery?" After Mom nodded, I turned to my father. "Dad, I've got it from here."

"No!" Hannah stared Dad down like she was the devil incarnate. The woman's voice was like something out of the *Exorcist*—she was scary as all get out. "Don't you fucking let me go, Doug. Ben, get behind me, my back is killing me."

So I did what she requested.

When my hands connected with her lower back and my thumbs started to dig in, she pushed back into me. I leaned forward into her and rubbed the side of her face with my cheek, cooing words of praise and reminding her of how much I loved her.

"God that feels so good," she said in an almost orgasmic way, which made my hands still. "Don't stop, Ben!"

Dad was trying not to laugh, but his face showed a

picture of a losing battle with how red it was getting. Within seconds, the man exploded in laughter.

"You're not helping, Dad," I said through gritted teeth.

"I'm sorry," he said around the same time Hannah let out another cry of pain.

Where the fuck are the EMTs?

The doorbell rang.

"I'll get it," Dad said and made sure that Hannah was holding onto my arms, as she was leaning fully into my chest, and my hands rested on her belly. The thing felt as hard as a rock.

When the next contraction hit, her nails dug deep into my forearms, but I dared not make a noise. I could take it. She was clearly in worse pain than I was.

"How are you, darlin'?" the EMT asked.

"Having a party in my uterus, want to join?" Her rhetorical words came through clenched teeth. Her head arched back onto my shoulder and she let out another cry of pain.

"Craig?" I groaned. "You mind rushing this?"

"Holy shit, Ben!" the man said and paused to look between Hannah and me. "You…you mean–"

"Not now, idiot," Mom said walking by him, smacking him in the back of the head.

"Mom, I don't think you want to do that to a man who carries tranquilizers around in the back of that rig of his."

"Would you all fucking just shut up and get my fat cow ass up into the back of that thing so I can push this devil child of yours out?" Hannah growled, and after a few breaths she added in desperation, *"Please!"*

Craig looked right at me. "Since you asked so nicely, ma'am."

"Don't call me ma'am," she snarled. "You're making me feel old. It's Hannah!"

"Hold my hands, Hannah," he said. "We'll walk slowly."

"Ben!" I could sense her panic. "Don't leave me." She let go of one of Craig's hands and reached behind her blindly feeling for me.

"Never, baby." I moved to stay pressed against her back. "I'm right here. I'm not going anywhere without you."

CHAPTER 65

I cursed out the doctor when we arrived as he wanted to take Hannah into examination without me. It was a good thing that Marie caught us arguing and assured the doctor that I wouldn't pose a disruption. By the looks of things, Hannah would have caused an even bigger one had they not given in.

The next best look of shock I received that day, aside from Craig's at the house, was Marie's.

By the time she was examined, Hannah was begging for an epidural. My worst nightmare came when the doctor announced that she was fully dilated and there was no time for the pain medication.

"Are you fucking kidding me?" Her jaw clenched as she squeezed the shit out of my hand. If any bones weren't crumbled to dust by the end of this experience, it would be a miracle.

"You can do this, baby, I know you can."

"You try and push something the size of a golf ball out or your cock and tell me how you feel," she spat on a wince as the health professionals readied the stir-ups and the rest of their equipment for delivery.

"Okay, we need you to calm down, Hannah. Your blood pressure is climbing too high. The baby's having a hard time," the doctor said. "Daddy, why don't you get in bed behind her? You can help massage the base of her back since it seems like that's where it hurts most, right, Hannah?" She nodded.

My do the tides change rapidly! One minute she was fine with the idea and when it came time for her to move and allow me to sneak in behind her, I got a, "Don't you fucking touch me!" and a, "You did this to me!" before she clutched at her belly with an, "Ah!"

"Sweetheart, I'll make it feel better, I promise. You want me to make it better, right?"

She nodded feebly and I could see the tears in her eyes. "I'm so sorry, baby."

"There's nothing to be sorry about, sweetheart. Calm down, and let's do this."

"Make it go away. Please make the pain go away."

"We'll do just that, sweetheart." I finally managed to squeeze in behind her. Hannah leaned back, leaving me with enough room to wedge a hand between us and massage her lower back. I never thought that she'd relax that much.

"I love you so fucking much, Benjamin Carpenter," she said mid-contraction.

I couldn't help the chuckle. "I love you too, soon-to-be Mrs. Benjamin Carpenter."

"Okay, you two," the doctor said as he looked up at us from between my woman's legs with a smile. "It's time."

"Let's meet our boy," I whispered in her ear, then kissed Hannah's temple.

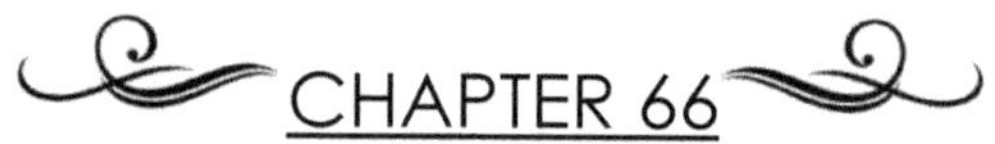

CHAPTER 66

After twenty-three minutes of pushing, Julian Doug Carpenter was born healthy, slightly under-weight, but with one hell of a set of lungs.

I was distracted, watching the nurses cart him away as they cleaned him up. I just wanted to see him up close again and kiss him, just like I knew his mother wanted to do.

It was Hannah's body's sudden shaking that brought my attention back to her. At first, it felt like a chill, but then it progressively got more severe, and before I knew it, I saw the crash cart get wheeled toward us, felt a porter pulling me from behind her and heard a shit load of yelling. The only thing I registered beyond the names of drugs called was the doctor's words. "She's seizing!"

I stayed rooted to my spot on the floor, the porter holding me back, as I watched from the foot of the bed while they did everything they could.

"Please save her," I heard myself say. "I can't live without her."

Within the blink of an eye, Hannah was wheeled off to surgery as the porter guided me to sit in a chair, and the nurse hunched down in front of me.

"Please tell me she'll be okay," I pleaded.

I know the nurse tried to tell me something, but all I

could do was repeat the same line over and over again. I was in shock.

Next thing I knew, my parents and Hannah's were in the room with me.

It was when Julian began to cry that I finally snapped out of it. The nurse brought him straight to me. "We're doing everything we can, sir. Why don't you try feeding him? He's hungry and with his weight, he needs as much as you can give him." She handed me a bottle of ready-mixed formula.

"Your mommy should be doing this right now, buddy," I said to him, "but she'll be back to take over."

I wished I felt as certain as my words sounded.

I fed Julian, burped him, then held him until he settled into sleep.

My son looked so much like his mother, except for his head of light brown hair, which was all me. I hadn't said anything to my parents or Hannah's as of yet. I was off in my own little world with my boy.

After an hour, Mom finally convinced me to lay my baby boy in his bassinet. As I did just that, the doctor that had been with us for the delivery walked in. It took everything I had not to jump the man for answers.

"How is she?" Adam and Anne both said at the same time as me.

"She's in recovery," the doctor said and turned to me. "She's lost a lot of blood. Part of the placenta ruptured, which sent her into shock. We found some scar tissue. Has she had a D&C before?" I nodded. "We think it might have caused the rupture."

"What does that mean?" I asked.

"For all intents and purposes, she'll recover and be fine. However, I do have to say that with the extensive rupture and the amount of new scar tissue that will be forming, future pregnancies will be difficult to maintain."

I walked to the chair I had been sitting in moments before

and let my ass fall to the seat. That wasn't so bad, right? Hannah was okay, Julian, aside from a low birth-weight, was fine, alive, and healthy…But why did I feel like my heart was breaking? "We can still have more kids, right?" The doctor hesitated so I pushed. "Right?"

The man sighed and met my gaze. "If she heals as we hope, yes. But that's not the hard part. As I've said before, maintaining the pregnancy is the problem. With Hannah's current bout of pre-term issues, I'd have to advise against it. I'm truly sorry."

"But the books say that each pregnancy is different. Is there nothing that can be done?"

I knew that Hannah didn't want to stop with the one child, and I would fight this doctor and find the answers that would satisfy both of us if it were at all possible. Hannah deserved the family she'd always dreamed about, and dammit, so did I.

"We have specialists that deal with this sort of issue, yes," he said.

"Then I want names and numbers. If anything can be done so Hannah can have more kids safely, she gets it."

"I'll see what I can do." Something in the way he said this made me feel like he disagreed with our entertaining the notion of having more children.

I ignored that feeling and asked, "Can I see her?"

"I can only allow one of you to go in, the baby is the exception," he said before showing me the way.

The rhythmic beeping of machines surrounded me, filling me with relief with its steady rhythm. I wheeled Julian's bassinet next to Hannah's bed where she slept.

She didn't look as pale as when they'd wheeled her out, and for that, I was optimistic.

I took the hand that was free of wires and probes and clutched it in mine, kissing it before leaning over her face.

"I thought I lost you. Wake up, please wake up, baby. Let

me see those bright green eyes. Baby, Julian is waiting to meet his mommy. He looks so much like you, sweetheart."

"Baby," Hannah mumbled as her eyes began to flutter open.

"That's right, baby." I smiled. "Our boy is here."

Hannah's eyes opened wide and the smile that took over her face made me so happy I could cry.

"I'm so sorry, Ben." Both her hands came up to cup my face, then pull it down. It was a quick kiss but one that showed me how much love she held for me. "I was such a bitch."

"Don't worry about it. I'm just happy you're okay and Julian's fine. He's right here, sleeping."

I picked up our tiny bundle of joy and brought him to his mother. I lay him on her chest, supporting him with one hand, and leaned over to kiss her forehead. "You did good, sweetheart," I whispered.

"No, we did great," she corrected, smiling up at me. "Now give me another kiss. He's so handsome like his father. I love you so much…the both of you."

"We love you too, baby. Please don't ever leave us. You scared the shit out of me."

"I did say I'd never leave you."

The events of the day had taken their toll on me and I broke down in tears. I gently wrapped my arms around her and our son and buried my face in her neck, taking in her familiar scent and letting it calm me, along with the one hand she had fanned through my hair, massaging my scalp. She always knew what to do to make things better. Julian sure had one hell of a mother.

CHAPTER 67

When the doctor came in and told Hannah the news about what had happened after the delivery, I would have thought that she'd lose it, what with the near impossibility to carry another baby full-term, but she didn't. In fact, she sat there, calm and cool as a cucumber.

After a quick check, the doctor cleared the rest of the family to be able to join us.

This is where the fun began, and I finally felt myself being able to relax and enjoy the simplicities of life again after the tumultuousness of the day.

Craig and Marie stopped by and accosted me with a series of questions along with their congratulations.

Deidra and Blake came as well with MJ in tow. Pictures were taken of the two babies and I had no doubt that growing up together, they'd most likely be either the best of friends or mortal enemies. Deidra was already talking about Julian as if he'd be the handsome boy knocking on their door twenty-some years from now, asking for their daughter's hand in marriage. Blake responded that his daughter wasn't marrying until she was at least forty.

Good luck with that!

By the time the day ended, Hannah had finally mastered the art of breastfeeding.

Cuddled low at her side, Hannah ran her hand down my

face after I yawned for the umpteenth time. "You should sleep."

My eyes strayed from Julian suckling at his mother's breast to the woman I love. "I'd rather watch this beautiful view I have in front of me."

"I'm serious, Ben." She leaned in to kiss my forehead. "You look like you've been awake for a week straight."

I held her gaze and was stern. "I'm not leaving you. I almost lost you today. I—"

"I'm not asking you to leave, baby. Just take a nap. Just like Julian will in a minute. I want my boys to cuddle me."

I leaned up and smiled against her lips before saying, "I like the sound of that." Then I kissed her sweet, long, and slow. When I pulled away, I sighed. "God, I can't wait to bring you guys home."

"Me too." She wagged her brows. "I guess I get extra time to lose all this weight before the wedding, huh?"

"You look perfect to me, Hannah. You've always been perfect."

"Charmer."

I yawned again before scooting up the mattress and settling my head beside hers on the pillow. "You know it."

CHAPTER 68

A few days and a couple of my burgers later, I was finally able to bring my family home.

Hannah was confined to the bedroom or the couch until her follow-up in a few days' time, but she was okay simply because she was out of that sterile environment. I couldn't blame her. It hadn't been long enough since her last stay.

The house had been filled with commotion since our arrival with people wanting to meet the new addition. I was looking forward to the day where it would be the three of us and peace and quiet.

Apparently our parents got the memo because that first evening, the phones stopped ringing, and so did the doorbell. I later found out that Dad had left a note over the door and they had taken off with our phones after turning the ringer off on the house phone.

Julian had been fussy over the last few hours with what seemed like gas. We had him lying on the flat of his back on our bed as both of us lay on either side of him.

"Will you sing to him?" Hannah asked. "It used to calm him down when he wouldn't stop gallivanting inside of me, maybe it'll work with this."

Hannah and I linked fingers above Julian's head as I began to sing softly to him. By the time I was done, we were all on the verge of sleep.

"Goodnight, Daddy," Hannah whispered on a teary smile.

My thumb captured an escaped droplet from her cheek. "Goodnight, Mommy." I leaned over to press my lips against hers.

It hadn't been the way either of us had envisioned spending our first night home together, but it couldn't have been more perfect.

When Julian stirred in the middle of the night for his feeding, I simply woke Hannah up and moved her so she cuddled with her back into my chest as she fed our son and I held both of them.

The next morning, I woke to my woman's delectable bottom tucked into my crotch as I listened to her talking to Julian. I smiled and kissed the back of her neck before leaning up and peering over her shoulder.

"Looks like we woke Daddy."

"Not at all, beautiful." I nuzzled her cheek. "I just don't want to miss a thing."

I heard a knock at the bedroom door and looked at Hannah with a furrowed brow. "Your mom told me she was coming over to fix us breakfast before she left last night," she explained. "Come in."

"I just came to steal the little prince away so you guys can have some alone time," Mom said. "I think you two can use a bit more sleep. I'll be back to wake you when breakfast is done."

"God love you, Mom."

Her eyes shone with pride. "Oh, I know he does if he's blessed me with you three and your father," she said and then shut the door. I could hear her cooing to Julian as she moved further away.

I reached out for Hannah and pulled her into my chest. She draped her leg over mine. I found that I actually missed the belly, but I was thrilled to have her that much closer again.

"Have I told you yet today how much I love you?" I asked.

"You haven't, but then again, you've been awake for all of fifteen minutes, and I love you too."

"Forever and always, sweetheart."

CHAPTER 69

It's been a couple of months since Julian was born and my little family couldn't have been better. Aside from the lack of sleep at night, I've never been more in love since laying eyes on my son, nor have I ever felt so complete as when I looked at the woman who birthed him.

Our wedding plans were finalized and in just under a month, I'd be whisking my woman away on a surprise honeymoon.

Things hadn't been quite the same in the bedroom, but I never pushed Hannah for more than what she was willing to give. It seemed that she had some self-image issues, though you wouldn't be able to tell with the outfits she'd worn on the few post-pregnancy outings we've had.

Julian started to lose weight again about three weeks after getting home, and boy did I have some consoling to do with Hannah regarding her feelings of inadequacy, with not being able to provide enough sustenance for our son. We've shared many sleepless nights with me holding her as she cried. I could only imagine how she felt, but I also listed the pros to the situation. No longer was she the only one to feed our son. Formula also sustained him longer, which meant fewer wake-up calls in the middle of the night. In just a few weeks, I could see that Hannah grew to enjoy watching Julian bond with friends and family while being fed. She finally started looking a bit happier and had voiced, just last week, that she enjoyed the time off.

Tonight was our first date night alone since Julian's birth. Every other outing had included our friends or our families. Suffice to say, I was looking forward to having a full uninterrupted night with my woman.

Anne and Adam had already dropped by an hour ago to pick up our son, along with the bag of necessities we had packed. I was sitting on the couch waiting for Hannah to finish up, and if she wasn't downstairs soon, I was going to march up those stairs and take what I'd been craving for months.

She'd been dropping hints all week long about wanting to get it on, and based on this morning's make-out session, I'd say she was open to my taking. If she wasn't, she sure as hell was sending me the wrong signals.

When my patience was lost, I went to find her.

Hannah's subtle perfume scented the air of our bedroom as I watched her put on a pair of earrings I had bought her on a whim.

"Just about ready," she said. "I'm sorry I'm taking so long."

"You can take as long as you need if you end up looking this good, baby."

Hannah snorted at my comment. She didn't believe me, and that stung.

I walked up to her and wrapped my arms around her waist, prompting her to lean back into my chest. I kissed her neck and felt her give way to me. "You look beautiful, sweetheart, and I know you don't believe me when I say it, but it's what you are to me. You're the only woman for me, Hannah, and that'll never change." She held my gaze in the mirror. "I love you and only you, and I'll spend the rest of my life making sure you get to feeling as beautiful, sexy, and desired for as long as you'll have me."

"If you keep this up, we might not make our reservation." She turned to face me. "I love you too, Ben. Forever and always."

"Then enough of this nonsense and let's get going." I kissed her quick. "I've got a hot woman, and I'm aching to show her off, aside from other things."

Hannah pulled my head down to hers and covered my mouth in a hungry kiss. She pressed her body into mine as I held her close. My hands roamed down her back to cup her butt, then squeezed it. I gave it a nice smack and she jumped back. The darkening of those green eyes of hers told me she liked it.

"Fine. I'll save it for dessert."

I grabbed her neck and pulled her in to give her bottom lip a nibble and eased its sting with a soft lick. She ground her hips into my crotch and I groaned. "Keep this up and we'll be lucky to make it through dinner. You have no idea what I'm hungry for."

Her sultry laugh filled the air and she kissed my cheek before moving past me to sit on the bed and put her shoes on. I hadn't seen her in strappy heels in far too long. Her legs looked endless in them, and it only made me want to wrap her around me that much more.

"I think I have a slight inkling." She winked as she got up to grab her purse. "Coming?" Without a backward glance, those hips of hers swayed from side to side as she started for the door.

You will be later.

CHAPTER 70

I made a point to remember to thank Paxton and Alissa for recommending Bocconcino. It was a beautiful and intimate Italian restaurant that served some of the best food in town.

To Paxton's advisement, I made sure to ask for seating near the back where it would be quiet, and the Maitre'D set us up in a rounded couch-like booth with curtained walls surrounding us and a fireplace across from our table. We could barely spot any of the restaurant's other patrons.

"Who'd you buy off to get in here?" Hannah asked.

"I had a little help from Pax. It turns out he's a regular, thanks to his editor who's obsessed with this place, so the moment I mentioned him, they did everything to accommodate us."

"I've been here once before, but I'm impressed. The food is amazing, but scoring this little section of peace and quiet makes this experience even better."

I jumped at the feel of her hand roaming up my leg toward my inner thigh. "Hannah," I warned.

"What?" Her leg pressed against mine.

I couldn't resist. If the woman wanted to play games, I was going to heat her up just to the boiling point and keep her simmering until we got home. After all, all was fair in love and all that.

I ran an open palm over the smooth skin of Hannah's knee, up her thigh and tantalized the skin just under the hem of her dress with my fingertips. "You really do look beautiful tonight." I leaned in to peck her lips.

Hannah had just gotten back from the women's room—the waiter having gone with our order—when I felt something drop onto my lap. I looked down to find a scrap of emerald green lace. My head snapped up and met Hannah's self-assured grin, a grin I'd missed so much over the last few months. It had disappeared along with our sex life.

I grabbed the underwear and hurriedly stuffed them in my blazer pocket, fighting the good fight that begged for me to get under our table and feast on her bared bits. Suffice to say, I doubted that the owner, the workers, or the patrons would appreciate my actions if I were caught. But it was tempting. Oh, so tempting.

Instead, I leaned close to Hannah's ear and nipped it, my voice coming out husky. "You're playing a very dirty game, baby. Open those legs for me."

Her eyes widened. "Y-you can't be serious?"

"As a heart attack. Two can play this game, and if I have it my way, you'll be coming long before we leave this place."

Hannah did as I requested and my dick got harder by her submission. I didn't think she'd do it.

I hitched the floor-length tablecloth slightly up onto our laps as I glided my palm up her thigh. When I moved my hand closer to the junction between her legs, she clamped them shut.

"Open," I ordered, then kissed her neck, feeling her pulse quicken. I slid a finger the length of her slit and pulled my face back to watch hers. "You like this."

She nodded. "Maybe a little too much." Her hand gripped my thigh.

"Then give in, sweetheart." I nuzzled her jaw. "Let me take care of you."

"Ben, we're in public."

"Then I suggest you keep quiet, because you need this, and I'm not stopping." She nodded her assent vigorously, as I pressed a finger into her, fusing my mouth to hers in time to capture her light moan. As I pulled away to take in her flushed cheeks, I spoke low, "You're so wet for me. I can't wait to taste you. And make no mistake, Hannah, I will be tasting you." Her whimper was the desired effect.

When I noticed the waiter come toward us with our dinner, my movements slowed. Hannah tried to clamp her legs shut at his arrival, but my hand was there. My fingers rubbed against her sweet spot before my thumb flicked her clit, making her gasp.

The young waiter eyed her curiously when she jumped and wiggled her butt in her seat to get away from my hand. I leaned forward in case the man grew more suspicious.

The minute his back turned and he walked away, Hannah grabbed onto my shirt and pulled me to her. She just pressed our foreheads together as my hand moved quickly over her slick pussy in a hurry to see the explosion in her eyes. Her heated breath fanned over my lips and I could tell she was close with the slight spasms that I felt clenching around my two digits.

As if craving the release, her hips began to ride my hand, while my thumb stroked her clit and my fingers played her g-spot like a fine instrument. "That's right, baby," I said. "Ride it out. You're so hot that I just want to lay you back on this table, and eat you up in front of everyone."

She squeaked around the same time I felt her first orgasmic tremor.

Her arms wrapped around my neck as she buried her face in the crook of it. I chuckled into her hair as I continued to stroke her heat, feeling her thighs twitch as I eased her back down to Earth.

"Ben…" She pulled away and seemed at a loss for words, so she crashed her lips to mine with what felt like gratitude.

"You're welcome, sweetheart." I gave her a quick peck. "Now, eat. I'd like to get you home sooner rather than later." I grabbed her hand and put it over my crotch. She squeezed. "Don't test me, you minx, or you might not like the surprise I have in store for you tonight."

"My, my, aren't we going all out this evening," she chortled.

"And you're a naughty girl." I attempted at pulling her hand away from my family jewels, but I couldn't.

All right, so I could have, but damn if she was taking the remainder of my control away.

"Let me know if someone comes to the table," she said.

Next thing I knew, she was gone. Hannah gripped me behind my knees and yanked my ass to the edge of the seat. Her hands made quick haste of the belt and zip to my slacks and with a gasp, her heated mouth covered my dick with a suction that made it hard for me to keep my eyes open.

She had me coming so hard and fast that had anyone walked by at that precise moment, I'm sure as hell that we would have been found out. A poker face could only do for so long when your woman knew just what to do to scramble your brain when she sucked you off.

Tucked in, pants redone, Hannah's hand rubbed over my relieved flesh before she peeked from under the table linens. I gestured with a *come hither* movement of my index finger to let her know the coast was clear, and she sat up beside me as if nothing had ever happened. Not even a hair out of place.

"All better?" she asked, leaning into me.

"I didn't know you had that in you." I smirked. "I have to say that it was one of the best damn surprises I've ever gotten, but that just sealed your fate for tonight."

She visibly shivered and her lids dropped, heavy with lust.

CHAPTER 71

By the time dinner was done, Hannah seemed ready to make a mad dash for it. I figured I'd have us a little more fun.

I stopped her by wrapping my arms around her waist as she attempted to get into the Range Rover. "I distinctively remember you saying something about the back seat never seeing more than cracker crumbs and spit up at some point," I said in her ear, nipping its lobe.

"Ben…" She groaned when I pressed my erection against her ass.

"You're going to get in there, let me strip you down, pay my respects, and then you'll ride my cock until we both explode." She moaned, but when she didn't move, I growled. "Now."

I don't think I've ever seen a woman move that quick on command before.

When both of us shut the doors, I locked them, and then quickly lifted Hannah to straddle my waist.

I kissed her hard and full of need, getting straight to business by pulling down the zipper at the back of her green dress. I pulled its strapless top down to her waist and took in the sight of her bare breasts.

"This is all you've been wearing all night?" I asked.

She smiled and pressed herself into me, nipping my bottom lip before licking it. I sucked her tongue into my mouth, taking over, feeling her velvety heat, tasting her unique flavor. The roominess of the vehicle was impressive, what with the car seat having been shuffled to Hannah's parents' car. I wasn't exactly a small guy, standing at six-two, but I had more than enough room to do what I wanted with her.

I laid Hannah back across the seat and pushed the skirt of her dress around her torso, driving my tongue into her depths and moaning in delight at her pungent smell and sweet taste.

"Fuck I've missed having you like this," I said over her moans, driving two fingers into her. After a few strokes, I had her coming undone, her juices flowing into my mouth as I drank as much of her in. I needed another one of those orgasms about as much as I needed my next breath. So I brought her over the edge again before pulling my pants low enough to sink into her heat with a hard thrust.

I sat us up with her over me and Hannah went wild, bucking, grinding and rotating her hips as I thrust up into her. "I love you, baby," I blurted into her neck.

"Oh Ben! I-I'm…Oh! I'm coming!" she screamed.

I thanked the higher power above for heavily tinted windows because when that knock on the back driver's side door came, my heart stopped.

"Take it home you two or I'll be forced to write you up," I heard. "Unless you're looking to be brought in, that is."

"Will do, thanks Shane," I said, no embarrassment despite knowing who it was. "Stop in some time."

The man chuckled. "Sure, but I should be thanking you, Ben. This is as much action as I've seen in weeks."

When Detective Shane Peters walked away, Hannah asked, "Do you know everyone in this damn town?"

Aside from avoiding a public indecency charge, and risking getting caught twice at the restaurant, I think it was safe to presume the eventual outcome of our evening.

"Now that we're home," I clicked the lock to the front door in place, "tell me how you want it."

"I want it hard, Ben. So very hard." She pressed her ass

into my crotch. "Fuck me good. Don't be gentle. I've missed this, I've missed you. I'm so sorry, baby."

I was abrupt in turning her to face me, then gripped her hair to tilt her head back. "I don't want your apologies, Hannah. I knew that you'd be ready in your own time. Now that you are, you better believe that I'll be all over you each and every day you'll let me have you. Now get that sweet ass of yours up those stairs before I bend you over that chair and fuck you until you come so hard you can't walk tomorrow."

Instead of walking toward the stairs, she made a bee line for the aforementioned leather sling-back chair.

"Like this?" She bent over and lifted her dress, thus framing her flawless and unclothed bottom.

I approached, letting my hand skim the surface of her ass. "Baby, I want you all over this fucking house right now." I pulled my hand away, and proceeded to drop my pants.

CHAPTER 72

I was calm, at peace with everything, and for good reason too. Today I was marrying the love of my life with no hint of nerves or anxiety—at least, not yet—and I wouldn't be shocked if they never materialized. I had never been more sure of anything in my entire existence.

The door to mine and the guys' room opened and Nicole—tiny baby bump and all—came in, dressed in a knee-length emerald strapless dress, her hair and makeup looking impeccable.

"Has Mike seen you yet?" I asked.

She shook her head, indicating the negative. "I take it you approve?"

"You look beautiful." I leaned in to kiss her cheek. "How is she?"

"Hannah's bouncing off the walls right now." Nicole laughed. "She's been ready for the last hour and a half. Dee had to hold her back from coming to find you."

"You mean to say it takes her hours to get herself ready for a date and she's ready this quick on our wedding day?"

"There's a difference, Ben. She was nervous that night, she's not today."

I reached up to try and do up my tie, but Nicole smacked my hands down and did the honors.

I chuckled. "Are you here to see if I'm freaking out?"

"Actually, I came here to drop this off and find my husband." She nodded her head toward the box she'd just set on the table beside us. "By the way, you look handsome."

"He took off with Jake and Pax just a little while ago. They should be back–"

A low whistle came from the door, and my gaze lifted toward it. Mike closed the door and eyed his wife from top to bottom. "Are you trying to outshine the bride, honey?"

"You should see her if you think this is hot." Nicole kissed her husband. "I have to get back, but Hannah wanted you to have this." Nicole smirked mischievously as she drummed a few fingers over the top of the box. "For your eyes only? Must be something good."

Nicole left with Mike and I found myself alone in the room once more.

I pulled the box on the table toward me and opened it. Taking the small piece of folded paper from it, I read before rummaging through the rest of the contents.

> *Ben,*
> *I would have worn these today, but I thought*
> *they'd be an inconvenience as the day wore on.*
> *As it is, so much can be said about easy access.*
> *Love you, forever and always,*
> *Your future Mrs. Benjamin Carpenter*

I had an idea as to what she meant, but I never expected to see it all.

My hands pulled each item out: garter belt, stockings, bra, and underwear. All of it white and all of it before me, which meant…

"Holy shit!" The door flew open, causing me to rush in stuffing the whole back into the box. My woman might be wearing white today, but she was going to be a far cry from angelic, despite her outward appearance.

"Something jump out and bite you in there?" Mike asked, which made Jake and Paxton start laughing.

"You dropped something." Jake walked up to pick the tiny scrap of lace off the floor and looked at it dangling from his finger. "Best keep those hidden. I've never seen a groom get his bride out of her underwear that damn fast before." Instead of handing them to me, he tucked them in my tux jacket pocket.

Mike busted out laughing. "She didn't."

"Oh, she did." I smirked.

"Damn woman is asking for trouble if you ask me," Paxton said.

"She's not asking for it, she's demanding it," I stated.

"Call me crazy, but I'm glad we're not hosting this wedding. I think my barn's seen enough action to last a lifetime," Paxton stated.

Mike let out a loud laugh. "It's not on the count of Nic and me. Who was it that we caught in there with his pasty white ass up in the air?"

Jake shook his head. "I never thought she had it in her, but after the pub incident…"

Paxton grinned. "I didn't lie when I said Allie had a kinky side."

The conversation was interrupted by Dad who popped his head in through the door. "Guys, let's get a move on. You can talk about your kinky wives when my son's married off for good this time." He winked at me.

CHAPTER 73

I could have sworn that I had died and gone to heaven when Hannah came out on her parents' arms. I mean, I knew she'd look good—better than that, great—but damn!

Mike put his hand on my shoulder and waggled his brows at me. I turned to look at Hannah, who stopped where I was to take her hand and she winked at me with that sly smile of hers.

"Hello there, handsome," she murmured.

"Hello, angel," I grinned before adding, "or am I marrying the devil today?"

"Remember, you're promising to take me as I am."

"And it's the best decision of my life," I said just in time to hear the Justice of the Peace clear his throat.

Vows were said, promises were made, and tears were shed.

When we were introduced as man and wife, I took my time. With one hand cradling the back of Hannah's head, the other went to her lower back as she grabbed on to my tux-covered biceps. I skimmed her soft lips with mine, barely making contact, then pulled back to utter those three little words before crashing my lips to hers.

Bending my knees, Hannah wrapped her arms around my neck, our lips still sealed, while whistles and applause filled the outdoor space surrounding us. With my bride in my arms, the wind off of the lake swirling around us, cooling us from the glare of the late afternoon sun, everything couldn't have been more perfect.

We laughed enormously, cried minimally, and enjoyed ourselves exclusively throughout dinner, the toasts, and the cake cutting, which I have to mention was Hannah's creation. How she managed to put together tiers of strawberry cheesecake and turn the whole thing into our wedding cake was beyond me, but she succeeded, and it looked great. It tasted even better.

I had gone to get Julian from his four grandparents, and brought him over to his mother.

"You're almost as handsome as your father," she cooed, cradling him close and dropping a kiss on his head.

"I think he wants a dance with his breathtaking mother." I pressed my lips to hers.

She pulled away but stayed close, cupping my cheek. "Only if his father dances with us."

I wrapped my arms around her, my front to her back, and she melted into me. Apparently behaving like a family draws attention and before we knew it, cameras were flashing in our direction again.

When the song ended, I motioned for Hannah's mother to come and get our little guy.

"I was just getting comfy." My wife pouted.

"Come get comfy with your new husband on the dance floor, but make sure to give our son extra kisses for the night, because your parents are taking him home now."

She didn't waste time.

CHAPTER 74

We'd been dancing for a few hours, and I was aching to get out of there with all the grinding Hannah had been doing against me. It didn't help my case either when I spent the entire afternoon knowing that she'd been bare under that gorgeous gown of hers.

I was sure as hell glad when Hannah mentioned a walk. I led her back up toward the lodge we had booked for the ceremony and reception. They had enough rooms for everyone to stay if they chose not to drive home.

"Where are we going?" she asked when I took her down another path to the other side of the property and away from the lodge itself.

"I want some real alone time with my wife." That's when the cabin came into view and Hannah gasped. "I figured the further from the lodge, the better, while my wife and I celebrate."

Hannah immediately dropped her clutch to the floor when she took in the canopied bed against a wall of windows, which opened up to a wrap-around deck that faced the lake where there was a small dock. It was a suite cottage that played host to mostly honeymooners and I figured, after seeing the abode for myself, that it would be perfect to spend our first night as man and wife, instead of being holed up with everyone else in the main building.

I pushed Hannah's hair to the side and kissed down her spine as I began to unzip the back of her gown, while she continued to take in the room.

"This is amazing," she said.

"You're amazing." I crouched down to finish with the zipper, allowing the material to fall, pooling softly on the floor.

My wife turned to face me and my eyes met their mark: a freshly shaved pussy I could barely hold off from sinking into, greeted me.

I got up and began to loosen my tie, but my high-heeled-wearing vixen of a wife walked the few steps to me and took the thing out of my hands, yanking back on it.

"I believe that's my duty, my loving husband." My heart sped up with the way she said my title. I loved hearing it on her lips.

She took her sweet time divesting me of my clothing, and believe me, when it comes down to this penguin suit of mine, the vest and cummerbund, the cufflinks and so on, there was more than enough for her to strip before getting to the goods. When she did though, boy did I enjoy her warm hands and soft lips as they kissed down my bare chest.

As soon as my pants hit the floor, her mouth was all over my dick. The soft curls to her hair framed her face perfectly, and her bright green eyes kept hold of mine while she sucked me off to bursting.

I picked her up by her arms and brought my very satisfied looking wife to her feet.

"I've been waiting all day to do just that," she said. "Along with a few other things. It's a good thing we have all night."

I nodded vigorously.

Her hands were rubbing my chest as she backed me up until my knees hit the edge of the bed. She pushed me down on top of it.

"About those other things?" I scooted back so my head lay on the pillows.

She slowly crawled toward me like a tiger to her prey.

"Stay put and I'll let you have a taste."

I arched my brow at her. "I plan on getting more than just a taste, sweetheart."

"Only if you–"

I grabbed her arm, pulling her on top, before rolling her under me. "I don't take orders, baby." I nipped her chin. "At least, not in the bedroom tonight. I give them, and last I checked, you enjoyed it."

"Well if you didn't want me riding your face, then–"

"You'll be riding my face, Hannah, just not from the top." Following my statement, I pounced.

CHAPTER 75

I had convinced Hannah of a midnight swim and we'd made it out to the lake.

The cool water felt great after the hours of lovemaking. The one problem was the lack of swimsuits, which ignited the never-ending blaze between us all over again.

Hannah was pinned under me as I held her arms above her head, thrusting into her with long, strong strokes. The wildlife around us had picked up and I could hear the wolves at a distance and the song of owls as Hannah's moans grew louder.

I rolled us over so she sat atop me and I let her have her way with me, guiding her hips up the length of my shaft, and letting her dictate the pace of the down-stroke.

"Those hips of yours are going to kill me," I said.

"You mean this?" She ground her hips in a circular motion, but threw in a little tightening action from within. I hissed. "I'll take that as a 'yes'. I wonder if I could ever get you to scream like you make me."

"Keep doing what you're doing and you might just get your wish."

So she did. And I did. In the distance, I could have sworn I heard some laughing…cheering…Hell, was that? Nah…

Yes, indeed it was what I thought it was. After a few

minutes of basking in the moonlight, regaining our wits. Sex noises.

Hannah kissed me softly. "Let's go to bed. Maybe I'll let you have another go before drifting off."

She got up and proceeded to leave me with the towels and walked toward the cottage in the buff.

I gave her a whistle. "With that ass, baby, you can damn well be sure you'll be getting more than just one more go."

"You do that, son!" I heard from a distance. Hannah was way ahead of me laughing. Had I spoken out that loud? And who the hell had that been earli–

Oh, fucking hell!

EPILOGUE

"Good morning," Hannah said in that husky sleepy voice of hers, while my fingertips played over her bare shoulders.

I'd been watching her sleep as I've often done when I woke before her.

"Good morning, wife." The grin that spread over her face never got old. "What are you thinking so hard about?" I pressed my lips to the top of her head.

"Me. You. Us…our family." She brought one of my hands up to kiss it before hugging my arms around her tightly.

"We've come a long way in a short time, haven't we?"

"Yeah…Are you happy, Ben?"

Was I happy?

I turned her to face me and kissed her nose before gracing her with a smile. "Let me put it this way…" I nuzzled her nose. "I had a life before you came along; a miserable one, but a life just the same. You make me feel alive. You give me more joy in all our time together than I could have ever hoped for in a lifetime alone. I can't say that there won't be arguments or moments of sadness in our future, because no one knows what the future holds, but I can say that never will I give up, turn my back, or walk away from us. I can guarantee you that I'll be giving it my all to keep that gorgeous smile on your face until the day I take my last breath."

"I love you, Benjamin Carpenter."

"And I you, Hannah Carpenter."

If the last year was any indication as to what our future held out for us, I'd have to say that we were looking at a damn great life together.

Something definitely has to be said about actually living life instead of existing.

When my head hit the pillow that night, I thanked my lucky stars just as I've done every day since I was gifted Hannah's love.

Fate had finally dealt me the best hand of all, and I finally won the pot in this crazy game of life. It may not have been millions in money, precious metals, or jewels, but it was better than that.

I had a home…not just a house.

I had a wife…not some random woman.

I had a son…not some crazy kid from up the street.

I had friends…not colleagues or patrons who think they know me.

I had a job…fatherhood definitely was the best title I ever held, in my opinion.

I had a life…a real one, filled with happiness, devotion and love.

With Hannah cuddled into me and my arms wrapped around her, I sighed my contentment.

Yeah, this is definitely a life worth being envious of.

ABOUT THE AUTHOR

Born and raised in small town Northern Ontario, Canada, Carey Decevito has always had a penchant for reading and writing.

More than a decade later, with weeks of sleepless nights, where exhaustion settled into her everyday existence, she finally gave in and put pen to paper (more like fingers to keyboard!) She submitted to the dreams that plagued her. And the rest, as they say, is history!

A member of the RWA, Carey Decevito enjoys spending time with family and friends, the outdoors, traveling, and playing tourist in Canada's National Capital region. When life gets crazy, she seeks respite through her writing and reading. If all else fails, she knows there's never a dull moment with her prolific storyteller of a daughter, her goofy husband, cat and dog who she swears are out to get her.

To Forgive & Hold Safe is the fourth book in *The Broken Men Chronicles* series.

FIND CAREY AT:

www.careydecevito.com
carey.decevito@gmail.com

ALSO BY CAREY DECEVITO

The Broken Men Chronicles series:

Once Written, Twice Shy
Almost Forgotten
Play Me to Infinity
To Forgive & Hold Safe

a heart's war

THE BROKEN MEN CHRONICLES

book five

excerpt

carey decevito

PROLOGUE

A *fiery blast came from our left. The vehicle I was crammed into took a sharp right before weightlessness set in; the deafening sound of crunching metal, shattering glass, and firing weapons making my ears ring. My head felt as if it was about to explode.*

Shouts, screams from the men around me, those I was responsible for, their sounds were what living nightmares were made of.

Suspended for eternity is how it felt when in fact, within seconds it was over.

"Donnelly," I coughed out, stuck sideways against my door. My vision was blurry, my head pounding. Everything was tinged with red. "Donnelly," I repeated, chocking on the dust and smoke floating inside the vehicle. I tried wiping blood from my eyes. Whether it was mine or someone else's, I couldn't tell. When I got nothing from Donnelly, I addressed the group. "Everyone okay?"

No answer.

I blinked a few times, the ringing in my ears dying down enough for me to be able to make out the horrific chaos that surrounded us outside. The erratic thumping in my chest, not to mention the prickling of the small hairs on the back of my neck, told me that danger still lurked.

I hoped that our Humvee was the only one in our convoy that had been hit, but with the size of that blast, I knew it was wishful thinking. We needed to get out, help whoever was left, and get the hell back to base.

I tried to move, biting my lip hard enough to taste the coppery flavor of my own blood as the debilitating pain in my legs manifested itself, letting me know that I was in bad shape.

"Damon." I leaned forward as much as I could, trying to get around his seat without blacking out, to rouse my teammate, one of my best friends. It wasn't until my eyes were firmly focused on him that I noticed his head hanging at an unnatural angle, his chest unmoving. I reached as far as I could, finding that spot by his carotid to make sure what I was seeing was right. My rations from that morning's breakfast began to weigh heavy and my gut clenched, bile beginning to rise, when I had my confirmation. "Oh fuck!"

The man lay against what should have been the window to his door—dead.

Beside him, the newest addition to our team—a woman we'd dubbed Tiny, for evident reasons—lay across the middle console, aortic blood spraying lightly as the last of her life force drained away.

Blood. There was so much of it. Keeping my sanity in check became harder as panic consumed me.

I can't be all that's left. I can't be alone in this hell.

So I turned to the last of my team members: Rick Donnelly. Just like with Damon, we'd been close, he and I. A true brother in this godforsaken sandbox, who'd kept me level-headed throughout our many deployments since BUD/S. He's a little crazy, but I suppose that's why he's a master with explosives.

"Rick!" At first glance, Donnelly appeared unharmed, as if he were sleeping. The sweet sound of his groan cut through the automatic gunfire around us enough to dispel my ever-growing sense of helplessness. Barely.

The sudden lull in weapon fire provided me with the opportunity to call his name out again. I knew insurgents were still around and we needed to get gone fast.

As I tried to rouse Donnelly, I became aware of approaching footsteps. I prayed for it to be our men but I knew that in all likelihood we might not be so lucky. The radio silence alluded to that fact.

"Dammit, Rick, wake the fuck up! We need to get out of here."

The man managed another groan but didn't move despite my grabbing on to his fatigues and shaking him.

I heard shouts outside our vehicle; both English and foreign. Just as another bout of gunfire hit, the distinctive sound of our M-16's against AK-47's, everything drew to a halt. The sound of gurgling close to the rear of our vehicle and the rapid fire of Pashto sent me into a full-blown panic. This felt too much like the end.

Seconds later, I was ripped from my seat, the searing pain in my legs escalating to a blinding level, making me scream.

As soon as two men laid hands on Rick, he kicked into action.

Fully extricated and now able to better see my surroundings, I heard weapons still firing intermittently in the distance, screams and pleas of mercy came from all directions, none of them in my native tongue though.

I tried to fight my captors but the injury to my legs had me useless against the two able-bodied men that held me. Before I knew it, my hands and ankles were bound with rope, a gag was shoved into my mouth, tied by a torn piece of cloth, and an old rice bag that smelled of sweat and mildew was slipped over my head.

In this moment, thoughts of my future, my family, my friends flashed through my mind. If I survived this ambush I knew before long, I'd be praying for death. I just didn't know how right I would be.

With a hit to the back of my head I fell into darkness.

"Welcome to Jacksonville, North Carolina, folks! The current temperature…" The flight attendant's voice startles me awake from my flashback. My breathing is erratic, my skin is crawling and clammy as I force myself to take in my surroundings and calm myself. Suffice to say, my nightmares were back. If I'm being honest, they hadn't really disappeared. But, with my imminent return home, they'd grown in frequency.

The elderly lady sitting next to me cowered in the furthest corner of her seat, her eyes wide, face pale. Her expression of fear morphed to one of sympathy as she eyed my fatigues, evidently processing my attire along with my behavior as soon as "I'm sorry," had left my mouth. Patting my arm, she turned to face forward without a word. It's too bad there weren't more people like her. I didn't need anyone claiming to understand what I'd been through. I didn't need their pity. And I certainly didn't need their praise and thanks.

I hadn't been home in ten years. Half of that time hadn't been by choice, either. I had owed it to my country to serve with distinction. Or, that's what I'd believed at one time.

A hero is what most everyone dubs me. The thought itself makes me cringe. Where's the honour, the glory, even the pride in it? Did anyone who killed, who witnessed death in all its violent forms, who slept every night with one eye open, wondering if they'd live to see the next day, think of themselves a hero? I can't speak for anyone else but the short answer for me is no.

Grabbing my rucksack, I head for the exit. The flight attendant sends a flirtatious smile my way. "Have an enjoyable stay, sir." I walked off the plane with only a curt nod as an acknowledgment.

After a quick stop at luggage claim, I exit the airport with nothing but my rucksack and a large duffle strewn over my shoulder, words of praise from passers-by having fallen on deaf ears. The pats on the back made me want to shrink away. It all made me want to scream, but those that haven't been where I've been, that haven't done what I've done, or seen what I've seen didn't know any better, did they? They held on to this romanticised version of what the media portrayed. If they only knew that the boogey man came in the form of a man, woman, or child and not with pins sticking out of their heads, or blades for fingers.

No, there was no glory in being considered a hero for my country. Those considered heroes in my book are the ones who fought and lost their lives, that have made the ultimate sacrifice. Those who were now six feet under, if their families were lucky enough to have a piece of their loved ones shipped back to them for a proper farewell.

My scars, both physical and emotional, run deeper than they appear. They serve as a reminder of those I've lost in the line of duty, those I had been in charge of, sworn to protect and bring back to their families. Alive. Those I had failed.

I hailed a cab and jumped in as soon as one pulled up in front of me.

"Where to?"

I don't know, home? Where the hell was home, really? Everyone thought I was dead.

"Hey buddy," the driver said. "Did you hear me?"

"Is there a bar around here? I'd kill for a cold beer and a decent burger."

"I know just the place." The mid-fifties man's eyes crinkled in the mirror.

Despite the curious looks the driver threw my way, the drive was made in silence and I was grateful. As the tree-lined streets and lights from oncoming traffic whizzed by, I found myself thinking about a plan of attack to reintegrate myself into what most people would call a normal life.

By the time the taxi pulled up to the curb, I still had no idea how to approach the situation that was my return from the dead. Perhaps my answers lay at the bottom of a beer bottle too many, or better yet, with my brother. He'd always been one to help me think things through in a rational and practical fashion.

But how will P take it?

I stood with my two bags, a summary of my life for the past decade, staring up at the pub in front of me. Fairfax. The place seemed fairly new. I didn't recall seeing it before leaving, that's for sure.

The sound of laughter, the smell of food and liquor assaulted me as I opened the door. The place appeared pretty quiet for a Friday night. It was just what I needed.

Starting toward the bar, I heard, "Son of a bitch!" making me freeze mid-stride. It might have been a little more than three years since, but that voice was one I'd never forget.

My head turned in the speaker's direction, the place having gone dead silent. A man came barrelling toward me, a flying fist connecting with my jaw before I could shield myself. My body rocked backward as I dropped my bags in shock.

"What the fuck are you doing here?" Paxton demanded.

"You're supposed to be dead!"

Not exactly the homecoming I was expecting. "Good to see you too, bro." I rubbed my jaw. *Fuck that hurt.*

Before I knew it, Paxton was on top of me, swinging like a mad man, yelling, cursing me out until I was forced to defend myself. Couldn't a guy catch a break? Couldn't I have at least had the chance to explain?

I was pushed onto a table, which collapsed, causing my brother and I to fall in a pile of splintered rubble to the floor.

"You just left!" Paxton landed a punch to my gut, knocking the wind out of me.

"I didn't have a choice!" I shouted back, blocking a hit before rolling us over so I was on top. I managed to get to my feet, swiping the back of my hand over my split lip to check for bleeding as I braced myself for another go, if that's what he wanted.

"Get the fuck out of here!" My brother picked himself off the floor, then came at me again.

I landed a hit to his jaw and another to his stomach. "I just got back and that's all you have to say? The least I deserve is a chance to explain."

W*e thought we buried you!*

My brother's words sent reality crashing through me. I hadn't forgotten about the heartbreaking news that had been delivered to my friends and family what felt like a lifetime ago. No one forgets that. But then again, I never gave thought about how my sudden reappearance would be taken either.

Next thing I knew, Paxton was being held back from another approach, and so was I.

When my breathing calmed, I said, "I'm cool," to the guys who had me restrained. Their grips loosened to release me altogether.

"What happened to you, man?" I recognized the guy on my left as Ben Carpenter.

Shaking my head in response, I rubbed the back of my neck, peering down at the floor before meeting Ben and my brother's gazes. Everyone seemed to have calmed down, but they were also awaiting my answer.

So I relayed my story. Well, the bits I could share, anyway. I told them about our ambush, how I had been captured, wished I had died, but had survived instead. When it came down to why no one was told that I was alive and well, I didn't have much in the way of an explanation because everything was classified to the *n*th degree. "It would have been too risky for everyone. You have no–"

"Don't tell me I have no idea!" Paxton spat. "*You* have no idea of the shit we've been through."

"Pax!" A woman came to stand beside him, her hands on his chest. According to the information that I'd been able to dig up, I knew this was Alissa, my brother's wife…and my new sister-in-law.

"Don't!" The pained look on his face had her eyes tearing up. "His own nephew nearly died and he wasn't here. He hasn't even met his niece. He knows nothing of our lives and he expects us to welcome him back with open arms?" Paxton's eyes bore into me. The betrayal they held was like a searing knife to the heart. "You deserted me!"

After a moment, I managed to choke down the ball of emotions that clogged my throat. "I knew."

His eyes widened. "What?"

Our gazes remained locked. "I said I *knew*. I know that you and Julie didn't work out… about the divorce. I know what happened with Jasper, Alissa coming into your life, and when that beautiful little princess of yours was born. Just because I didn't stay in touch doesn't mean I don't care. I've kept tabs on my family the entire time I was away because that's the only thing I could do. I don't think I would have survived if I hadn't been able to do that."

The look of shock and relief in my brother's eyes filled me with hope. "As messed up as this all is, I believe you." He sighed, pinching the bridge of his nose between his thumb and forefinger as if trying to rid himself of a sudden headache. "I need a drink after this bombshell. Want one?" That classic Lowell grin spread onto his face before he took his wife's hand and led her toward the bar. "It's the least I can do for that busted lip. When did your face get so hard?"

I chuckled, falling into step beside them. *Same old P.* I was glad he hadn't changed. "Training." I patted him on the back. "By the way, your left hook could use some work, it's weak."

"Two Jack's and a raspberry martini for my wife, Derek." Alissa curled into Paxton's side as he eyed my face, that sure-of-himself grin still present. "Let me know if I still need practice when that jaw barely opens tomorrow and you can't see out of your right eye."

Only when Paxton headed toward the men's room with his wife did I swivel my barstool and look around. I felt like a fly on the wall, content to observe the festivities without partaking in them, recognizing a few faces, most of them from high school, while others were new.

Earlier, my brother brought up a few points that had me thinking. I needed to see my parents. I needed a job. And my younger sibling also saw it fit to tell me that I needed a woman.

Well, I couldn't agree more with the first two, but the last one was debatable.

To be honest, I don't want a night of hot fun where I sink my cock in some willing stranger. To have that would be like never having evolved from my old ways. And I wasn't the old Theo Lowell. Far from it, in fact. I wanted a simple life with a partner—much like my brother and his friends seem to have acquired, if tonight was anything to go by. What I wanted was a woman to call my own.

No one will have you once they know everything.

That pesky internal voice was always there, reminding me of the things I have done, or better yet, the things I failed to do during my deployments, things that no woman would overlook for the kind of long haul commitment I yearned for.

"Just as well," I said to myself as I tilted the remainder of my beer back.

Cat calls and hollers sounded from the area where the gents and ladies' rooms were located. I turned to see what the women were going on about to find none other than my brother blushing while the women high-fived his wife.

Derek waved another bottle of *Bud Light* at me and I nodded. Catching wind of what had gone on had me smirking as I took a large gulp of my fresh brew. I guess my brother had finally found himself someone to keep up with his wilder side after that frigid bitch of an ex he'd been married to had left him.

Alissa settled herself on the stool next to mine having left Paxton to deal with the guys razing him.

"So, Theo," she eyed me, "where are you spending the night?"

"I was thinking of the Sunset Inn on Western Boulevard."

I was met with a disapproving look. "I'm not going to let you hole yourself up in a hotel when we have a perfectly well-made-up room at the house."

I harrumphed. "That tiny townhouse only has two rooms."

Paxton nudged my shoulder with his as he leaned against the bar on my other side. "We're living in Mom and Dad's old place now."

"The ranch?" Alissa nodded. Something inside me ached to see the old place again. "You're sure?" I knew that it would be fine with my brother, so I aimed my gaze at his better half, who nodded once more. "Okay. Thank you."

The look of approval in my brother's eyes told me that accepting his wife's invitation had been the right move.